Tall Cool One

A-List novels by Zoey Dean

THE A-LIST
GIRLS ON FILM
BLONDE AMBITION
TALL COOL ONE
BACK IN BLACK
SOME LIKE IT HOT
AMERICAN BEAUTY
HEART OF GLASS
BEAUTIFUL STRANGER

If you like THE A-LIST, you may also enjoy:

Bass Ackwards and Belly Up by Elizabeth Craft and Sarah Fain
Secrets of My Hollywood Life by Jen Calonita
Haters by Alisa Valdes-Rodriguez
Betwixt by Tara Bray Smith
Poseur by Rachel Maude

Tall Cool One

An A-List Novel #4

by
Zoey Dean

poppy

LITTLE, BROWN AND COMPANY
New York   Boston

Poppy

Little, Brown and Company
Hachette Book Group USA
237 Park Avenue, New York, NY 10017
For more of your favorite series, go to www.pickapoppy.com

First Edition: April 2005

The Poppy name and logo are trademarks of Hachette Book Group USA.

Produced by Alloy Entertainment
151 West 26th Street, New York, NY 10001

Cover design by Marci Senders
Cover photography copyright © Andrea Balena/Photonica

ISBN 978-0-316-73508-7

10 9 8 7 6 5 4

CWO

Printed in the United States of America

For my friends in Aruba

"If I'd observed all the rules I'd never have gotten any where."
—Marilyn Monroe

Female Perfection

Anna Cabot Percy was very good at a wide variety of things: Conjugating irregular French verbs. Putting together the perfect understated outfit. Memorizing the poetry of Emily Dickinson. Ballet. Any and all forms of analytical left-brain thinking. Looking tan and gorgeous in her white racer-back Polo Ralph Lauren bathing suit. So okay. She was not without talents. But as she shivered on her surfboard in the ocean at Zuma Beach, Anna realized that surfing was not going to be one of them.

She felt like a bedraggled, waterlogged wreck. Who knew a person could wipe out so many times in one afternoon?

"You good?" asked her friend Danny Bluestone. He bobbed on his own board a few feet from Anna. Danny was on the short side, but he was still cute and quirky and funny and extremely talented. He and Anna had met on *Hermosa Beach*—the new hit TV show where he was the youngest writer and Anna had interned. A native Californian, Danny had assured Anna that he could teach her how to surf in a single afternoon.

"I'm great," Anna lied, trying to will herself into a positive mind-set.

"Hey, did I mention the peeing thing?"

"What . . . thing?" Anna asked, refusing to blush. It wasn't easy, though. According to the *This Is How We Do Things* Big Book (East Coast WASP edition), the apocryphal bible by which she'd been raised, urination was not a bodily function to be discussed in polite company.

"Basically, don't pee in your wet suit," Danny explained. "Gives you a rash from hell. You won't be able to sit down for a week."

"Good to know," Anna replied gamely. But memories of the carafe of Jamaica Blue Mountain coffee she and Danny had shared at the 17th Street Café in Santa Monica three hours ago suddenly became a pressing issue. She willed herself to ignore them. When she'd moved from Manhattan's Upper East Side to Beverly Hills six weeks before, hoping for new adventures, a severe rash in unmentionable regions had not been one of them.

"I learned the hard way," Danny said with a grin. "Anyway, you ready to give it another go?"

Anna nodded with determination. Because that's just the kind of girl she was.

"Perfect. I'll be behind you. We'll pick the wave, I'll help turn your board, you'll paddle like hell, and I'll push you from behind. Then stand up. Hey, take this one!"

Anna saw a decent wave coming her way. Not too big, not too small. She swung her board around so the nose faced the beach and paddled as the wave swept toward her. Then she felt an extra surge as Danny shoved her board from behind.

"Get up!" he yelled.

Anna rose to her feet just like Danny had taught her on the beach—knees bent, left foot ahead, arms spread for balance—she was surfing!

For about a nanosecond.

Then she lost her balance, the board flipped out from under her, and she somersaulted headlong into the breaker.

"Woo-hoo!" shouted a guy on a surfboard who rode past her when she surfaced. "Nice wipeout!"

Humiliating. Even Anna knew it was time to pack it in. Five minutes later she and Danny floated in to shore.

"I think I missed getting the surfing gene," Anna despaired as they carried their boards up onto the beach.

"That's a good thing." Danny cut his eyes at her and smiled.

"Does that remark come with an explanation?"

"Let's just say that female perfection can be highly intimidating. This is our spot. Dig your board in here."

As they pushed the boards into the sand by their woven rattan beach mat, Anna noticed that two long-haired burnouts in crud-encrusted tie-dye shirts had plopped down on their spot without asking. But before Anna could say anything to them, they stood and scuttled away. She was about to tell them to go ahead and use the mats. But after Danny's crack about "female perfection," she was probably better off keeping her inner Mother Teresa . . . inner.

Danny closed his eyes and raised his face to the sun. "Man, I'm glad to be out of the office while it's still daylight."

"You might want some of this for your face." Anna handed him some Clarins 30 UV sunblock for his fair skin.

He nodded, squirted some into his hand, and spread it on his face. "You can't do this in New York in February, that's for sure. What's the temperature there right now?"

"Probably twenty-something."

"Perfect surfing weather. For polar bears."

Though it was a Saturday afternoon in February, here at Zuma the weather was perfection and the beach crowded. Up and down the sand, sun lovers frolicked with their dogs, tossed Frisbees, played volleyball, built sand castles, and picnicked. Out in the water, there were still dozens of surfers doing their thing. Anna had to agree: Except for her inability to get up on a surfboard, this was about as close to nirvana as real life could get.

Danny reached into the cooler he'd brought and plucked out two bottles of pear-apricot juice. He handed one to Anna. She opened it as she scanned the ocean. A girl surfer had just caught a humongous wave and was riding it with elegant perfection.

Anna cocked her head toward the girl. "What's she got that I haven't got?"

"Me?" Danny quipped.

Anna gave him a confused look.

"I mean not now. But in theory I could probably go chat her up, give her the old 'yeah, I write for a hit TV show' routine, and next thing you know, we're getting our freak on."

Anna playfully swatted his arm. "Very funny."

He shrugged. "Just want you to know what you're missing."

She laughed because he was joking. Sort of. She and Danny had formed a fast bond since they'd met at *Hermosa Beach.* They'd had some adventures and shared some kisses. She liked him a lot. But in the last few weeks, Anna had come to think that this was a time in her life when it would be best just to focus on herself. After her fling with Ben Birnbaum had flamed out, she didn't want to make things too complicated, too fast.

"We're *friends,* remember?"

He winced. "The F word—kiss of death." He took a long drink of his juice. "Would it help to mention how hot you look? A tall blonde in a wet suit? Can't beat it."

Then his gaze shifted to a gorgeous redhead who was carrying her board up from the surf line. She was poised and slender and wore a blue wet suit. Her thick red hair glistened in the afternoon sun. "Wow," Danny commented.

Anna knew that the tiny stab of jealousy she felt was utterly ridiculous. After all, she'd just reminded Danny that their relationship was strictly platonic. But men never ceased to amaze her. Danny could flirt with her one minute and "wow" after a complete stranger with great hair the next.

She smiled at him. "You're wasting your time, Danny. You're not her type."

"On the contrary," he replied, "I know her. But I never thought I'd see her here."

Oops. Anna did a mental rewind. Danny's "wow" had been a "wow" of recognition. She took a casual sip of her juice.

"How's that?"

Just then the girl noticed Danny and waved. Danny waved back.

"She lives in Santa Barbara. We hooked up at a party in Ojai last summer."

Anna watched the girl, trying to picture her with Danny. "You mean, just for one night?"

He nodded. "You shocked?"

Anna shook her head.

Danny laughed. "Yeah, you are. Because you are the last girl on the planet to go for a hit-and-run."

He took another slug of his drink and patted her hand. The gesture struck her as patronizing, even if what he'd said was true.

"I don't think casual sex is necessarily bad," she insisted.

Danny cocked an eyebrow at her. "Yeah, you do."

"No. I really don't."

"Really. Okay, then. Check out the beach." Danny

propped himself up on one elbow. "Point to a hypothetical one-night-stand candidate. Myself included."

"You're my friend; I already know you," Anna pointed out. "So by definition you don't qualify."

"Ever hear of friends with benefits?"

She frowned—he mimed sticking a dagger into his heart, then extracted it. "Just covering my bases. Anyway, it's better when you don't know the person too well. Out of town is primo." Anna took a moment to ruminate on the concept of sex for its own sake.

Danny just chuckled at her. "But don't worry about it, Anna. It's not everyone's style," he said as he pulled on his Ray-Bans and lay down on his mat.

Okay, maybe it hadn't been her style in the past. Back in New York, she hadn't even had the guts to flirt minimally with Scott Spencer—the object of her most intense crush. But that was then, this was now. And from a purely intellectual point of view, she had no problem with mutually consenting people having a mutually satisfying . . . whatever.

Fine. She'd accept Danny's challenge.

Anna stood with new resolve and scanned the crowded beach. Danny was right. There was no lack of local talent. A guy in a Dodgers baseball cap, with a golden six-pack that ended in red surfer jams, was playing catch with his German shepherd. Guys being maternal with their dogs were always a turn-on. Another guy—lean and cut, with multiple tattoos on his arms and a red bandanna—caught her eye as he jogged along the shoreline.

She pictured herself making idle chitchat with one of them and then heading off to . . . where? His car? His apartment? Surely a one-night stand didn't pony up for a night at Ma Maison Sofitel, did he? And the girl wouldn't be the one to pay for such a thing, would she? She was pretty sure this wasn't covered in the Big Book.

"Success?" Danny asked. He was leaning on his elbows, peering up at her.

"Him." Anna pointed to the jogger.

"You like tall guys."

She heard the regret of being five feet, eight inches in his voice and shook her head. "It's really more about the person, Danny. When you get to know someone and they interest you—"

"Ha!" He pointed at her.

She sat next to him again. "What's that mean?"

"You don't *want* to get to know a one-night stand, Anna. That's the whole point. Face it, you suck at this."

Anna sighed. Maybe she did. Maybe her aptitude for casual sex was right down there with her aptitude for surfing. Then she noticed the redhead from Danny's past parked on a green beach blanket a hundred feet away. She was chatting with two guys, both blond surfer types in black wet suits, and another pretty girl with short, jet-black hair and a maroon wet suit. Four longboards stuck into the sand cast shadows over them.

"What's her name?" Anna asked. "The redhead."

Danny shrugged and reached for another bottle of juice. "I forget."

She winced. "Ouch."

"Why 'ouch'?"

"I'm sure she'd like to think of herself as more memorable than that."

He shrugged again. "Trust me, Anna, some girls don't care. They're in it for the boo-tay just as much as the guy is."

Anna thought about that for a moment.

"So, did you regret it afterward? Sleeping with her?"

"Nope."

"It didn't feel sleazy? Empty? Meaningless?"

Danny wriggled his eyebrows. "That's the fun part."

"She told you that?"

"I'm just being honest. If both people know exactly what the expectations are—"

"Meaning, none?"

"Exactly. Then no one gets hurt. Want another juice?"

Anna shook her head and studied the redhead, trying to picture her with Danny. Had they danced, had a few drinks, flirted? Did they end up having sex in the wet sand, with the surf spraying their naked bodies?

God, how cheesy romance novel was *that*?

But maybe it had been different. Maybe they'd met at the Ojai getaway of Danny's television agent, shared a bottle of Dom Pérignon, and then attacked each other in the agent's overdone bedroom, with a mirror on the ceiling over the bed.

God, that was just as cheesy. But what if instead they'd talked intimately all night, driven back to

Danny's place in Santa Monica, and made love as the sun rose?

Made love. But it wasn't love. That was the whole point. Danny was right. She even sucked at *imagining* a one-night stand.

"Does my hollow and sordid sex life shock you?" Danny teased.

A little, Anna thought. Which was puzzling. She should have been used to it by now. Cynthia Baltres, her best friend back in New York, regaled Anna with her wild exploits and open-door policy with guys of all shapes, sizes, and sartorial leanings.

But she wasn't about to tell Danny that.

"Your sex life couldn't shock me, Danny. *Shocking* would be me actually getting up on a surfboard."

"Or you having a one-night stand," he shot back.

Maybe he was right. But it really annoyed her that he was so sure of himself.

The R Word

Back on New Year's Eve, the night Anna had first arrived at her father's Beverly Hills mansion, she'd walked in on him with his girlfriend, Margaret Cunningham.

Anna had rarely seen her father since her parents' divorce many years earlier. And she had certainly suffered through her mother's serial boyfriends—mostly young artists of the Eurotrash variety. But it had still been a jaw-dropper to see her father tangled up with a half-dressed woman she had never seen before. Anna had been so startled that she'd accidentally broken a priceless Ming vase.

Now, as Anna—still gritty from the beach—opened the front door lock of the mansion, a sight shocking enough to shatter the replacement vase, plus every other antique heirloom in the place, greeted her.

It was her father. Jonathan Percy. And her mother. Jane Cabot Percy. Together on the living room couch.

Thankfully, they weren't doing anything more than drinking martinis from crystal stemware and chuckling over some private joke. But not only were Anna's parents divorced, they also—at least as far as Anna knew up until this moment—didn't speak to each other. In fact, they hadn't been in the same room in approximately five years, and the last time they were had been at a Manhattan divorce judge's chambers, flanked by their batteries of high-priced lawyers.

After the divorce, her father had returned to Los Angeles, his birthplace. Anna and her older sister, Susan, had stayed in the Upper East Side Manhattan town house with their mother, end of story. Anna had last seen her mother seven weeks before, when Jane had gone to Florence to visit a twenty-eight-year-old Italian sculptor of whom she'd become a "patron." What that patronage entailed, Anna had never wanted to ask.

But here was her mother, the one and only. In Beverly Hills. In her ex's living room. Drinking martinis.

That part was familiar. So was her mother's patented Jane Cabot Percy outfit: a straight black vintage Chanel skirt that ended just below the knee, a three-ply gray cashmere sweater, and a pearl choker that she had inherited from an eighteenth-century ancestor. Her glossy blond hair was parted down the middle and fell just below her perfect jawline.

"Come in, Anna dear." Jane beckoned, as easily as if they'd had breakfast that morning. She offered Anna her cheek; Anna dutifully kissed it.

"What are you doing here, Mom?" Anna asked, trying to match her mother's even tone. "You're supposed to be in Italy."

"It's a surprise, sweetie," Jonathan explained. "Susan's being released from rehab today."

"She *is?*"

This was news to Anna. Her older sister wasn't supposed to get out of the world-famous Sierra Vista drug-and-alcohol rehabilitation facility in Arizona until next week. This was her second stint in rehab in as many months—Susan had come to Los Angeles in January after she'd checked herself out of the Hazelden rehab facility in Minnesota. It had only taken a few days before she'd reimmersed herself in her drugs and alcohol of choice, California style.

Finally, after Susan had done an inebriated near-naked dance in an outdoor fountain at a swank Hollywood industry party, Anna had persuaded her to try a different facility.

"Her doctor called yesterday," Jonathan continued. "He described your sister as 'a changed human being.' So I phoned Jane in Italy. She decided to fly in and share a family moment."

Family moment? They weren't a family, and they hadn't had a moment in years.

"The doctor suggested that having us present a united front might be helpful," Jane added. "According to your father, he almost insisted on it, which is really rather rude. But I only want what's best for Susan."

Anna was dubious. Susan and their mother did not get along, to say the least. Meanwhile, relations between Susan and her father ping-ponged between scratchy and disastrous.

"Are you sure this is the best thing?" Anna asked. "It might be kind of . . . intense."

"Nonsense," Jane decreed with divine assurance. "If my elder daughter is clean and sober, I call it a minor miracle I'd like to witness." She sipped her martini and frowned at Anna. "What have you been doing with your hair?"

Anna touched her head. Still wet from the ocean, she felt sand beneath her fingers. "I was at the beach. Surfing."

That got a trout-like rise out of her mother; a slight skyward movement of the eyes. "Surfing?"

"Yes, Mom," she replied. In the olden days—aka almost two months ago in New York—Anna would have wilted under her mother's thinly veiled disapproval. But she wasn't that girl anymore. "Actually, I love surfing. Want to go with me sometime?"

"Interesting," Jane murmured.

"Well, I'm going to take a shower. And get changed." Anna headed for the stairs. "What time do we have to be at LAX?"

"Her flight gets in at seven," Jonathan said.

"We'll leave at six," Jane decided, glancing at her Cartier watch. "Sharp. That's in fifty-seven minutes. I know you tend to run late. You'll be with us?"

"Of course."

Anna gritted her teeth as she headed upstairs to her room.

In her palatial marble bathroom, she turned on the

shower and peeled off her grungy clothes. No matter what Susan's shrinks had or hadn't said, Anna knew her sister better than they did: Sending her the Jonathan-and-Jane airport greeting committee was about as helpful to Susan's cause as handing her a Grey Goose and tonic.

Exactly fifty-six minutes later, hair in a ponytail, dressed in Seven jeans, a white Juicy Couture tank top, and a white terry hoodie, Anna returned to the living room. She expected—even hoped—that her new low-key West Coast–style clothes would irk her mother. Jane raised her eyebrows; silent Mother Percy–speak for disapproval. Mission accomplished.

Anna noticed that the crystal martini pitcher was now nearly empty. She doubted the most encouraging way for her parents to reunite with newly sober Susan was with Tanqueray gin and vermouth on their breath.

"Would you like coffee before we go?" Anna asked pointedly.

"You worry too much, Anna," her mother replied tersely. "You always have."

"Your sister has to live in a world where people drink socially," her father added, "even if she can't."

"We can do the drive-through Coffee Bean on the way if ya'll want," a voice drawled from just inside the front door.

Anna turned to see Django Simms, her father's driver and all-around assistant, standing at the hallway entrance to the living room. His short dark hair, tips bleached white-blond, set off perfectly chiseled features; his sexy baritone voice betrayed his southern roots. Django lived on her father's property in a guesthouse just behind the main house. Anna liked him. A lot. He was, in four words, a man of mystery.

She smiled at him. "Great idea."

"I told you, Anna, it's not necessary," her mother insisted. "But thank you, Django. That's a very gracious suggestion."

He tipped an imaginary hat to her—a signature gesture—and glanced at Jonathan. "I've got the Beamer waiting, sir." Then he opened the front door and ushered the family out. As Jonathan and Jane strode to Jonathan's car, he put a gentle hand on Anna's arm. "You turn into a surfer girl today, Miss Anna?" he asked playfully.

"I was terrible," she admitted. "Do you surf?"

"I've been known to catch a wave or two."

"Where'd you learn?"

He flashed an enigmatic smile. "Let's not keep your big sister waiting." He dropped his voice even lower. "Though I don't know that she'll be all that pleased with the greetin' party. "

It was a surprisingly perceptive remark, but Django always surprised her. Like when she'd heard him playing a magnificent concerto on the living room piano. Or when she'd discovered a photograph of him as a boy, wearing a tuxedo and standing by a Steinway grand piano in front of a full symphony orchestra. It was clear that he was the featured soloist at that concert. But Django wouldn't talk about the photograph. He barely talked about himself, ever. Which only made her want to know even more. Why was a guy that musically talented hiding out from the world in a Beverly Hills guesthouse?

Someday, she vowed to find out.

As Anna headed out the front door, she got another Django surprise. A stunningly beautiful woman with auburn hair floating around her shoulders and a model-type build stepped out of Django's guesthouse. She wore a very short black Yamamoto skirt and a velvet Louboutin blouse. Anna recognized the designers, having inherited from her mother an appreciation for exquisitely created clothes.

"Hey, Lisa," Django greeted her warmly. "Meet Anna Percy."

"Hi," Lisa said, barely registering a glance at Anna. "So Django, listen, I'll probably be gone by the time you get back."

"Cool. I'll call you."

"Great." She kissed him on the lips, then headed back to the guesthouse.

"Secret girlfriend?" Anna asked. She just couldn't help herself.

He cocked his head at her. "Just what are you getting at, Miss Anna?"

"Nothing," she answered quickly. "I just didn't know you had a . . . whatever she is."

"She isn't, actually," he said, being his usual enigmatic

self. "Except when she happens to be in town and calls me, and I happen to be footloose and fancy free."

"Oh."

Anna said "oh" because it seemed rude to say nothing but even more rude to pepper Django with questions that he obviously didn't want to answer. She'd never thought of Django's personal life. But the Lisa scenario made her think of her earlier conversation with Danny.

Danny and the redhead. Django and this woman. No mention by either of them of the L word. Or even the R word: *relationship.* Just a good time had by all.

Django held the car door open for Anna, and she slid in next to Jane with Jonathan on the other end. Then he shut the door and went around to the driver's side. As he pulled the car out of their massive circular driveway, Anna mused. Maybe everyone was running around having meaningless encounters except her. Maybe she'd be happier if she didn't try to find the magic she'd felt with Ben Birnbaum. Her first. A guy she'd fallen for in the matter of a six-hour flight from New York to L.A. A guy she'd ended up sending back to the East Coast, though he was more than willing to blow his entire Princeton education just to stay with her. Maybe in the end she really didn't understand anything at all about sex, or love, or how the two of them did or did not fit together.

The ride to the LAX was a Kafkaesque experience—more because of what her parents didn't do than what they did. Jonathan didn't ask about Jane's latest sculptor in Italy. Jane didn't ask about the state of Jonathan's love life in Beverly Hills. Instead they chatted in the backseat like old friends who hadn't seen each other in five years instead of a divorced couple who had parted badly. No, not badly. *Horrifically.*

Her mother even seemed to show interest when her father rambled about some upscale resort in Mexico. Apparently he was representing a syndicate of investors on the verge of acquiring it. Jane actually asked probing questions about the purchase. It struck Anna as hypocrisy of the worst kind, as the downfall of their marriage had been her mother's constant complaints about how work-obsessed he was.

Anna tried to tune them out by thinking about Susan. If only there were some way to prepare her sister for the welcoming committee. She had Susan's cell number, of course. But she'd have to call just after the plane landed, before Susan spotted the family trio; she'd also have to find a way to do it out of her parents'—

"Anna?" Jonathan asked, interrupting her thoughts. "Would you like to go along?"

Anna craned around toward her dad. "Go along where?"

"To this resort. I'm sending an associate next week to do a final inspection."

Anna was taken aback. "Why me?"

"I could use another set of eyes that I trust. Didn't you say you have Friday off for teacher conferences? It wouldn't hurt to miss a few days of school."

She was shocked that he remembered. Then she hesitated. Getting away from the Jonathan-and-Jane show would be a pleasure. But how could she possibly go to Mexico just when her sister had gotten out of rehab? Susan was going to need Anna's help to stay sane and sober, especially if both parents were within visual disapproval distance.

"I think I'll stick around and hang out with Susan. But thanks," she finally responded.

LAX was uncharacteristically empty. Django dropped them at the Delta terminal and went to park the car. They made it to the bottom of the arriving passengers' escalator near baggage claim just as the monitor announced that Susan's plane had landed.

Once again, her parents were chatting amiably in their bubble of blissful ignorance. The perfect time for Anna to steal away and call Susan's cell. Her sister didn't pick up. *Oh, well.* Susan would just have to see all three of them—two-thirds of whom were still loose from their afternoon martinis.

When Anna returned from the bathroom, she was met by a visibly stressed Jane. "Anna? Where could your sister possibly be?" Anna looked at her watch and was astonished to realize they'd been waiting for almost twenty minutes.

"Just be patient," Jonathan assured his ex-wife.

Jane shook her head. "No. She should be at that baggage claim already; that's the one for the flight from Tucson. Look at all those people." She pointed to the second Delta carousel. There were plenty of passengers gathered around it, and the last of their baggage was coming down the chute. "Jonathan, I don't think Susan was on that plane."

"That's impossible." He took a sheet of paper from his breast pocket and checked it. "Flight 345 from Tucson, Delta Air Lines. Today. That's her flight."

"Well, you obviously made an error, Jonathan."

"Why do you assume it's *my* error, Jane?"

Anna remembered how her parents always tacked on each other's names to sentences when they got irritated or anxious; she knew she had to step in before the bickering began to get out of control. "Let me go check at the Delta desk," she suggested. "Stay here in case she comes down."

Three minutes later, Anna was on the airport second level, near the ticket counters. She tried her sister's cell again. No answer. Damn.

"Can you check the passenger roster of Delta 345?" she asked the counter clerk, a jovial-looking Asian guy with short dark hair and glasses. "I'm waiting for Susan Cabot Percy. I'm her sister." She flashed her passport to establish her identity.

The clerk smiled broadly. "You look pretty safe." He typed something into his computer. "Yes, your sister boarded that flight in Tucson."

"Thanks." Anna exhaled with relief. "Can you page her, please? Tell her that her family—no, scratch that— her *sister* is waiting by the baggage claim?"

"Right away."

By the time Anna got off the elevator at the baggage claim level, she could hear the announcement for Susan over the airport public address system. It made her feel instantly better. There was undoubtedly a mix-up; her sister had probably forgotten her iPod on the plane and had to go back for it or something.

After ten more minutes, Django, who'd tired of circling the airport, parked the car and checked in for a progress report.

"It's none of my business," he drawled. "But I think we could go to the concourse and check on her."

"That's a good idea," Anna agreed. "Mom, Dad, stay here in case she comes down, okay? If she does, call my cell."

Thankfully, her parents didn't insist on coming along as Anna and Django went up to the security checkpoint on the main level.

"Where do we look?" Django asked once they were past the metal detectors.

"Everywhere, I guess." A knot of anxiety was forming in Anna's stomach as she surveyed the vast concourse. There were more than seventy gates, dozens of shops, and several restaurants. Susan could be in any of them. They fanned out and Anna checked the women's bathrooms, the Delta executive lounge, the food court, even—yes—the bars. No Susan. Her nervousness grew. Where was her sister? She strode through the rows of plastic seats at every gate at the far end of the concourse.

Nothing. She was about to ask a custodian to check the men's bathroom when her cell rang. She snatched it open.

Please let it be Susan.

"Hello?"

"It's Dad. Anything?"

"Zero."

"Zero back here too. I heard from Django. He's got nothing. Looks like your sister has done it again."

"Let's not jump to conclusions," Anna said, even though she'd already jumped pretty far into conclusion land herself. "She was on the plane. She's *got* to be here. I'll check everything one more time."

"Good luck," Jonathan replied. He had clearly given up.

Anna gave it one more halfhearted try. But she was merely postponing the inevitable. There was no escaping two truths: Susan had definitely boarded the plane. And now, she was definitely gone.

Ruby Hummingbird

Tired but also exhilarated, Samantha Sharpe trudged through the white oak double front doors of her father's palatial Bel Air estate, laden with packages from a Saturday afternoon shopping expedition to Fred Segal.

Over the past three weeks, a miracle had occurred. She'd actually gotten on the treadmill every single day and consumed nothing but soy shakes and raw veggies. It had resulted in a five-pound weight loss. She looked better, she really did. Sure, she was stuck with fat calves—thank you, maternal grandma dearest. (It was the cruelest fate: When it came to calves, genetics trumped liposuction.) But she'd battered herself down to a size ten in a town where a twelve was a felony. Once she got a fresh blow-out and new streaks at Raymond's, and maybe the caviar facial at Marabella's, she'd look . . . well, not quite beautiful. Even with all the effort she put into her appearance, she knew she'd never be beautiful. Maybe more in the vicinity of pear-shaped cute.

It would have been nice if someone in Sharpe world had noticed Sam's efforts. Fat—ha ha—chance. Sam's father, Jackson Sharpe, one of America's most beloved movie stars, didn't notice much beyond his own reflection. Sam would have to be hooked up to a feeding tube in a top-secret Four Seasons hotel suite next to an Olsen twin before her father would pay her any mind.

Well, screw him. Sam was psyched that she'd lost weight. When she'd awakened that morning and the scale reported that she'd dropped another pound, she'd decided to celebrate in the way that she knew best: spending money. Copious amounts of it.

Shopping was best accomplished as a group activity, so she tried to rally the troops. First she called Anna but only got voice mail. Then she tried her backup choice, Cammie Sheppard. Cammie had been Sam's best friend since kindergarten. But lately their relationship seemed to be cooling. Sam wasn't sure if this was due to her budding friendship with Anna or in spite of it. Either way, Cammie was out. She had plans with Adam Flood for the afternoon and evening. With the emphasis that Cammie had placed on the word *plans,* Sam assumed said plans involved La Perla lingerie and a canopied bed.

Adam and Cammie. Talk about your unlikely couples. Adam was part of a rare species: the truly good guys. It wasn't very long ago that he had kissed her, Sam, at her impromptu New Year's Eve party. Then he and Anna had had a thing that had lasted about a millisecond. And *then* gorgeous Cammie, the cold-hearted vixen—a label Sam held in high esteem—had gone after Adam. What Cammie wanted, Cammie got. Sam just hoped she wouldn't use him and then throw him out like last year's Sergio Rossi green alligator pumps.

With Anna and Cammie off the list, Sam dialed Dee Young. Dee, the third member of the Cammie, Sam, Dee triumvirate, was always good for a shopping expedition, even though her burgeoning New Age woo-woo spaciness tended to drive Sam nuts. But Dee's housekeeper said that Dee was at the Kabbalah Center for a special lecture by a visiting scholar from Israel. Maybe Sam would want to meet her there?

Uh, *no*. Sam had zero interest in Jewish mysticism. So she went solo to Fred Segal, where she purchased three cropped and fitted Christian Lacroix jackets that would look cute with jeans, a Tracy Reese wrap skirt that hid her hips, and a pair of red leather Valentino boot-cut pants. Since she needed new footwear to go with the red leather pants, she picked up some Via Spiga brown suede boots and a lethal-looking pair of black studded leather Armani heels fit for a dominatrix.

Sam rushed home to try on all her new clothes. As she padded through the endless white marble foyer lined with black marble pedestals holding her father's various movie awards, she heard faraway laughter coming from the massive, rarely used living room. Rousing ancient Jewish klezmer music wafted from the in-home sound system. She dumped her bags and boxes at the bottom of the spiral staircase to go see who was having fun without her . . . to such a bizarre sound track.

In the white-on-white living room, she found her very pregnant, twenty-one-year-old stepmother, Poppy Sinclair Sharpe, on the white leather couch with her friend Dee Young. Weird. Poppy and Dee didn't really know each other beyond a hello/goodbye/Sam's upstairs kind of thing.

But here was diminutive Dee, baby face and blue eyes shining, sitting in the lotus position. Dark-haired Poppy was doing a half lotus, barely manageable due to her very pregnant belly. They were both giggling like twelve-year-olds.

"Hi, Sam!" Dee sang out when she saw her friend. "I've been trying to help Poppy into position. But Ruby Hummingbird keeps getting in the way."

Ruby Hummingbird was the name Poppy had selected for the soon-to-be-born bundle of joy, after much consultation with a spiritualist-numerologist in Topanga Canyon. Sam found the name very affected but knew the kid would fit in fine in a town where girls were named Rumer, Coco, and Apple.

"You know, Poppy, I don't think crushing the baby because you want to get into a yoga position is necessarily a good idea," Sam said.

Poppy popped out of her lotus. "Sam, that's a mean thing to say."

"It was a joke, Poppy. Remember humor?" Sam looked at Dee. "So. You came over, Poppy let you in, and you're waiting for me?"

"Nope," Dee said. "Poppy invited me over."

Poppy invited her? Why would her dimmer-than-a-burned-out bulb of a stepmother do that?

"And how did this come about?"

"Well, I was at the Kabbalah Center for a lecture after Shabbat services." Dee unhooked her legs. "A really famous rabbi from Safed, Israel. I want to go there this summer; it's, like, so mystical and everything. Anyway, he was fantastic, and I don't even speak Hebrew. He was talking about the different names of God, and that's when I realized that God isn't really God's name at all."

"It's amazing," Poppy chimed in. "Because I realized the exact same thing."

They shared a look of profundity, and Sam tried to keep down her two slices of ahi. "Wow," she deadpanned.

"I know," Dee agreed. "Anyway, I turned to my left, and guess who was just three seats away from me? Poppy! So after the Havdalah service, we got to talking. And Poppy said—"

"I said that I finally understood how we're all the fusion of the spirit and the physical," Poppy took over. "Even you, Sam. Because God made us from of the dust of the earth. Isn't that just so *immense*?"

"Oh yeah. Rocks my world."

Sam was vaguely up to speed about Kabbalah—the study of Jewish mysticism that involved parsing hidden meanings out of sacred Jewish texts. She recalled something she'd read by the philosopher Elie Wiesel that discussed Kabbalah. He'd said Kabbalah should never be studied by young people—that age, maturity, and wisdom were required to plumb the depths of its secrets.

None of which applied to either Poppy or Dee.

"Elie Wiesel says that too many people take Kabbalah too lightly," Sam told them.

"Who's he?" Dee asked.

"A fashion designer," Sam deadpanned.

Dee scrunched up her precious little face. "What would a fashion designer know about—?"

"He's a writer," Poppy interjected. "I'm not stupid, Sam. Jackson met him at a Federation dinner."

Dee folded her arms. "You know, Sam, a little more spirituality in your life might make you less hostile."

"I totally agree," Poppy said. Then a look of pleased surprise came over her face. "Oh my God! The baby just kicked. Come feel."

Instinctually Sam went to her young stepmother, truly excited to feel the baby in motion. But before she could take two steps, Dee had slid over on the couch and placed her hand on Poppy's enormous belly.

"Whoa," Dee marveled. "That's amazing."

For the next few moments Dee and Poppy were in their own private world of the baby in the womb. It was like Sam didn't exist. They started talking about Poppy's upcoming baby shower and whether or not Poppy should hire Yanni to play piano. Poppy was concerned that Yanni would be the only male at the shower.

But Dee related that she'd read an article on the Internet about how unborn babies appreciated music right through the amniotic fluid, which sealed the deal for Poppy.

"I don't know what I'd do without you." Poppy put a hand atop Dee's. "I'm so glad we were both at that lecture."

Dee beamed. "I'll do whatever I can to help you with the shower. My parents are going to New York for the week, so I'll have plenty of time."

"Oh, wow, do you want to stay here?" Poppy asked eagerly. "There's plenty of room."

To Sam's relief, Dee shook her head. "I'm fine at home. But I'll come over all the time, I promise."

"Well, if . . . hey! Ruby kicked again!" Poppy exclaimed. "Come touch, Sam. Put your hand on top of mine and Dee's."

Sam shook her head; it was a bit too late for Poppy to get all-inclusive. Honestly, Poppy and Dee deserved each other. They were two of a kind. This month they'd bond over a Chassidic rabbi from Israel and a baby shower. Next month it would be Bikram yoga and a birthing pool. The month after that, it would be something else. Whatever the latest celebrity trend, they'd latch onto it, even if that trend changed as often as Nick Lachey's Q rating.

But Sam had known Dee a long time. She'd largely come to terms with Dee's quirks. Dee might be wacky, but she was loyal. In this town—the village inside Los Angeles that the world thought of as glamorous

Beverly Hills but which Sam knew was a treacherous pit of fame-hungry vipers—loyalty counted for a lot. A hell of a lot. When push came to shove, when you had to fit your size-eight foot into your size-seven Manolo Blahniks, she knew she could count on Dee.

Probably.

Quite Possibly a Virgin

Cammie Sheppard was in love. Which just sucked so hard.

In Cammie's opinion, everything about love sucked, unless she was the object of someone else's unrequited affections, in which case love could be mildly amusing. But to be the one in love? It gave Cammie an anxious, itchy feeling, like trying on a sweater at Target. At least with a Target sweater you could laugh at how ridiculous it was and take it off. But the jones she felt for Adam Flood was something she just couldn't seem to control. When she allowed herself to think about it, she had to call it what it was.

Love. Shit.

Standing on the crowded dining deck of Geoffrey's restaurant in Malibu, overlooking the jagged cliffs and the broad, white sand beach below, not to mention a glorious Pacific sunset off in the distance, Cammie ruminated on how she'd sunk to this sorry state. Here she was, at a Saturday night movie wrap party given by her father in honor of his client Kyle Raye, a hot young rock-'n'-roll star who'd just finished *Taster's Choice*, with Mandy Moore and Beyoncé. There were gorgeous guys everywhere, all clad in some variation of hip. With her looks, body, and pedigree, Cammie knew she could get any of them. But she only had eyes for this high school boy who was quite possibly a virgin—a status Cammie hadn't had even a winking acquaintance with since she was fifteen.

Love with a virgin. Double shit.

Adam Flood. He'd been in Beverly Hills for two years, having moved from Ann Arbor, Michigan, with his parents. More an alt type than a club kid, he played basketball on the school team and had a huge CD collection that he'd burned himself. He had a reputation for being one of the nicest guys at Beverly Hills High School. But Cammie never went for nice. That is, until several weeks ago, when she'd started to feel this *thing* for him. He was just so genuine. And he seemed to bring the extremely underdeveloped, very latent niceness out in her. They'd been hanging out since they'd shared a kiss on the beach at an after-game party. But it hadn't gotten any further since then.

"Here you go." Adam edged through the boisterous crowd, sidled up next to her, and handed her a Coke. Cammie could bet there was no rum in it, because Adam didn't have a fake ID. Nor was Adam the type of guy to slip a bartender a few twenties to get him to overlook the fact that he was seventeen. He was far too honest for that. In another guy, Cammie would have found such rectitude ridiculous. In Adam, she found it incredibly attractive.

Triple shit.

He offered Cammie her fitted white Italian leather DeMarco jacket. "I got this from coat check," he explained. "I figured it might get chilly."

"Very thoughtful," Cammie said. She meant it. With the sun going down, the temperature would drop quickly, so she slung the jacket over her arm.

Adam gazed out at the horizon. "Fantastic sunset, huh?"

Cammie nodded and turned to study his strong profile. The fading light of day brought out the orange highlights in his brown hair. She could see the tiny star tattoo behind his ear and fantasized about running her tongue around the edges. Then she decided it might freak him out. So she demurely sipped her Coke instead.

"Hungry? I can get you something from the buffet. It's killer."

Cammie shook her head. "I already ate."

That much was true. Breakfast. She'd skipped lunch because when she'd gotten on the digital scale after her early morning workout at the Century City Sports Club, she hadn't been happy with the last digit. The one that came after the decimal point. Cammie was used to looking perfect, and she wasn't about to settle for anything less.

The question, though, was did Adam think she looked perfect? She knew they had chemistry; she could feel the sexual tension. But Adam wasn't acting on it. And it was driving her crazy.

"I had some seafood gazpacho. Awesome." He patted his taut stomach.

"Glad to hear it." She wondered what it would be like to run her fingernails up and down those abs. Right here on the deck at Geoffrey's.

He put both elbows on the railing that separated them from the long drop to the beach below and scratched his chin. "Something bothering you, Cam?"

Yes. Every guy drools after me but you.

"No." She shook her strawberry blond curls off her face. To her right, she caught a glimpse of an actor from *Hermosa Beach.* He was eyeing her with obvious interest. But she couldn't care less. All her attention was on Adam. "Why?"

He shrugged. "You don't seem like yourself."

Cammie did a rapid-fire mental inventory of the reasons why she should seem exactly like herself. Last time she checked, she had fantastic reddish blond curls cascading down her back and a fantastic body with the best breasts money could buy. She was easily the hottest girl at Beverly Hills High School, an institution that overflowed with hot girls. And she had one of the most feared fathers in Hollywood—Clark Sheppard, a powerful entertainment agent at Apex.

She also had the trendiest clothes by the hottest designers. Tonight she was wearing an Alexander McQueen black chiffon wrap dress with a black ribbon tie at the waist. By next week, some suck-up starlet wannabe like Lindsay Lohan would be photographed in the exact same dress. America might ooh and ahh at the pictures in *Us* and *Star,* but real insiders would know that Cammie had worn it before it was even available in stores. And that it looked a lot better on her, too.

She could get any guy she wanted, anywhere, anyplace, anytime. So why the hell did she have to want *this* guy?

"Something *is* on your mind, Cammie." Adam's soft voice interrupted her thoughts.

"Maybe." She cleared her throat and tried to sound nonchalant. "Tell me . . . have you ever been in love?"

She immediately wanted to bitch-slap herself for sounding so needy. Cammie Sheppard didn't *do* needy.

He scratched the stubble on his chin again. "Maybe. You?"

"I don't know. I wonder—if there was no such thing as love, would they have to invent it for the movies?"

Adam grinned; Cammie felt pleased that she'd been able to divert the conversation away from such dangerous turf as her feelings. She took a long sip of her Coke, pushed more curls off her face, and edged closer to the railing. The deck was getting crowded—a DJ had started spinning records, and the beautiful people were drifting outside to dance. Standing gas lamps had been fired up so that the temperature stayed comfortable, and tuxedo-clad waiters circulated around the deck offering snifters of brandy and Belgian dessert beer. Meanwhile, laser light beams danced against the side of the restaurant and over the crowd on the deck.

"I definitely believe in love," Adam mused aloud,

raising his voice over the pounding music. "I mean, take my parents. They're still in love."

Cammie raised her eyebrows dubiously. "Please. Next you're going to tell me they've never cheated on each other."

"Well, it's not like they'd tell me. But if you love someone, really love them, why would you ever do something like that?"

Cammie could see that Adam meant what he said. His innocence was so un–Los Angeles that it touched her. "You really need to move out of Beverly Hills."

"Oh yeah? Why?"

"Because if you stay too long, you'll become as jaded as the rest of us."

A gust of sea breeze washed over them; Adam gently pushed some hair from Cammie's cheek. "You're full of it."

"Which means?"

"Which means you want to believe in love just as much as I do."

He was right, of course. But Cammie couldn't decide if that was good or scary.

"How do you know?" she asked him.

He draped an arm around her. "You're here with me, aren't you?"

True. It was all true. It was like he saw past all her bullshit. Cammie didn't know how, but he managed it. Once again, she realized she had to change the subject.

"Here's the star of tonight's show," Cammie announced.

Kyle had just stepped onto the patio. He waved to Cammie, then beckoned to her in a way that asked whether she wanted to dance. Cammie shook her head and leaned into Adam.

"I feel I should point out that you just turned down a guy who's going to be really famous in about four months," Adam said.

"I feel I should point out that he's got nothing on you."

He tilted her chin up to him. "How many people know you, Cam? I mean, really know you?"

"One-half," she whispered. "You half-know me."

He held her closer. "The other half of me is still in the learning curve."

Amazing. He even got that.

Another gust of wind blew some of Cammie's curls dangerously close to her MAC lip gloss. "That's sweet."

Adam laughed. "Did the word *sweet* just pass Cammie Sheppard's lips without sarcasm attached?"

"Funny." She gave Adam a friendly punch. Just then, a jocular voice sounded behind her.

"Cammie, my dear."

She turned to see her father, Clark Sheppard. He looked tanned and rested, and though he was dressed far more formally than anyone else at the party—an impeccable hand-tailored-in-Hong-Kong jacket with a white Yves Saint Laurent shirt underneath and a maroon and silver tie—he still looked cool and relaxed. Which made sense. The movie was still months away from being released. There were no box-office numbers yet to deal with, no pirated editions of *Taster's Choice* available on the Internet, no crooked distributors in Malaysia who weren't paying for their prints, no critics with vendettas ready to rip his client a new sphincter.

"Hi, Dad," Cammie replied, on her best behavior in front of Adam. "Great party. Thanks for having us."

"Sure."

Cammie could see that her father's eyes were already flicking over the crowd of dancers like a hyperactive metronome—to see if there was someone more important than Cammie who he should be talking with.

"I bought a pound of cocaine in Echo Park today," Cammie said, her tone conversational, just to see if her father was listening.

His eyes went back to her. "Very funny. Just remember where you got your sense of humor," Clark quipped. His eyes rested on Adam for a moment. "So who's the date?"

"Adam Flood, sir." Adam extended his hand. "I go to school with Cammie."

"Nice. And will you be graduating this—hold on." Clark's eyes bounced twenty feet past Adam's right shoulder. "There's Quentin. Shit. I've gotta talk to him about Kyle's next movie. I'll check back with you. Nice meeting you, Alan." Clark moved off and within ten seconds had his arm around the slouched shoulders of one of the hottest directors in Hollywood.

Cammie grimaced. "Sorry about my dad, *Alan*."

"Yeah. He's kind of lacking in the listening department.

If he ever paid attention to what you had to say, he might just learn something."

God. Adam was just so . . . so everything. The more time she spent with him, the harder she fell for him.

"I've got an idea," she whispered, leaning toward his chin. "Let's get out of here."

She crooked her elbow, and Adam took it. Together they headed for the weather-beaten wooden staircase that led from the Geoffrey's dining platform down the rocky cliff to the Malibu beach below. As they descended the staircase, the raucous sounds of the party faded almost to nothingness; ochre light from the rising moon illuminated the beach.

They walked north a few hundred yards or so until the music from the deck became a whisper that merged with the slap-slap of the waves on the sand.

That was when Cammie slid her arms around Adam's neck. "Kiss me," she murmured.

He did. Softly at first, but the kisses quickly heated into the torrid zone. Cammie tugged off his well-worn Levi's jean jacket, placed it on the sand, and then sank down on it. So did Adam—he ended up half atop her, kissing her neck. She let her hand drift under his black cotton T-shirt and up his buff chest, then over his tight six-pack like she'd imagined just a few minutes before. With an easy and practiced flick of her fingers, the top button of his 501s was open.

He pulled back a moment so that he could look into her eyes. "You sure?"

"Yeah," she whispered.

This was it. Her and Adam. The call of the sand, the moon, and the wild. She lifted her dress and touched the top of her white lace thong. If he wasn't a virgin, he'd never want anyone else. If he was a virgin, he wouldn't even *think* of anyone else. No matter what, she'd be the one calling the shots. She would make him so insane with lust that—

Suddenly Adam rolled off her and buried his head in his hands. "Shit," he muttered.

Cammie quickly sat up, thong still slightly askew. "Meaning?"

Her heart was pounding, her mind racing. What was it? Why didn't he want her right now? What had she done wrong?

He fumbled with his jeans and re-buttoned them. "I'm sorry, Cammie. I know I sound like a character in some lame chick flick, but this is moving a little too fast for me."

"You mean . . . you don't *want* to?"

"God, yes." He reached for her neck and caressed it with his thumb. "I'm totally into this, Cam."

Cammie exhaled. "Good. So let's roll back thirty seconds and—"

"I don't know if I can. . . . I mean, we're at a party. On a public beach. Anyone could see us."

Ah. Now she got it. It was cute, in a way, how he was so worried about being caught.

"Trust me. That's part of the fun." She gave him a

lingering kiss on his cheekbone. And then headed for his neck. But he pulled slightly away.

"Uh . . . Cammie? My body doesn't agree with that opinion."

Okay. Fair enough. It was the right time, but not the right place. She could deal with that. As long as she knew he wanted her.

"It's not important. We've got all the time in the world," she whispered, giving him another kiss.

Then he wrapped her leather jacket around her slender shoulders and held her as they listened to the gentle waves. It felt good, both to be in his arms and to understand what was going on. Adam was an intimidated probable virgin. But now it didn't faze her, because she knew exactly how the story would end.

An Icy Martini

"I'm sure Susan will get in touch with us eventually," Anna told her parents. Not because she believed it, but because she thought it was what they needed to hear.

"It's Susan," her father cautioned. "You can't be sure about anything with her."

All the way back home in the car, they tried everything they could to figure out where Susan could be. Called Sierra Vista. Called Delta. Even called the Beverly Hills Hotel, where Susan had taken a bungalow on her last visit to Los Angeles. Anna had tried her cell again numerous times. Nothing. It was like Susan had disappeared into thin air.

In a way, Anna found it upsetting. In another way, it was just . . . Susan, who never did things the normal way and had taken the fast route to the bottom of the slippery slope so many times. But she always managed to land on her feet. More or less. Anna was reasonably confident that this was just going to be another one of those bizarre Susan Percy episodes.

Now they were once again in the living room of her father's mansion, two hours after they'd left LAX. The martini pitcher had been refilled—one of the maids must have done it—but no one was drinking.

Jonathan drummed his fingers on his thigh. "Maybe we should try the police."

"And report what?" Jane asked in a low voice. Anna knew that the decibel level of her mother's voice dropped in direct proportion to her level of unhappiness. And when she started picking invisible lint off her skirt—like she was now doing—it meant that Jane Percy was on the verge of fury. "That our adult daughter didn't meet us at the airport when she was supposed to? That she didn't have the common decency to inform us of her alternate plans? Jonathan, I'm ready for a cocktail."

As Jonathan poured an icy martini into his ex-wife's glass, Anna closed her eyes for a moment and recalled what it used to be like in the Percys' town house on the east side of Manhattan, back in the long ago days before her parents had divorced. It had been a sort of Upper East Side WASP version of *Who's Afraid of Virginia Woolf?* Her parents had all the drinking, the bickering, the loathing. But unlike the characters in the Albee play, they never yelled. Anna had learned well that a whisper could cut more sharply than a knife.

By the time Anna reached middle school, Jonathan and Jane had reached what they called "a civilized arrangement"—they'd spend most of their time apart and come together when social niceties required that they be a presentable couple. This had worked for a year or so. After that, they headed straight for divorce court.

It all made Anna wonder about the idea of one man, one woman, forever. Was marriage just another kind of peculiar institution? Maybe it was impossible to expect to love someone forever. Just because Jane Austen and Tolstoy and the Brontë sisters waxed poetic about eternal love didn't mean that such love really existed; it just meant that they were excellent writers. Unfortunately, literature was not life. Right?

Jane sipped her martini and sighed. "Evidently, our elder daughter will never take responsibility for her own life."

"We should find out what happened before we—" Anna was interrupted by the chime of her cell phone. She took it from her jeans pocket. "Hello?"

"Don't freak, Anna, it's me."

"Susan!" Anna saw her mother sit forward on red alert while her dad sagged back on the couch in relief.

"Where *are* you?" Anna asked her sister. "We came to meet you at the airport. You weren't there!"

"I'm on another plane. Using the air phone."

"You're *what?*"

"On my way to Albany."

"Albany, *New York?*" Anna asked.

"No. Albany, Georgia," Susan snapped. "Of course Albany, New York. I got off the plane in L.A. and got on a different flight twenty minutes later."

Anna was completely bewildered. "Why?"

"Because fucking Dad *and* Mom are with you, that's why," Susan declared. "I just couldn't do it, Anna. Don't be mad at me. I'm trying to protect myself."

"Hold on a sec," Anna told her, and put a finger over the mouthpiece of her cell. "She's on a plane. She's going to Albany, New York. Mom? She knows you're here. Somehow."

Jonathan looked sheepish. "I told her doctor I'd get Jane to fly in—it was his suggestion, after all."

"Your sister has still not dealt with her issues," Jane stated. "Don't let her blame it on the rest of us."

Anna exhaled slowly. No wonder Susan had changed destinations. Then she spoke into the phone again. "Sooz? Why Albany? There's nothing up there."

"I'm going to the Berkshires. I'll rent a car and drive across."

"What's in the Berkshires?"

"The Kripalu Yoga Institute."

Anna knew the place she was talking about. It was a yoga retreat perched on a hillside above the Stockbridge Bowl, directly across from the Tanglewood concert grounds. Kripalu catered to spiritually minded visitors.

On the hierarchy of places where Susan could have been headed after rehab, with a crack den in Philadelphia at the bottom and her grungy apartment on New York's Lower East Side someplace in the middle, Anna thought Kripalu was actually not a bad option. At least they weren't selling glassine bags of smack on the nearest street corner. If only Susan had chosen to announce her destination in a somewhat more conventional fashion.

"That's nice," Anna said guardedly. "How long do you plan to stay there?"

"Forever, maybe. I got a job. Working in their kitchen."

Anna had to let that one sink in. Her sister had a lot of interests, but yoga and Eastern religion had never been among them. Nor was she a particularly spiritual person, except when it came to distilled alcohol. Plus Susan had an eight-digit trust fund. She didn't need to work, period.

"This guy Raji I met at SV turned me on to it," Susan continued. "He said it's the perfect place to be after SV. He was a cook there."

"You don't know how to cook."

"So I'll peel a few potatoes or something. I was going to go there after L.A. anyway. I'm just moving up the timetable. And don't worry. I'm alone. Raji went home to Bombay."

"I wish you'd have stopped here first," Anna said. "To let us know. At least at the airport."

"I just couldn't, okay? Dad triggers me. Mom triggers me. Mom and Dad together, it's like stepping in front of a machine gun with a fucking target on my chest."

"Uh-huh," Anna replied, just to keep her sister talking while her parents looked at her pleadingly. They were desperate for some information. But Anna stayed focused on Susan.

"Anyway, Raji says Kripalu totally changed his life."

"Then why was he in rehab?" Anna asked.

"Hey, chill on the judgments, Anna," Susan admonished. Then her voice softened. "People like Raji, like me . . . there's this thing inside us that we've got to fight our whole lives. Sometimes we don't win that fight."

"I understand."

Anna didn't, really, but God knows she was trying.

"Understand what?" Jane asked impatiently. She held out a slender arm. "Give me the phone, Anna."

Anna shook her head at her mother. "You do what you have to do, Sooz."

"I can think up there, Anna. I think. I hope." Susan laughed nervously. "Hey, listen, do me a favor? Can you explain to Mom—?"

"You should talk to her, Sooz. She came all the way from Italy."

"Forget it!" Then Susan softened. "Later. I promise, Anna. Tell her that. I'll call you in a week or so, okay? And them, too."

"Okay. I guess."

"Love you, baby sis."

"Love you, too." Anna clicked off, turning to her parents. "She said she promises to call you guys in a week."

Her mother rubbed her temples with elegant French-manicured fingers and sighed. "Her promises are meaningless, Anna. Surely you know that by now."

"If that's how you feel, then why did you bother to come?" Anna asked her. Defending her big sister was habit. Anna had always been the dependable one, Susan the flake. But even at her flakiest, Anna still loved her.

Jane's chin jutted upward. "I was willing to give her another chance. Are you going to fault me for that, Anna?"

"No," Anna replied, chastised.

Jonathan patted his ex-wife's arm. "I'm glad you're here, Jane. Why don't we just give Susan a little time to sort things out?"

"Sure. Why not?" Jane asked rhetorically. But Anna could see that she wasn't at all convinced.

Tired from the surfing and the drama, Anna dozed off on her bed. Her cell rang a couple of times; she tried to ignore it. But when she couldn't get back to sleep after the second time, she decided to check her messages.

The first one made her snap wide awake.

"Anna, hey. It's Ben."

Ben. His voice always managed to hit her somewhere south of her navel. She'd been glad when he'd returned to Princeton. But hearing him now gave her instant second thoughts.

"So, I'm calling from Princeton. I waited, you know, a long time to call. But I think about you. A lot. You were right, though. About school. It was a good idea for me to come back. I was all fucked up, I know. Too much pressure, maybe. The whole thing with my dad and all.

"Anyway, I just wanted to let you know I haven't forgotten about you. If you come back east, let me know. And if I come home for spring break—I don't know, I might go skiing at Jackson Hole. Maybe you'd want to come. We could be together away from all the insanity, you know? So . . . that's it. I'm still thinking about you."

His voice still made her heart pound. Maybe she and Ben were star-crossed lovers, like Anna and Vronsky in one of her favorite novels, *Anna Karenina*. That story didn't end very well—her namesake fell head over heels for the Russian count but was much more in love with him than he was in love with her. In the end, she died under the wheels of a train barreling down the tracks. If that wasn't a Freudian notion, what was?

Ben. Their lust on an airplane had quickly turned into . . . so much more. But it couldn't be love, could it? Wasn't love something that happened over time when you really got to know the other person? Everything with Ben had been so tumultuous and had happened so quickly. Maybe they were a fire destined to burn each other out, intense lust masquerading as more.

Honestly, Anna didn't know.

Ari Something-or-Other

"What is this place?" Cammie asked as Adam led her into the open-air square that was teeming with people. "And what smells so good?"

"Watch and learn," Adam told her with a grin. "You wanted to eat, right?"

"Yeah. But I was thinking the Beverly Hills Hotel." Cammie looked around the crowded plaza, which Adam had told her was the Buddhist temple complex of North Hollywood. There were many Asians and hippie-looking American kids who probably professed to believe in the principles of the Buddha. But the crowd was by and large eclectic. The plaza had a few redwood and metal tables, but most folks had set up picnic blankets in the shade of the big eucalyptus trees nearby.

"Think outside the box, Cam," Adam told her as he led her to a money-changing booth, where people were lined up to exchange their American dollars for the plastic chips that were apparently the sole approved currency at the venue. An old man with craggy skin and

an impossibly long last name on his name tag super-
vised the operation.

Cammie looked ashen. "Don't worry," Adam said,
tapping his daypack. "I'm completely prepared. You'll
dine like a princess."

*A princess who dines at a place like this must have had
her kingdom overthrown*, Cammie thought. But she
didn't say it. Because, God help her, she wanted Adam
to like her. More than like her.

When they'd parted the night before, Adam had
suggested they meet for Sunday brunch; a good sign.
He couldn't be too upset or embarrassed about their
little incident in the sand if he wanted to be with her
the very next day, right? Cammie had suggested a couple of possible restaurants, the Beverly Hills Hotel at
the top of her list, with Encounter (located in an ultra-
modern structure above LAX, it had an amazing view of
arriving and departing jetliners) being a close second.

But Adam had insisted on surprising her, promising
that it would be well worth it. So he'd brought her to
the Wat Thai Theraveda Buddhist temple in North
Hollywood. He explained how, during the week, this
temple complex served much of Los Angeles' sizable
Thai community. But on weekends, it was transformed
into an oversized outdoor food court, with a good per-
centage of all sales going to the upkeep of the temple.
Adam was no Buddhist, but he'd come here with his
parents a few times and loved it.

Cammie was actually impressed. Not because she

was about to dine in some multicultural mosh pit, but because he hadn't been too embarrassed to admit that he'd eaten here with his parents. She entwined her fingers with his as they waited to change their money.

As for the nonevent on the beach, she had no doubt that he'd be ready for a rematch at the soonest possible moment. Every guy Cammie had met since eighth grade wanted to get his hands on her. Adam might be a great guy, but he was still a guy.

"I don't know anyone else in Los Angeles who would have brought me here," she told him.

"Yeah, I'm up for anything," Adam joked. "That is, if we don't count last night."

Cammie shrugged. "Already forgotten," she lied.

He grinned at her. "If at first you don't succeed . . ."

She stood on tiptoe to kiss him. "My sentiments exactly."

Ten minutes later, armed with the plastic money chips, they'd visited several of the open-air food vendors arrayed around the plaza and loaded up on pad Thai, meat satays, papaya salad, and sweet pancake rolls. By the time they found some unoccupied space on the grass under a huge eucalyptus tree, Cammie's mouth was literally watering at the luscious aroma from the food. Meanwhile, Adam extracted a thin ground cloth from his backpack, along with linen napkins, silverware, and two small thermos bottles.

"The fair lady said something about a mimosa?" he asked, offering Cammie one of the thermoses.

"You're kidding. You mixed mimosas?"

"I'm a guy of many talents."

Cammie bit into a forkful of pad Thai. "Delicious. But I don't get it. You moved here last year from Michigan, I've lived in L.A. my entire life. Why didn't I know about this place?"

"Umm . . . because there are no waiters and no valet parking?" Adam quipped.

"That must be it." She leaned over to kiss him. What started out as a peck turned into the real, pad Thai–flavored thing. "Yum."

They ate for a while, watching the passing parade. When Cammie recognized two cast members from *Saturday Night Live* with an Endeavor agent named Ari Something-or-other who had once threatened to put out a hit on her father, she knew this had to be an actual Hollywood insiders' hot spot. Eventually she put her food aside half eaten; there were only so many calories she was willing to ingest while the sun was still up.

"So, what would you like to do *now*?" she asked, keeping her tone low and suggestive, though there was a definite answer she was looking for. From their spot under the tree, she could see the tops of both the Universal City Hilton (decent, though it catered to too many tourists) and the Universal City Sheraton (somewhat less nice, but hey, for what she had in mind, they wouldn't be spending a lot of time in the lobby). It was a Sunday; people checked out early to catch their planes, so there would certainly be a suite available.

Adam took way too long to answer. "I don't know how to ask you this," he began, "but . . ."

"Ask," Cammie commanded. She could already picture them inside a suite, already imagine the look on his face when he realized he'd just lucked into the sexiest girl on the planet.

"I do some work for Habitat for Humanity," Adam went on. "They're building houses for two homeless families on this vacant lot in South Central. How 'bout we go down and help out? I've got a few hours before I'm supposed to run hoops down in Venice with some guys from the team."

A house? He had a few hours, and he wanted her to help build a *house?* Was there something wrong with him? Maybe he was gay. No. Couldn't be. Cammie's gaydar was better than that. Her friend Dee was the one who hooked up with gay guys. What could the problem possibly be? Her? What if it *was* her? What if he'd decided that she wasn't a charitable enough human being or some such shit? Well, she would change, if that was what it would take to get this guy to want her.

Pushing aside thoughts of what hell would be wrought upon her French manicure, Cammie smiled and did her best to look enthusiastic. There was something touching about a guy sincere enough to believe that pounding nails in the hot sun would save the whales, the redwoods, Tibet, and the universe. She kissed him again and told the second lie of the day.

"I'd love to."

Had Kabbalah Reprogrammed Her Neurons?

S am was confused. The noxious smell that had awakened her was paint. Fresh paint. But fresh paint made no sense. Her father and Poppy had flown in Harry Schnaper, the famous New York interior designer, only three weeks ago. Under Harry's meticulous direction, the whole upstairs had been redone and repainted. Everything: the bedrooms, the new nursery, even the hallway. So Sam rolled over, buried her nose in her pillow, and pulled her Yves Delorme rose-colored combed Egyptian cotton four-hundred-thread-count sheets over her head.

But it was no use. The smell was overpowering. Reluctantly, she got of bed, her Sunday morning sleep ruined. As she brushed her hair, she saw her new clothes from Fred Segal hanging in the closet, though she'd left them in the foyer the night before. But the evening housekeeper, a recent immigrant from Belarus named Svetlana, had left the closet doors open. Sam closed them. She was not going to walk around all week smelling like acrylic.

Then she left her room, following the strong odor to Ruby Hummingbird's new nursery. Even larger than Sam's bedroom, it had a small room attached for the soon-to-be-hired live-in nanny.

"Morning, sleepyhead!" Dee chirped as soon as she saw Sam. "Want to help us?"

Sam was aghast. There were cans of paint, brushes, and rollers everywhere. All the new furniture in the nursery that Harry had brought in was now covered by drop cloths. Ditto the floor. Two of the walls, which yesterday had been a hand-mixed off-white blend, were red.

Fire-engine red.

"Isn't the color great?" Poppy asked. Like Dee, she held a red roller and wore crisp denim overalls. A smock speckled with red paint ballooned over her belly.

"For the seventh rung of hell, yes; for a newborn baby's room, no," Sam replied.

"But Ruby Hummingbird resonates with red," Poppy explained. She showed off her slender wrist, which was encircled by a red Kabbalah string that supposedly warded off evil energies.

Dee lifted her own wrist and displayed a similar string.

Suddenly Sam felt a bit dizzy from the paint fumes. "Are you sure this is okay for the baby, Poppy? It reeks in here."

"It's fine," Poppy assured her. She pointed to an open window. "There's plenty of ventilation."

"Does my dad know about this?"

Poppy nodded. "Jackson is fine with it. Go ask him, he's

out in the lap pool. You really are going to have to get used to the idea that this house is as much mine as it is yours."

Sam rolled her eyes. She knew there was already a betting pool run by assistants around Hollywood over how long the Jackson-Poppy marriage would last; the over/under was fifteen months.

"Focus on the work, Poppy," Dee urged. "You don't want to upset the baby."

"Why not? She's already asphyxiating her," Sam growled.

"That is mean and untrue," Pop retorted. "But Dee is right. It's important to be serene."

"Thank you, Poppy." Dee practically blushed.

"Thank *you*. I'm glad Ruby has you, Dee. You're going to be like a *real* older sister to her."

"That's so sweet, because . . ." Dee's voice trailed off, and she fixed her huge blue eyes on Sam. "You don't mind if Ruby Hummingbird has two big sisters, do you, Sam?"

"Why would I mind?" Sam asked, plotting strategy as she spoke. As little interest as she had in the soon-to-be-born evil spawn, it did tweak her that her step-mother had formed a bond with Dee. Ditzy as Dee might be, Sam was not about to give up one of her chosen friends to the Pop-Tart.

"Dee, can I talk to you for a sec?" Sam asked sweetly.

"Sure."

"Out here, I meant."

Dee smiled at Poppy, put down her paintbrush, and

stepped over to the edge of the drop cloth closest to the doorway. Sam kept her voice low so Poppy wouldn't overhear. "So, I bought all these new clothes yesterday."

"That's nice."

"Want to come see? They're in my closet."

"Um, I'm kind of busy."

Sam swallowed her frustration. "Well, how about lunch, then? I'm going to ask Anna to meet me at Marcos Fresh at the Farmers' Market in Hancock Park. We can go over to Melrose after that and shop. I'll help you pick something out. I saw this DeMarco tapestry jacket at Masque that'll be perfect on you."

Dee nibbled on a hangnail. "Gee, I don't know if we'll be done by then. Also, I promised Poppy I would lead her through a guided prenatal meditation this afternoon. Maybe another time. Okay?"

It was impossible but true. She'd just given Dee every possible opening to display her vaunted loyalty, and Dee had turned her down flat. It made no sense. Sam had always had more power in their friendship than Dee did. Sam led, Dee followed. Had her infatuation with Kabbalah reprogrammed her neurons?

But Sam knew better than to show any sign of vulnerability or weakness. "Have a great day painting, then. I'm going to eat breakfast."

She headed down the hallway. She'd have some oolong tea and an apple and read the weekly *Variety*. She stopped downstairs and asked the cook to bake her a Granny Smith apple with Splenda and to add a dollop of fat-free, sugar-free whipped topping. Then she went upstairs to her room and began trying on her new clothes. First on was her new cropped jacket—pale pink and silver suede.

Shit. Yesterday she'd thought the jacket looked great. Now she saw in her three-way mirror that it only emphasized her pear shape. She tugged on the new red leather pants. Ugh. Why not just stand on the Getty Center roof and holler, "Wide load!" What alternate universe had she been living in when she'd bought this stuff? It never did pay to go shopping by herself. If Dee or Cammie had been with her, she would have been too intimidated by their size—or lack of size—to buy something as assholian as size-ten red leather pants. And if she *had* been on the verge of such a brutal fashion error, Cammie would have made some bitchy but all-too-true comment about the circumference of Sam's ass, and Sam would have dropped the pants as if they'd just been endorsed by Ashlee Simpson.

Her empty stomach rumbled. She had a sudden craving for a Sunday morning feast at the most famous showbiz deli in Beverly Hills, Nate and Al's. Lox, eggs, and onions. A buttered everything bagel fresh out of the oven, laden with poppy and sesame seeds and garlic chunks. Fresh coffee with real cream and real sugar. Then maybe a slice of fresh Nate and Al's cheesecake after—

Stop, she told herself. As her celebrity shrink Dr. Fred always said: "Sam. Ask yourself—what's the real issue?"

Well, that was a no-brainer. The real issue was fifty

feet down the hall, very pregnant, and wearing a wedding ring from the father that Sam hardly ever saw. From the moment that Poppy had entered Jackson's life, she'd been a completely disruptive force. Everything in the Sharpe mansion changed, even the food in the refrigerator. Now Poppy was going even further, remaking one of Sam's best friends into her new surrogate daughter. As for Jackson Sharpe, he'd always been long on material gifts and short on time and attention. He was either at the studio, on location, doing publicity, in a meeting, getting Botoxed, working out, or now fawning over his young wife. She couldn't count on him for anything

So who could she talk to? Not pompous Dr. Fred. She'd been seeing him for two years, but the only progress Sam had made on what she saw as her main issue—food— she'd had to do on her own by starving herself. The more she thought about it, the more she realized that there were really only two people she knew who might understand the absurdity of the clichés that passed for her life: Cammie or Anna. Both co-sufferers of the poor-little-rich-girl syndrome. Though in completely different ways.

And even though she'd known Cammie for most of her life and Anna for only six weeks, Sam opted for Anna. Cammie would never understand why the Poppy-Dee thing was so upsetting to Sam, because Cammie apparently hadn't allowed herself a moment of vulnerability since her mother had died in a boating accident nine years ago. But Anna was a genuinely feeling and caring individual.

National Oversharing Day

Anna came back from a quick morning run to find her parents on the couch again. This time, her father's hand was on her mother's knee. There was a heather gray Christian Dior flannel trouser leg between said hand and said knee, but still. Her parents were sipping tea from her great-grandmother's bone-china tea service while light classical music wafted through the sound system.

"Good morning, Anna," her mother announced, uncrossing her legs so that her ex-husband's hand slid from her knee. She smiled broadly at her daughter. "I was just about to get some more scones. Would you like one?"

Anna nodded as her mother moved off. When Jane was safely in the kitchen, she stared at her father, a question in her eyes.

"Don't look at me like that," her father demanded. A man who never put his feet on the coffee table, he kicked them up and leaned back, resting his head against his own palms.

Anna shook her head. "Something is wrong with this picture."

"What makes you say that?"

"You. Like that. And Mom. I've never seen her like this. She's almost . . ." Anna searched for the right word. "Relaxed." Anna stopped. The *why* of this dawned on her. But no, it couldn't be. She cleared her throat, feeling extremely uncomfortable.

"Um . . . where did Mom sleep last night?"

Suddenly Jonathan seemed decidedly uncomfortable. He pulled his legs off the coffee table and sat up straight. "Uh . . . here," he replied, leafing through the newspaper that was scattered across the coffee table.

"But didn't she book a bungalow at the Beverly Hills Hotel?"

"Yes." Jonathan fixed his eyes downward. "But by the time we got back to the house, she didn't feel like driving all the way to her hotel, so it just made sense for her to stay here."

"Okay," Anna said slowly, even though it made absolutely no sense at all. The Beverly Hills Hotel was about a five-minute drive from Jonathan's home. A five-minute drive that Django would have been happy to make.

Without letting herself fill in too many of the details, Anna felt reasonably sure that her mother had not only spent the night in Jonathan's house, but in Jonathan's room.

It made no sense. Her parents *loathed* each other.

"You two aren't getting back together. Are you?" Anna asked cautiously.

"One never knows."

One never knows? Her parents could barely have a civil conversation, but evidently they'd found other ways to communicate. God, the irony. Back in middle school Anna had spent hours trying to figure out the perfect scheme that would bring her parents back together and make them live in peace.

If only she had realized then that all it required was a daughter getting out of rehab, a crystal pitcher of dry Tanqueray martinis, and a flimsy excuse of some sort or another.

"Dee and Poppy have bonded in cosmic heaven," Sam told Anna, stopping long enough to sip her fresh-squeezed pineapple-papaya juice. "Poppy wants Dee to be Ruby's role model. It borders on the unbearable. The poor kid is going to have nightmares. It's a girl, by the way. Did I tell you that they're naming her Ruby Hummingbird? I plan to call her the Hummer."

They were at Marcos Fresh, one of the many open-air restaurants found in the labyrinth that was the Farmers' Market in Hancock Park. Recently renovated after decades of decay, the market featured dozens of outdoor shops that sold succulent fresh produce, designer foods from around the world, exotic flowers, and upscale tourist trinkets. Interspersed with the shops were the restaurants. To the east of the market was an office complex and one of Los Angeles' best multiplex theaters, the ArcLight. It frequently featured world premieres of big-budget films that drew crowds of star-gazing gawkers.

Anna chuckled, then lifted her glass of Italian mineral water to propose a toast. "Here's to dysfunctional families. You're not alone. I think my divorced parents hooked up last night."

"As in, rekindled a love flame? Or as in, fuck-buddy?"

Anna winced. "Please, you're talking about my parents. My father wouldn't say. I asked him if they were getting back together and he gave me this cryptic response. But trust me, world peace will come before Percy family reintegration."

"It can't be as bad as dear old dad and the Pop-Tart because—oh, great." Sam stopped mid-sentence and gazed over Anna's shoulder. Then she groaned. "Guess who's heading this way?"

Anna craned around; Dee and Cammie were snaking through the crowded tables, Cammie's arms laden with shopping bags.

"How did they even know we were here?"

"I mentioned it to Dee," Sam admitted. "But I told you, she and Poppy were in drop cloth heaven. I never figured she'd show."

Sam stood to greet her friends. After the mandatory air kisses, Dee and Cammie slid into the two empty chairs. Dee held a massive bunch of scarlet roses, wrapped in red-and-white tissue paper. "They're for Poppy," she explained.

"Right," Sam agreed, her voice deadpan. "Because red resonates for her and for the Hummer."

"The Hummer." Dee looked thoughtful. "That's kind of a cute nickname. Unless Ruby turns out to have a weight problem. Then it would be kind of mean. Oh, wait. I didn't mean that she'd have a weight problem because it runs in your family or something. I mean if anything, she only has half of your genes. I mean—"

"Let's stick with Ruby," Cammie interrupted, shaking her curls off her face. "I'm really glad we could join you for lunch. I've been missing you, Sam."

"Yeah, me too," Sam admitted.

Anna kept her face neutral. She didn't trust Cammie's sudden burst of apparent sincerity. She'd learned from experience that Cammie Sheppard was out for Cammie Sheppard. Cammie had tried to ruin Anna more than once—she'd even tried to get her fired from her internship on *Hermosa Beach* before Anna decided to quit. She was certain that if Sam bought into Cammie's Glenda the Good Witch routine, it would only be a matter of time before the Wicked Witch of the West would emerge again. And while Sam had perhaps a dozen pairs of ruby red slippers—from Prada open-toed to Moschino snakeskin—none of them could keep her safe from Cammie's malice.

Cammie smiled. "So. Anna. How are you?"

"Fine," Anna responded cautiously but politely.

"Adam sends his regards," Cammie told her. "We had breakfast together today. Then we went to build houses for Habitat for Humanity, but thank God he had the day wrong. Then we went to Venice Beach before he had to go play basketball."

"That's nice," Anna said noncommittally.

"It was great." Cammie lifted her hair and fanned the nape of her neck, then dropped the heavy curls back in place. "Actually, I'm more than great. Much more."

Asking why Cammie was more than great would be an exercise in futility. Cammie was obviously setting something up, because Cammie always had an agenda. So Anna patiently waited for the other Ferragamo to drop.

"I've been spending a lot of time with him," Cammie went on. "Last night we went to this party in Malibu—some movie-wrap thing. Then we ditched the bad food and boring company and went down to the beach." She leaned in close, eyes half closed. "The boy is *amazing.*"

Amazing, as in . . . well, it was obvious what she meant. So, Cammie and Adam were having sex. Making love. No, it couldn't be love. Sweet, smart, good-guy Adam and Cammie the viper? Anna knew she had nothing to say about it. She'd dropped Adam. At the time things had been so mixed up with Ben: They were together, then they weren't, then they were. She had to tell Adam the truth. He was the last guy on the planet who deserved to have a girl cause him pain. But why had she lusted after the bad boy instead of the good guy? Why was nature so perverse? Now she wasn't with either Ben *or* Adam. So if Adam wanted Cammie, well,

Cammie probably couldn't hurt him any more than Anna herself had hurt him. She really hated that.

"So Anna," Cammie continued. "You know all about Adam, in every way. Right?"

The question hung as the waitress brought Anna her prawn-and-avocado salad and Sam a fruit platter. Cammie and Dee ordered without even looking at the menu—a spinach salad for Cammie, a bowl of the restaurant's signature squash soup for Dee.

"Not really," Anna replied when the waitress had moved off. The truth was, she and Adam hadn't shared more than a kiss or two.

Cammie smiled. "Take my word for it. *Insatiable.* Want to know why sandpaper is made out of sand? Check out my butt."

Anna wondered if it was National Oversharing Day and someone had forgotten to send her the memo.

"I'm happy for you," Anna said evenly, forking a bite of shrimp into her mouth.

Cammie laughed. "Honestly, Anna. You sound like a woman who has cobwebs growing—"

"Cammie. *Enough,*" Sam warned. "Don't be so bitchy."

"It wasn't bitchy," Cammie insisted, then stretched languidly. "It was an honest assessment of a condition that I hope changes as soon as possible. For Anna's peace of mind and happiness. Anyway, a girl can't be as happy as I am and be bitchy. Who has the energy?" She fixed her gaze back on Anna. "Honestly, you quit on him too soon. You can't imagine what you were missing."

You can't imagine what you were missing.

As Anna parked her Lexus in front of her father's house, she wondered why Cammie's words bothered her so much. She didn't want Adam back. And if he was happy with Cammie and they were having sand-blasting sex together, fine. So be it.

Anna glanced toward Django's guesthouse and wondered if he was home. She could use some of his southern charm right about now. But what about the girl, what was her name? Lisa. Was Lisa still there? Were they together, doing what everyone in the world—Cammie and Adam, Danny and the redhead, even her mother and father—except Anna seemed to be doing?

She decided to let discretion rule and opened the enormous black door to the main house. The first thing she saw was a note tucked under the Ming vase in the foyer.

Anna—
Your mother and I took a drive up the coast to San Simeon. Please think about doing the Las Casitas trip for me, if only to keep an eye on my associate. You'll miss only a few days of school because of the conference on Friday. You could use a break.
—Love, Dad

So what was this, then? What were her parents doing? Did her father want her to go to Mexico just so he and her mother could be alone?

She lay down on her oak canopy bed and stroked the pink silk quilt that had been handmade by a seamstress in Kentucky. It was beautiful. The whole room was beautiful: hardwood floors dotted with museum-quality, hand-knotted tapestry rugs, antique oak furniture, carefully preserved. In fact, the whole house was as lovely as this room. But none of it seemed to make her father happy. Not happy in the way he'd looked that morning on the couch.

Maybe there were some people you could never get out of your heart, not completely. It wasn't love; it was . . . what? Something she just didn't understand. Like how she felt about Ben.

Anna did have his number at Princeton. Before she could think herself out of it, she impulsively picked up the phone and dialed the number. One ring. Two. Three. She was glad that he wasn't picking up. This way she could leave a message. Something casual that still left open the possibilities for—

"Hello?"

Holy shit. He'd answered.

"Hello?" he said again.

Anna couldn't speak.

"Hel-lo?" Louder now, and irritated.

Anna quietly hung up the phone and lay back on her bed. Of all the infantile things to do. She was acting like she was in fifth grade or some crazy stalker out of Lifetime TV. If she didn't want to talk to him, she shouldn't have called him. What the hell was *wrong* with her?

Maybe in her heart of hearts, it wasn't talk she was after. Maybe she was after something more . . . carnal. In which case, she didn't really need Ben.

Lust could just be with someone you didn't know and would never see again.

Anna sat bolt upright, almost smiling as a truly daring notion raced through her chronically overactive mind. That *someone* sounded like someone she might meet at a highly upscale, all-inclusive Mexican resort.

Right Gender, Wrong Person

S am spent the first part of Sunday night lying on her bed, reading William Goldman's *Adventures in the Screen Trade*. She was preparing for the big time. After already making a few student films, now she was ready for the real thing. Few fantasies were sweeter than the one where every thin, blond, perfect girl at Beverly Hills High was groveling to be in a Sam Sharpe movie.

"Sam?" Svetlana was standing at the open door to her room, arms folded across her black housekeeper's uniform.

"Yes?"

"Friend said to tell you she has moved into room down hall."

"Fine, great . . ." Sam mumbled, too deep into her reading to care. But something told her to rewind and play back. "Wait. What are you talking about? What friend?"

"Small one," Svetlana replied.

"What small—?"

Sam never finished the sentence. Instead she jumped

up from her bed, tossed William Goldman on her pillow, and bolted past Svetlana and down the hall to the
last room in the wing. There was barefoot Dee, in size-
zero Earl Jeans and a pink Zac Posen ribbed tank top
that could have fit a twelve-year-old, sitting on the
floor next to an open and brimful Louis Vuitton suitcase. She was in a lotus position, her eyes closed. It
took a moment for Sam to take in all of this, because
the room was lit only by two fat votive candles; their
vanilla scent overpowered the room.

"Dee? What are you doing?" Sam flipped on the
overhead lights.

Dee opened her eyes. "Oh. Hi, Sam. Can you turn
off the lights? I have seasonal affective disorder. My life
coach says I need a certain lamp from Light Bulbs Plus
in Sherman Oaks, or I'll get really depressed. Poppy said
she'd have one delivered tomorrow. Isn't that sweet?"

"Diabetic," Sam opined.

"The lights?" Dee prompted.

"Focus here for me, Dee. Please. Did you just
become our houseguest?"

Dee nodded. "I changed my mind and accepted
Poppy's offer. Isn't it great?"

"Great" wasn't the first word that came to mind.
Sam wasn't just bothered that Dee had shown up with a
suitcase. After all, she and Dee were still friends. But
this bedroom was special, reserved for family members
only. Like when Sam's favorite cousins came three
times a year from New York. Or her grandparents on

her dad's side—in December and for the month of August. In fact, there were two dresser drawers full of her grandparents' clothes and personal items so that they could travel to visit without lugging suitcases.

The Sharpe estate was big enough to have a guest room reserved for family. For everyone else who might be asked to spend the night, there were three guest-houses out behind the main building: a whitewashed three-bedroom cottage near the winter heated pool and twin two-bedroom log cabins down the path from the tennis court.

"Why aren't you staying in one of the guesthouses?" Sam asked.

"I *could* move into one of them, I guess," Dee had agreed. "But I thought this would be more like a pajama party."

Sam had to admit that would be fun. She and Dee had had many memorable slumber parties when they were younger.

"Did you know that Poppy never had slumber par-ties when she was little? She shared her bedroom with two sisters, and there was no room for her friends. Isn't that sad?"

"No," Sam retorted. "She had *sisters.*"

"She really misses them," Dee went on. "That's why she wants Ruby to have a sister so much. You know, me."

"What am I, a blow-up doll?"

Dee did her patented wide-eyed look. "I just thought we could share."

Sam waved a hand in the air. "Share away."

Dee pulled her knees up to her chest and circled them with her arms. "I had the most amazing dream last night. I heard a baby cry, and I wandered all through this house—*your* house—trying to find her. Finally I found her in one of the log cabins. *She looked just like Marilyn Monroe.* Only with a baby's body. Isn't that amazing?"

"More like bizarre. Can we get back to the moving-in thing?"

"It's simple. I decided that I didn't want to be home alone." Dee's round blue eyes grew huge. "I think our house is haunted, seriously. My dad says that Marilyn slept there with Bobby Kennedy, you know."

"Dee. Stop and think. Marilyn Monroe had three different husbands. She had sex in a lot of places. She is not haunting *your* house."

"Spirits return to where they have unfinished business. There used to be a vintage movie poster from *The Seven Year Itch* in our attic. I remember it from when I was little. But last week, when I went to look for it, it was gone."

"Someone threw it out. That's all."

"Or maybe Marilyn came back for it," Dee whispered. "I heard she didn't like that movie very much. Anyway, I think I know what all of it means."

This was beginning to hold a sick fascination for Sam. "I'm hanging on every word, Dee."

"I think that *Ruby Hummingbird is the reincarnation of Marilyn Monroe.*"

"I don't think so, Dee. Though that is a provocative theory. Listen, have you ever considered psychotherapy? Because—"

Dee scrunched up her forehead. "You don't believe me. Poppy believes me."

Of course Poppy believed her. That was just *perfect.* No wonder Dee wanted to live under the same roof as her new mentor. The two of them could spin off into New Age paradise hand in hand. But Sam decided to work on grounding her friend back into reality another time. For now, she shifted to the matter at hand—reclaiming her home, or at least her grandparents' special room.

"Back to the home-alone thing, Dee. Are both your parents in New York?"

"Well, my dad had a recording session there. Mom decided to tag along and keep an eye on him. Last time he went, he had a fling with one of Usher's backup singers."

"He cheated on your mother again?"

"Yep. But he says it's not really cheating unless he becomes emotionally involved."

"But your mom didn't used to care," Sam recalled.

"I think she's going through menopause or something and she gets unhinged about everything. Listen, can I unpack?"

Sam sighed. Maybe this was a time to take some pity on her friend. "Sure."

"You know, Sam, you are so lucky. To have Poppy as your stepmom."

"Dee, she's only four years older than I am. Who has a stepmom who's only four years older than they are? No, wait, forget I asked. That would be about half of our friends."

"Love doesn't go by the numbers, Sam," Dee murmured solemnly.

"My father does not love her, Dee. He screws the young hottie in all of his movies. This one happened to get pregnant."

"That is a really mean thing to say," Dee choked out, her voice stricken. "If he didn't love her, he would have just written a really big check and made her go away. That's what everyone does in this town. He loves her, Sam. Deal with it."

"Fine, Dee. I'm wrong. He does lo—"

Just then, Sam noticed an open box of disheveled clothes on the far side of the bed and recognized one of the red flannel shirts that her grandfather habitually wore. Someone—Dee or Poppy—must have taken her grandfather's clothes from their drawers and dumped them in this ratty cardboard box. Presumably to make room for Dee's copious wardrobe.

"Dee, please tell me you didn't touch those clothes." She pointed to her grandparents' stuff.

"No. Poppy did. I think Svetlana is bringing them to the Goodwill when she leaves this afternoon."

That did it. Without another word, Sam strode out of the room.

"Wait!" Dee called. "Wanna go to Au Bar later?"

Too late. Sam had already flown down the spiral staircase to the main level of the house. She was going to find Poppy and let her have it with both barrels. But all she could find was Svetlana, who told her that Poppy was getting a "special maternity massage" at Blooming Mama.

"Iverson fakes left, spins right, and goes with the fadeaway jumper!" Adam used his best announcer's voice to narrate his own play.

Tonight on the white concrete driveway of the Flood house just off Coldwater Canyon, his opponent was merely his father. Ninety-nine percent of the time, his dad was no match for his younger, faster, and taller son. In fact, Adam would spot his dad ten points in a game to twenty-one just to make it interesting.

Tonight, though, was a one-percent night. Jeff timed his leap perfectly, blocked the shot, then grabbed the ball and drove for an easy layup that Adam barely made an effort to defend.

"Twenty-one to eighteen!" his dad chortled. "Score one for experience and cunning over youth and innocence."

"Good game, Dad," Adam said, retrieving the basketball. It had rolled under a big rhododendron.

Jeff used the bottom of his faded college T-shirt to wipe some sweat from his forehead. "Not really. You played like you were half asleep." He tossed his son a quart bottle of iced Gatorade they'd brought out with them. Adam cracked it open and drank greedily. "I haven't beaten you like that in two years. And that was when you were recovering from mono."

"What, I'm not allowed to have a bad game?" Adam asked, trying to keep his tone light. He knew he'd played poorly. Distractedly. More than that, he knew what was distracting him. Or rather, *who* was distracting him.

"Maybe you were just going easy on me," his dad suggested.

"Nice out, Dad. But you really won." Adam expertly spun the ball on one finger. "Got stuff on my mind."

His dad dropped down to the front step of the entryway to their house and motioned for his son to join him. Adam did, and for a few moments they sat in the Sunday night quiet together, no sound but the rumble of the occasional car on Coldwater Canyon heading from the city to the valley or vice versa. The Floods lived in a beautiful three-thousand-square-foot, two-story traditional home on a side street just off busy Coldwater Canyon. In any other neighborhood in America, it would be considered large. In Beverly Hills, it was considered a starter home.

"You want to talk about it?" Jeff finally asked.

Adam shrugged. He was one of the rare kids who sometimes really did confide in his father. Like the time in eighth grade when he'd lived through his unrequited crush on Betsy Cousins. And the time in ninth grade when he and all his friends had gotten wasted on Jack Daniels and grape juice at Nicholas Pacheco's house; even though he'd been completely polluted, Adam had

been the one to call his father to come and get them.
The next day, it had been Jeff Flood who'd nursed him
through a brutal hangover. After that experience, Adam
had barely ever gotten even mildly drunk.

But how could he possibly tell his dad what had happened with Cammie on the beach? Way too personal.

"Nah."

"Is it about Anna?" his father guessed.

Adam spun the ball again. "Right gender, wrong person."

"Yeah? Is Anna out of the picture?"

"It's all about Cammie now."

"Ah, Cammie," Jeff repeated. "You mentioned her
last week."

"I guess I did. The g-girl is . . ." He stammered,
searching for the right father-friendly word.

"A vixen?" his father suggested.

Adam laughed. "Yeah. Times infinity. I mean, every
guy at school dreams about her. And she's into *me.*"

Jeff took a long swallow of Gatorade. "You two
sleeping together?"

"Uh . . ." Adam could feel his face burn. They'd had
the big safe-sex lecture before they'd moved from
Michigan to Los Angeles. Jeff had talked about how
things were different in California, how kids grew up
faster, how Adam might well run into kids who had a
lot more experience than he did. But in the past year
and a half in Beverly Hills, his parents had never come
right out and asked him if he was having sex.

"Can we not have this conversation?"

"No. It's in my job description." Jeff put his hand on Adam's arm. "You're using protection, aren't you?"

Adam edged away from his father. "Time out, this is excruciating. If Cammie and I are doing anything—and I'm not saying we are—then I would be smart enough to, you know, take care of things."

"Good to know." His dad looked out into the darkness. "You know, I don't think I ever told you this, but before your mother, I had this girlfriend back in Grand Rapids. Erika Ackermann. Man, I was crazy about that girl."

"We're veering into major TMI," Adam warned.

"TMI?"

"Too much information," Adam explained.

"Oh, it's not what you're thinking. We never had sex. Erika went away to Albion, and it was over. Anyway, there I was at orientation at Kalamazoo, and this girl from Wilton, Connecticut—I don't even remember her name—decides that I'm *it.*"

Adam was fascinated in spite of himself. "What happened?"

"There's this knock on my dorm room at three in the morning—my roommate hadn't showed up yet—and there she was. You want to know what happened?"

"Damned if I do and damned if I don't," Adam joked.

"Nothing. I mean, I tried. But . . . zip. Same thing the next night. I thought there was something wrong with me."

Holy shit, Adam thought. Like father, like son. Maybe it's genetic. But obviously his dad got over it eventually.

"Well, it's not like there's anything wrong with you, Dad," Adam said rhetorically. As absurd as it was, he just wanted to double-check. "I mean, I'm here, and I look just like you."

"Exactly." Jeff ruffled his son's hair. "I think the problem was that my body was trying to tell me something. Like, 'Whoa, there. Maybe this isn't the right one to share this with.' So if you're having a problem with Cammie—"

"I never said I had a problem," Adam interjected.

"I said *if.*"

"Trust me, Dad. My mind and my body both want to share."

His father stood, took the ball from Adam, and bounced it once. "I don't doubt it, son. But maybe it's not your mind or your body you should be listening to. Maybe you should be listening to your heart."

Adam shook his head. "Too deep for me."

"That I highly doubt." Jeff bounced the ball again. "You love this girl?"

"I don't know."

"Well, when you have the answer to that, all else will follow."

Turkey-Breast Sandwich

Anna checked out her reflection in the mirror over her antique dresser. She'd chosen a simple cotton-and-silk Graham and Spencer pale blue skirt with a white Cynthia Rowley sleeveless blouse. She wore no makeup and tied her hair back in a ponytail. Then, deciding she didn't look like a girl ready for torrid climes, she unbuttoned two of the blouse buttons, slicked on some Chanel lip gloss and mascara, sprayed herself with the Jo Malone perfume she loved, and took down her hair. Ah. That was more like it.

Mexico. A place where a girl could safely be whoever she wanted to be, if only for a day. But the doorbell still hadn't rung. Which meant that Lloyd Millar, her father's associate, was already twenty-five minutes late.

When Anna called her dad on Sunday evening to tell him that she decided to go to the resort, his response had been greatly enthusiastic. Ten minutes later, Lloyd had telephoned to make plans to leave on Tuesday. When he considered how long it would take to get to LAX, go through security, fly to Mexico, and get a shuttle van to the resort, he decreed that they should drive down in his BMW E90 3 series roadster. By the time Lloyd showed up, Anna was already waiting for him in front of the house. He was a tall, slim guy, mid-twenties, she guessed, with short dark hair and a faux hipster goatee. He wore mirrored wraparound Ray-Bans, a 1950s black-and-white sports shirt with dice running down the center, and classic water buffalo sandals.

"Hi, I'm Anna." She extended her hand politely as he approached her. She saw that he had hairy arms. And hairy toes. Anna had a thing about hairy toes. They made her gag. She mentally chided herself for being so superficial and slapped a pleasant grin on her face.

"Lloyd Millar. Hey, sorry I'm late. The 405 was bumper to bumper."

"No problem."

Lloyd lifted his sunglasses and did an exaggerated eyebrow wriggle that Anna assumed was meant to convey approval. "You're even more beautiful than the photo in your dad's office." Then he licked his lips.

Ick. Why had she unbuttoned those two top buttons? She managed a thank you, then draped her summer Madeline Weinrib leather-trimmed tote over her arm.

Lloyd reached for her compact classic Hartmann suitcase. "A beautiful woman should never carry her own bag," he announced.

"Hey, Miss Anna."

Django. He'd come out of his guesthouse and was heading for the main house, looking as hot as only

Django could look. Anna wished she were going to Mexico with him instead. She waved.

"So you decided to take your dad up on the Mexico thing, huh?"

Anna nodded, only mildly surprised that Django knew about her decision. She started to introduce the two men to each other and then stopped, realizing that they must already be acquainted.

"Hey, Lloyd," Django drawled, confirming Anna's realization.

"Django," Lloyd responded stiffly. There was ice in his voice.

Django opened the BMW door for Anna, and she impetuously kissed his cheek. "Thanks. See you in a few days."

"If school calls, do I tell 'em you're in bed with consumption?"

"They won't. Seniors at Beverly Hills High take off all the time and claim college tour. No one keeps track."

"Will do. I'll keep the home fires burnin'," Django drawled, and tipped an imaginary cowboy hat.

With that, Lloyd peeled out of the driveway like an aggressive sixteen-year-old who'd just gotten his license. "I don't trust him."

Anna jumped to Django's defense. "I do. We're friends."

"All that 'gee shucks' crap is a load of horseshit. You know that, don't you?" Lloyd glanced at Anna, then back at the road. "I'd tell your father to watch him if I were you. I already did. I think he's a spy for Warren Buffett."

"Well, you're not me," Anna replied pleasantly, hoping this would end that particular line of conversation. Django had been nothing but terrific to her. All she knew about Lloyd was that he worked for her father. And that he already grated on her. And that he had hairy toes.

It would be a three-hour drive to the Mexican border and then another three and a half to Las Casitas. Anna wasn't sure she'd last. Lloyd was smart—it was immediately obvious why Jonathan Percy had hired him—but it was the kind of intelligence that made Anna wish he'd develop an instant case of meningitis. He fancied himself an expert on everything and felt an undying need to share his encyclopedic abundance of knowledge with her. The stock market. Politics. The relative strength of the dollar and the euro. Hollywood. Los Angeles restaurants. Life, with a capital *L*. He never stopped talking.

When they made a pit stop north of San Diego to use the restrooms, Anna found Lloyd in the connecting restaurant, where he informed her that he'd already ordered them Diet Cokes and turkey-breast sandwiches. Anna didn't want turkey, but she also didn't want to get their elderly waitress in trouble by canceling food that was in the process of being made. So when the waitress brought the sandwich, she just said "thank you" and asked for an iced tea with lemon and an English muffin. Which prompted Lloyd to expound on how turkey's uniquely efficient balance of amino acids made it the definitive power sandwich.

Anna allowed how she felt quite powerful already and preferred to order her own meals.

Fortunately, Lloyd had brought a book on tape for the ride. Unfortunately, it was Donald Trump's *The Art of the Deal*. But at least it allowed Anna to doze off until they reached the border crossing between the United States and Mexico, just north of Tijuana.

"The hair thing is a ruse, you realize that," Lloyd informed her. She'd awakened just in time to hear the New York real estate magnate expound on how he'd developed the parcel of real estate that ultimately became the garish Trump Tower on Fifth Avenue in Manhattan.

"I have no idea what you're talking about."

"The Donald. The hair. He deliberately goes for this weird hairdo thing. The hair makes people think he's got a weak spot. They underestimate him, which he uses to his advantage. I've been studying the guy for years."

Well, that would explain your weird-hairy-toes weak spot, Anna thought.

Traffic was heavy at the border crossing between San Ysidro, California, and Tijuana, Mexico. It took Lloyd nearly an hour to roll his BMW up to the checkpoint. The Mexican border guard peered at Lloyd and asked politely for identification. Anna handed her passport to Lloyd; he passed it to the guard along with his own.

"We were stuck in line for an hour," Lloyd complained as the man scrutinized their passports. "Not a very organized system. If you'd simply create two lines, delegating one for small cars and motorcycles and the other for SUVs and trucks, things would flow far more easily, amigo."

Amigo? Anna winced.

The guard looked down his sunburned nose. "I am not your amigo, sir," he said in excellent English. "I am an official of the Mexican government. Are you traveling to Mexico for work or pleasure?"

"Both," Lloyd replied.

"Where will you be staying?" the guard asked.

"Las Casitas. The resort in Baja. Thinking of buying the place. Resorts down here do a lot better when they're owned by Americans."

Anna was ready to flee and run all the way back to Beverly Hills. Anything to separate herself from this overeducated social klutz. Did he really have no clue how his comments and demeanor would come off to an overworked, underpaid, carbon-monoxide-choked Mexican immigration official? She scrambled to say something, anything, to improve the rapidly deteriorating situation.

"Lo siento para mi amigo; el tiene muchas problemas sicológicas," she said, which basically meant, "I'm sorry for my friend's behavior, but he has a number of serious psychological problems." Unfortunately the comment didn't seem to make a dent in the guard's impassive expression.

Lloyd whirled around on her. "I caught that. I speak five languages fluently, Anna. Spanish is one of them."

"Too bad tact isn't," she muttered.

The official waved Lloyd's car to the right toward a

covered pavilion and a low-slung brown building. "You will need to pull over there, sir."

"Why?"

"Official business. Inspection. Your car and your person."

"I'd appreciate a specific reason," Lloyd persisted.

"Because I am an official of the Mexican government, and you wish to enter my country, sir." Anna got a sinking feeling. Searching Lloyd's "person" undoubtedly meant searching her person, too. How detailed that search might be was a big fat question mark.

Lloyd reluctantly pulled the BMW into the covered area. While two customs agents methodically went through all their baggage and the vehicle itself, Anna and Lloyd were escorted to the adjacent, modern two-story building, the second story supported by huge concrete columns. Just inside the doors was an American-style bureaucratic waiting room, with people working behind Plexiglas and all the signs in English and Spanish. Anna and Lloyd waited for ten minutes. Then Lloyd was taken away, presumably to a different room for a more thorough personal examination. Anna waited, nearly trembling, for an escort to come and spirit her away for her own version of the Lloyd treatment.

"Follow me, please," said a chunky middle-aged woman who appeared before Anna.

Anna rose and followed the uniformed woman out of the room, up a steep staircase and into another smaller

room. It was barren save for two vending machines,
three wooden chairs, and a portable metal table.

"Um, a body cavity search isn't really necessary, is
it?" Anna asked, steeling herself for the worst. She kept
her eyes locked on the woman's meaty hands; if she
donned rubber gloves, she knew she was in trouble.

"Wait here." The woman pointed to a coffee
machine. "There is the coffee, if you want."

"You brought me in here to wait? That's all?" Anna
exhaled with relief.

"*Lo siento,* the coffee is not very good, but machine
takes American money," the woman explained, and
then lumbered out of the room.

Anna sagged into a chair, grateful that she was not
going to pay for Lloyd's boorishness—her person and
her Weinrib tote would remain untouched. But the
notion that he was probably undergoing a certain
degree of indignity at that very moment cheered her
considerably. She skipped the coffee and flipped
through a Mexico City newspaper to pass the time.

Two hours later, the customs officials finally released
Lloyd from custody. He looked ready to chew nails but
kept silent until they were back in his car and under way.

"I'm sorry you had to go through that," Lloyd apolo-
gized as they finally pulled away from the border crossing toward the entrance to the toll road that would take
them to Ensenada and then points south. "Fucking ass-
holes. These low-level guys are power crazed. Everyone's
just pissed off at everyone else."

"I'd agree with that, Lloyd."

"What?" He was incredulous. "You're mad at me? You think that was *my* fault?"

"*Sí. Muchisimo,*" Anna replied. "Now, *por favor,* shut up and drive."

Las Casitas

Mexico. Anna had no idea what to expect. But she marveled at the landscape as she and Lloyd drove south, first on the spacious toll road that hugged the coast between Tijuana and the resort city of Ensenada and then inland toward San Quintin. For a long time, the Pacific Ocean had been to her right, glistening in the sunshine for as far as the eye could see. Its beauty lulled Anna into a zone-like state that lasted through the wild terrain of Ensenada and up until Lloyd chose to ruin it by opening his mouth.

"Are we there yet?" Lloyd mock-whined like an impatient child on a long car trip. Then he winked at Anna. "I'm just teasing you. Only a half hour or so more."

"Good to know." As the miles had passed, it had become increasingly difficult for her to remain civil.

"So, you planning to follow in your dad's foot-steps?" Lloyd asked.

Now he wanted to make pleasant chitchat?

"I really have no interest in business or in money."

Lloyd guffawed. "You know, it slays me when people born rich say they have no interest in money. I grew up in Lake Balboa. Know what that is?"

Anna shook her head.

"The Valley. Lake Balboa. Van Nuys, really, but the people there voted to change the name because Van Nuys has such a bad rap. You know, gangs. But anyway, not a millionaire in sight. Want to know how I made it?"

Not really, Anna thought, but she was much too polite to say it. She waited for him to continue, knowing that he would.

"I kicked butt at Birmingham High School—that's in Van Nuys, too. Lettered in soccer and tennis, president of the debate club. I was all around 'the man.' Got a full-ride scholarship to Williams. You know it?"

She nodded. Of course she knew it—Williams was one of the best small colleges in the country.

"Four years there," Lloyd continued. "Full of thoroughbreds like you. Guess who was the only kid from Lake Balboa?"

"You?"

"Yep. And the cream always rises. I had a four-oh average. An alum recommended me to your dad. I started out as a flunky at the firm; your dad had no clue who the hell I was, which wasn't gonna fly. So I snuck into this VP's office—the guy was working on this top-secret acquisitions plan, right? He's pulling down six figures, easy. The thing sucked. I took it home on a Friday night, worked all weekend rewriting it, slipped that beauty on your dad's desk, saved the company about five mil, the rest is history."

"What happened to the vice president?" Anna asked, fascinated in spite of her dislike for him.

"*Former* vice president," Lloyd replied. "Like I said, the cream rises."

Anna didn't respond, so Lloyd restarted the Trump book on tape. Fifteen miles later the road turned south, once again paralleling the ocean. Then, as if someone had hit a switch, the landscape changed suddenly from rocky and brown to lush and green.

"Irrigation," Lloyd expounded. "We're on Las Casitas property. Just another half mile or so to the entrance."

Thank God. Anna didn't know what had been more difficult to stomach, Lloyd's pontificating or Donald Trump's audio self-aggrandizing.

"That's good," she replied evenly. "It's been . . . quite a drive."

Lloyd nodded. "Even with the ridiculous delay at the border, this was still more time efficient than flying."

With a smile that was almost human, he turned off the highway onto a two-lane road that appeared to have been blacktopped the day before; the white stripe down the center was freshly painted. There was a speed limit sign in English that said ten miles an hour but no other indication that they were approaching one of the world's most exclusive resorts.

"Excellent. See the security cameras?" Lloyd cocked

his head toward small cameras mounted on tall wooden poles, all camouflaged by lush foliage. "Unfortunately, Mexico's had quite a few kidnappings in recent years. Some of the world's biggest power brokers frequent this resort. What they don't need is an unexpected interruption of their vacation."

"Come on," Anna chided. "Americans visit Mexico all the time and don't get kidnapped."

"You know where the secretary of state likes to vacation?"

"No."

"How about the chief justice of the Supreme Court? Or Tony Blair?"

"Here?"

"That's why they need the security," Lloyd explained. "If you motor in, you have to inform the management in advance what you'll be driving. If we'd just showed up from out of the blue, they'd meet us in a Bradley Fighting Vehicle."

A few hundred feet farther along, the landscape opened up, and a magnificent golf course came into view, dotted with a few golf carts and golfers enjoying a late afternoon round. Then the road dipped to the left and tunneled under the course. Anna realized it was so the golfers could safely cross the road without any danger from passing vehicles.

When they emerged from the tunnel, they passed a driving range where a few more golfers were hitting buckets of balls, then a tidy ocean-side tennis facility where a singles match was in progress, and a low-slung wooden stable where a sleek white Arabian horse was being hot-walked by a young groom.

Finally they came to a white-gabled, low-slung building with a small copper sign announcing that this was indeed Las Casitas.

"How much did you say this place was worth?" Anna asked.

Lloyd smiled. "Let's put it this way. A famous hotel guy with a very overexposed granddaughter once bid two hundred and seventy million for it. The owners here turned him down flat. Your father's syndicate"—he said the words "your father" with something approaching reverence—"has an offer on the table that's sweeter than that. A lot sweeter."

As Lloyd stopped the car, a battalion of valets, car parkers, and attendants was upon them.

"Welcome to Las Casitas." The eldest of the valets greeted them with a huge smile. He wore black pants, a long-sleeve white golf shirt with the words *Las Casitas* embroidered in red thread, black shoes, and white gloves despite the warm late afternoon sun. The intended effect was understated elegance, and Anna thought it worked perfectly. "Miss Percy, Mr. Millar, it's a pleasure to have you with us. Check-in is arranged; your escorts have your keys. Mr. Millar, Miss Rodriguez will be available to escort you to your casita. Miss Percy, Mr. Phelps will do the same for you. If you want a look at the premises, just phone the front desk ten minutes before you'd like your tour to begin and then simply wait for your guide to arrive. If there's anything we can do to make your stay with us more pleasant, just ask. Your bags will be in your casitas by the time you arrive. And remember: No tipping, gratuities, *propinas,* or *pourboires* are accepted at Las Casitas. It is our pleasure to make sure you have everything you need or desire, twenty-four hours a day."

Lloyd nodded. Meanwhile one of the valets—dark-skinned, with short dreadlocks; his name tag said Trevor—bowed slightly to Anna. "I'll bring you to Casita Las Brisas." His voice had the lilt of a Caribbean island. Barbados? "That's where you'll be staying."

As Lloyd was escorted in the opposite direction, Anna followed Trevor through the main building, where a white-jacketed waiter handed her a flute of chilled champagne with floating raspberries. She was thirsty and took it gratefully. One sip told her that this was no ordinary champagne.

"Louis Roederer Cristal 1995," Trevor commented. "Shipped by refrigerated container from France to San Diego, then by refrigerated truck to us. It's a little obsessive, yes. But our sommelier demands it that way."

"It's wonderful," Anna declared as she took a serious swallow.

"Very good," Trevor told her as he continued them on their way. "It's all we pour at Las Casitas. Have as many as you like."

Five minutes' walk took them through a lush

garden—Trevor pointed out hedgehog cactus, poppies, and Indian paintbrush flowers, all native to Baja. A few moments later, they were in front of Anna's casita.

"*Casita* means 'small house' in Spanish," Trevor told her as he handed her a key to her home for the next several days. "As you can see, we've taken some liberties with the language."

As Trevor used another key to open the door to her casita, Anna took in the immaculate exterior: front porch with a slate floor and two white rocking chairs, big picture window, and a gently sloping roof to shield the rockers from afternoon showers. She pictured herself curled up on one of those chairs, reading a book, listening to the birds and the distant ocean. Nice.

Then she stepped inside. Nicer.

The interior was as breathtaking as the exterior was inviting. There was a large living room with pale wood furnishings accented in sunny yellow. A ceiling fan turned slowly in the center of the room. The sliding glass doors at the rear opened to a magnificent view of the sapphire ocean, seemingly close enough to touch. There was a sitting room with a stocked library, a bedroom with a massive white iron bed fluffy with white and yellow pillows, and a huge bathroom with a two-showerhead shower, a jetted Jacuzzi tub, and a bidet. The thermostat read sixty-seven degrees, the humidity less than twenty-five percent. Yet Anna couldn't hear an air-conditioner or a dehumidifier at work. She did hear beautiful classical music coming from hidden speakers.

Trevor led her into the kitchen and opened the refrigerator. "As you can see, it's been fully stocked with the foods you requested."

"It's lovely," Anna said. "But I didn't request food."

"Perhaps your escort did, then."

"Let me guess. Turkey."

The valet looked confused.

"Sorry, never mind."

Trevor nodded. "Internet access is available between ten A.M. and ten P.M. That's when we have access to the satellite. In the living room cabinet is a TV, VCR/DVD, and CD player. We've brought in a selection of movies and music. If there is something you like that isn't there, let us know. Outside, you'll find a hot tub and a small cooling pool."

Anna smiled. "It's lovely, thank you."

Trevor gave a slight nod of thanks. "Your private maid and butler are available twenty-four hours a day. Simply press the yellow button on your phone and explain your needs. Shall I have your maid unpack your suitcase?"

"No thanks. I'll do it myself."

"Very good. Is there anything else I can do for you at this time, Miss Percy?"

"Not a thing. This is fantastic. Can I ask you how many square feet it is in here?"

"Two thousand seven hundred twenty-four. Like all our one-bedrooms," he said confidently. "Well, if there's nothing else . . ."

Trevor departed; Anna toured the amazing casita one more time. She'd stayed at high-end guest bungalows at Sans Souci in Jamaica, Caneel Bay in the Virgin Islands, and Deer Valley in Utah. But this put them all to shame. No wonder her father was interested in helping some clients acquire the place.

The first thing Anna wanted to do was swim in the ocean. But before she could find her bathing suit, a bell chimed discreetly. Anna had no idea what it was. The front door? No one was there. Ah, the phone.

"Hello?"

"Hey, there, it's Lloyd. Nice place, huh?"

"Fantastic," Anna agreed.

"How about we hit the beach?"

"I have other plans, but thanks."

"What other plans? I'm flexible."

Couldn't he take a hint?

"I'd like to just relax on my own for a while."

"You'd have more fun with me, guaranteed," Lloyd assured her. "But we'll just hook up later. Tell you what, I'll be at the poolside bar." He hung up.

Yuh. The only place they were doing any kind of hooking up was in his dreams.

Forty-five minutes later, after a refreshing solo swim in the crystalline ocean, Anna was in the lobby. She'd asked for a tour of the resort; a guy in his early twenties was waiting for her. He looked Hawaiian and very handsome, with dark hair and broad cheekbones. His muscular physique was clad in blue tennis shorts and a white Las Casitas shirt like the one the valets wore, except with short sleeves. He wore a name tag introducing himself as "Kai."

"Anna Percy?" he asked, striding over to her.

"Yes, hello. Are you my butler?"

"No, actually. Name's Kai. I'll be showing you round." Whoever Kai was, he was gorgeous and had an Australian accent.

"I was told to look for Regis," Anna explained.

"Ah, yes, your butler. Apologies. I'm the surfing instructor. Filling in for your Regis."

Anna was confused. Not in a bad way, considering how adorable this guy was. "I'm sure I can look around myself if you've got something else to do," she offered.

"No, no, it's my pleasure," Kai insisted. "Plus I feel responsible for Regis's absence." He leaned close. "Confidentially?"

Anna nodded.

"I took the bloke out surfing yesterday, his day off. He'd just pounded some margaritas, and he insisted on wearing a wet suit. Once he got out there—"

Anna laughed. "I know the rest of this story. A friend warned me about the hazards of nature and wet suits."

"A rash so fierce it'll make a man wish for scabies," Kai declared, grimacing. "So you surf, do you?"

"Not really." Anna was not about to share the details of her failed efforts.

"We've got some of the best waves between Zuma and Peru. If you'd like to give it a whirl, come on down to the Surf Shack. It's not really a shack—you can order a full meal and eat it right on the beach, at a table with a linen tablecloth. Let's shove off, shall we? Walk or golf cart?"

"Let's walk," Anna decided.

"Your wish is my command."

For the next half hour, Kai showed Anna around the magnificence that was Las Casitas resort. The beach and water sports area, complete with fishing boat, kayaks, water skiing, parasailing, a scuba center, and wakeboarding. The five different restaurants—seaside buffet, sushi bar, Mexican with a roaming mariachi band, French haute cuisine, and Atkins-friendly. Two of them—the seaside buffet and the Mexican one—stayed open twenty-four hours a day. One could also order room service round the clock or hang out at the Surf Shack.

Kai took Anna through the luxury open-air spa. It rivaled anything in New York or Los Angeles. There were four different types of outdoor massage, including a two-hundred-pulsating-jet hydrotherapy variety, eucalyptus body wraps, Diamond Perfection exfoliation, wherein the entire body was rubbed with skin-smoothing ground gems, and the very popular seaside manicure-pedicure, complete with fourteen-karat gold polish.

Next came a walk through the two boutiques: one for goods made exclusively in Mexico, the other for very upscale designer clothes and accessories—Prada,

Chanel, Marc Jacobs, and the like. It was obvious to Anna that the boutique's buyer had excellent taste.

Then they toured the sports facilities: The possibilities were endless. There was a running and biking track that made a two-mile circuit around the property, with Segway machines as a low-impact option. An Olympic swimming pool featured high and low diving boards plus two swim-up bars that Kai reported poured only premium beers and liquors. A smaller, more out-of-the-way pool (Kai termed it "the relaxing pool") featured a man-made, perfumed waterfall. It was surrounded by a riot of Mexican flora.

The pièce de résistance of Las Casitas, though, was the re-created crossroads of an actual Mexican village, complete with craftspeople and stores. Kai told Anna that the famous Las Casitas street party happened right there every Wednesday night.

"Margarita fountain, lobster barbecue, dance contests, and general bacchanal. The rich and famous and splurging accountants from the world over throw off their inhibitions here in paradise. Always a good time."

"I'm looking forward to it," Anna told Kai. "Not the accountants, but the rest of it,"

Kai grinned. "I'm sure your escort will swat them off."

Escort? He had to mean Lloyd, Anna realized. That's right; this resort kept perfect tabs on all their guests.

"Um . . . for the record? The guy I arrived with isn't my escort."

Kai's eyebrows rose. "Companion?"

"Only in the sense that we arrived in the same vehicle."

Kai seemed to be waiting for further explanation, but Anna didn't really want to go into it. Then she'd have to explain why she was traveling with someone she disliked. And then it would come out that her father was trying to buy the resort. Not that it was a secret, but it could still make things awkward.

"So, have I completed the tour?" she asked, changing the subject.

"Hardly. Ready to visit the au naturel side?"

"Pardon me?"

Kai grinned. "There's a whole wing of this place that's clothing optional. You'd be surprised how much of our clientele ends up there. Accountants and all."

"You mean a nude beach?"

"Much more than a beach. It can be quite wild. It's the no-cameras policy, I think, that does it."

"I don't understand."

"This resort has a strict no-cameras policy. If we see a guest with a camera, we take it away and expose the film. If it's a digital, we take away the internal media. And we don't return it. It's in our contract. We want our guests to feel safe . . . no matter what they choose to do. We've got excellent security." He pointed to the sky. "The last time some tabloid from the States sent a flyover helicopter, the Mexican government launched two fighter jets. I'm sure they scared the bejesus out of the poor fellow."

"That seems a bit extreme," Anna commented.

"Hardly. The gossip rags will pay millions for a nude photo of either of the Jennifers. We have to protect their privacy."

"Has anyone ever snuck in a camera?"

"We had one guy try to scuba in with one."

"What happened?"

"If I told you, I'd have to kill you," Kai joked.

The tour ended at the Surf Shack. Kai gestured to the Pacific; the waves were rhythmic and well spaced. "The water temp is seventy-six. Sure I can't get you out there?"

"Not now. Maybe later. Thanks for the tour, though. It was great."

"Definitely my pleasure."

Kai gave her another one of those sexy, crinkly smiles. Her conversation with Danny about one-night stands suddenly flew into her head. Someone hot she'd never see again.

Then she stopped herself. She was only seventeen years old. She'd only been with one guy, Ben. Who did she think she was kidding?

Anna, a voice inside her said. *If you aren't at least going to try it, you should go back to Beverly Hills. Now.*

"Kai?"

"Yes?"

Anna cleared her suddenly dry throat. "Would you like to meet for a drink later?"

For a moment, he didn't answer, which made Anna feel like an idiot. What if he wasn't allowed to fraternize with the guests? What if he wasn't attracted to her? He probably had a girlfriend. Probably ten women a day came on to him, like he was just another perk of paradise. He might even be married. How could she be so—?

"I'd love to," Kai answered.

Tens and Near Tens

"Who's in charge here?" Sam asked pointedly. She'd just left her house for about an hour or two to shop for her diet at Whole Foods, and when she returned, unexpected mayhem greeted her inside the front door. Skinny men flitted around the cavernous interior hall, guiding a small nation of workers in the fine art of hanging strands of tiny lightbulbs entwined with ropes of red and pink wildflowers. Other workers were gluing twenty-foot panels of red washed silk fabric to the stone walls in some manner that would allow them to remove said fabric without a trace. Another work crew fastened a scarlet velvet carpet runner to the slate floor. And amongst this mini-cast of thousands, not one person responded to her question.

Suddenly Dee trotted into the hallway, trailed by a man in red monk's robes. "Can you bless this area, too, please? Thanks." Then she skittered over to Sam and enveloped her in a hug. "I was wondering when you'd get here. Isn't this going to be the best baby shower?"

Poppy's baby shower. The next day. Sam had done

her best to erase it from her mind. She hadn't even bought a gift yet.

"Wait," Sam recalled. "Isn't it supposed to be at House of Blues?"

"Yeah. But Poppy had a dream in which Ruby Hummingbird told her that she needed to be in a more nurturing atmosphere. So we decided at the last minute to have it here. Isn't that sweet?"

"Ruby Hummingbird makes a habit of showing up in dreams," Sam uttered, absolutely deadpan.

"She's preparing us for her arrival," Dee said, missing Sam's sarcasm. "Besides, Baba Yaga has blessed the entire house, room by room. We tried to get a rabbi from the Kabbalah Center, but no one would volunteer. We even called Chabad. No luck."

"Well, you got . . . Baba," Sam intoned, as the spectacled bald guy in the diaphanous robes went from corner to corner of the hallway, shaking a silver beacon filled with smoking incense. "He looks like he knows what he's doing."

"Excuse me," said an older man in workman's coveralls. "Coming through!"

Sam and Dee had to edge against the wall to make way for him and his helper, who were carrying a ten-foot-high framed photo of naked Poppy, in profile. Sam saw the photo as it went by: Poppy's head was turned toward the camera, her arms wrapped around her very pregnant belly. A single ruby-throated hummingbird flew overhead.

"Um . . . whose idea was that?"

"Mine," Dee said proudly. "What, you don't like it?"

Sam gritted her teeth and ignored Dee's question. "Look. I'm going to have the cook make me a soy shake and a salad. You hungry?"

Dee patted her nonexistent stomach. "Nah. I just had half a sweet potato and I'm superstuffed. I'm only eating orange food today."

Whatever. Sam wandered into the kitchen and gave her instructions to the cook but then caught a glimpse of herself in the mirrored refrigerator. The mirror was a dieting ploy of her father's—in an interview with *People* he'd explained how every time he went to the refrigerator to get something to eat, his reflection would guilt-jerk him into leading man shape.

I am so not leading lady shape, Sam thought. *I'm still fucking fat.*

She told the cook to cancel her order. Then two more workers came into the kitchen and started moving around furniture. It gave Sam an instant headache, and she knew she had to escape. The alternative was homicide.

Sam dug her new cell phone out of her jeans pocket—platinum coated, with her initials encrusted in diamonds. It had been delivered last week from Tiffany, courtesy of her father. She pressed speed dial.

Cammie was having a crisis.

No one could tell by looking, of course. She sat at the bar of the Spider Club in Hollywood, sipping her cranberry

martini and awaiting Sam's arrival. She knew she looked
fantastic in her Gucci denim miniskirt and Boy Scout shirt
that looked like it belonged to her little brother—if she had
a little brother. But it had been designed, in fact, by a former porn star named Lydia Cherry   mock scout-
ing and bowling shirts for a   Beverly
Boulevard. Cammie had chosen it to match the interior of
the club: a striking red lighting scheme, oversized Chinese
lanterns suspended from the ceiling, and Spanish-Moorish
tiling on the floor and around the doorways. Acid green
walls, golden bar stools, a huge mirror from the 1950s
behind the bar, and an arachnid theme in the artwork. And
that was just the dance area—there was an indoor smoking
patio as well.

Spider Club was private, but Cammie had been
offered a free membership the week the club had
opened, on the theory that hot girls hanging out would
help ensure that the club was a hit. The club concierge
tracked her favorite drink; the cranberry martini had
arrived without her having to ask for it.

Cammie took a sip—perfect—and watched a hot
young model-turned-actor whose last movie had tanked
slip out the door with an older actress. It was rumored
that she had had so much work done by Dr. Birnbaum,
plastic surgeon to the stars (Ben Birnbaum's father—
formerly *her* Ben, then for about a millisecond *Anna's*
Ben, and now probably doing-half-the-girls-at-Princeton
Ben), that she had a zipper all the way from her butt to
her neck, due to the massive removal of hanging skin.

Cammie figured the couple was going next door to Avalon, where they would pretend they wanted privacy while in actuality they'd put on a spectacle. First they'd make out on the dance floor. Then she'd give him a topless lap dance and—w e it would make the rumor rags because they we th desperate for publicity.

Cammie took another sip of her drink. Sam had called that afternoon to ask Cammie if she wanted to go clubbing. It had been a salve to Cammie's bruised ego. So were the guys all checking her out. For kicks, she was keeping a running tally of how many had mentally undressed her. Five. Eight. Eleven. It boosted her self-confidence, which had been recently been slipping like a Telemundo actor's bad hairpiece. How could the hottest girl at the hottest high school in the hottest city in the world be in love with a boy who couldn't get it up for her? Why wasn't Adam Flood calling her day and night, pining for her, insane for her, when every other male of wet-dream age went deaf and dumb—but never blind—in her magnificent presence? And the most pressing question of all—

If Adam had been with Anna on that beach, would he have been ready, willing, and very able?

Without saying a word or even being in her presence, somehow Anna Percy had managed to screw her over again.

"Hi, sorry I'm late," Sam said, sliding onto the gold leather seat next to Cammie. "Did you happen to notice that like half of our class is in the next room at Twyla Bonet's birthday party? Mischa Barton's in there, too. She's Twyla's cousin, I think. Can you believe Twyla didn't invite us?"

Cammie drained her martini. "And I would care because . . . ?"

"Because we always get invited everywhere."

"Everywhere *important.*"

A young bartender with a shaved head discreetly slid a Cosmopolitan in front of Sam. "No thanks, Remy. A Diet Coke."

He whisked the cocktail away.

"Don't tell me you quit drinking." Cammie scoffed.

"No, I'm—" Sam stopped mid-sentence.

"What?" Cammie pressed. She hated it when Sam didn't tell her everything.

"Never mind. Anyway, I had to escape the Poppy and Dee show. They're all atwitter over Poppy's shower tomorrow. I suppose you'll be there. Ugh. I don't want to think about it. How's it going with Adam?"

"Ah, here's a subject near and dear to my heart," Cammie murmured, sipping her drink. "Not to mention many other parts of my anatomy. The boy's a stallion."

Sam looked surprised. "Adam?"

"Yes, Adam. I mean it, Sam. I can barely *walk.*"

"Gee, he seems like he'd be such a gentle—" Sam began.

"What can I tell you? I bring out the beast in men." Remy set a Diet Coke with lime in front of Sam and another martini for Cammie, who raised her glass at him. "Here's to unbridled lust."

"Right back 'atcha," the good-looking bartender replied.

"You had lust with Ben, too," Sam reminded Cammie.

Cammie flashed her patented cat-got-the-canary grin. "Would you like to know how good Adam is? He makes me ask, 'Ben who?'"

The DJ fired up some Beanie Man and the girls went to dance. Boys instantly surrounded them. As usual, though, the ones who came on to Sam were never more than six-point-five on the heat-o-meter that put, say, Orlando Bloom at nine-point-nine. Or if they were higher than six-point-fivers, it was only because they recognized Sam and wanted to suck up to her in hopes of ingratiating themselves with her famous father.

After a couple of songs, Sam signaled to Cammie that she wanted to return to the bar. But Cammie merely waved and kept dancing, gratified to see that she was surrounded by tens and near tens, with a few nines who had an inflated view of their own good looks.

If only Adam could see her now.

Back at the bar, Sam nursed her Diet Coke. If she'd hoped that an evening with Cammie would pull her out of her funk, seven minutes on the Spider Club dance floor had destroyed that notion.

"Hey, Sam!"

A guy so handsome that he didn't look real slid onto the stool next to her. His short, spiked black hair set off sexy deep-set green eyes, and he wore the regulation young-actor November-to-March uniform of low-slung blue jeans, black button-down shirt, and white T-shirt underneath. She knew him, vaguely. Lars Something-or-other. He'd played a fresh-scrubbed young cop in a Jackson Sharpe film called *Street Hero*. Sam recalled he'd died in the teaser before the credits. She'd seen him recently in an underwear ad in the *Los Angeles Times*. Evidently, the acting thing wasn't working out.

"Wow, you look great!" he told her.

What an asshole.

"Thanks, Lars."

"So, what have you been up to?"

"I'm having a sex change." Sam said first thing that came into her head.

"Wow, cool," Lars said, nodding, which proved Sam's point. He hadn't heard her, didn't think she looked great, and didn't care a flying fuck about her. "So listen, I've gotten into Scientology. It's the bomb, really. It's helped my acting like you wouldn't believe."

"Uh-huh."

"You should check it out—go to the Dream Center building in Hollywood; you can see it from the 101. They're really good people. Tell your dad I sent him my regards, okay? Tell him Scientology really helped me get in touch with my core. I'd love to read for him for his next project."

"Right. As soon as I get home," Sam lied. "In fact, if he's asleep when I get home, I'll wake him and tell him, okay?"

Sam went back to her Diet Coke without even bothering to wait for a response. For all she knew, Lars believed her. How depressing. Everyone was a user or a poser. Everyone had an angle.

The more she thought about it, the more she wanted to eat.

Fuck it. What difference did it make if she weighed five pounds more or less? She could turn into a Sherman tank for all anyone cared. She surrendered herself to Remy and ordered one of every single appetizer on the bar menu: fried Brie with water crackers, prawns in chutney butter, confit duck bites wrapped in miniature Mandarin pancakes, charred vegetable crostini, and Asian pear with candied walnuts.

"Hungry, Sam?" he joked.

"You can't even imagine."

Within five minutes, as if by magic, plates surrounded her in a gluttonous semicircle. People rushed past, flirting, dancing, tripping; no one noticed the brunette surrounded by a meal for six.

Sam knew that if she took a single bite, she wouldn't stop. And she realized there were probably photographers lurking at the club—there were always photographers. She'd likely end up in a tabloid spread: SUPERSTAR'S DAUGHTER TURNS INTO SUPERPIG. Was she willing to risk *that*?

She edged back from the bar. She had to change locations. Someplace away from everything that could make her want to eat. Not just from Cammie, but also away from Dee and Poppy—all the day-in, day-out usual suspects. The question was, Where to go? Money was no object. But what fun would it be to go to Paris or Tokyo or Maui by herself? Sam wasn't very good at flying solo and she knew it.

And then, the lightbulb moment. She knew exactly what to do.

"Remy?" She got the bartender's attention.

"Yeah, Sam?"

"Put this all on my tab and give it away to the next person who sits down." Then her face brightened. "Better idea. Bring it into Twyla's birthday party and tell them it's a present from Sam Sharpe."

Remy grinned knowingly. "She'll appreciate it."

"I know."

As Sam pushed away from the table, she wondered if she wasn't the first person at Spider Club to tempt fate and then walk away. She was actually proud of herself. One quick wave to Cammie, and Sam was outta there.

Eenie, meeny, miney, mo, Cammie thought as she raised her arms over her head and swiveled her hips to the music. *Which cute boy should I take home? This one?*

"This one" was a curly-haired guy named Uzi who told her with the cutest Israeli accent that he lived in Tel Aviv but was in Los Angeles for a week to train with the American Olympic judo team. Objectively speaking, he was way hotter than Adam. Older. More worldly. Most likely able to function in the junction.

After an hour of dancing with Uzi and two more

martinis, Cammie told him she'd be right back and tottered off to the ladies' room. Her path took her right by the doorway into Twyla's little party. Something made her want to go in and waggle her fingers at Beverly Hills High's B-list.

So she did. Twyla spotted her immediately.

"Cammie! I didn't know you were here!" She whirled around to her friends. "Hey, you guys, look who's here!" Then back to Cammie. "Come party with us!"

"Gee, can't," Cammie said, her voice oozing faux regret. "I have to meet Adam."

"Adam Flood?" Twyla asked.

"The one and only," Cammie confirmed. She let her index finger trail from her clavicle down to her cleavage. "We are so hot for each other, it's unreal."

"Wow," Twyla breathed. "I always thought he was a nice guy, but I didn't think . . ."

"Trust me," Cammie purred. She moved closer. "Confidentially, if I keep him waiting too long, he'll spontaneously combust."

Twyla giggled the most annoying and imbecilic giggle, and Cammie remembered all over again why, even though Twyla's father owned half the BMW dealerships in Southern California, she would always be second tier.

"Tell him I said hi, okay?" Twyla asked.

"Sure. Oh, one more thing." Cammie leaned even closer to Twyla and whispered in her ear, then spread her hands apart. The space between them was approximately the length of a tennis racquet. Twyla gaped in awe.

Cammie sashayed out, feeling great. One more cranberry martini and she might even start to believe her own lies. In the meantime, she realized, she'd already forgotten about Uzi. Which meant that Adam had *really* gotten under her skin.

Now if only he'd get on top of it.

The Paradise Clause

"Thanks for meeting me."

Kai grinned. "It wasn't exactly onerous."

Anna and Kai were sitting at a table with a white tablecloth that had been set up in the sand a few feet from the water. Each had the Surf Shack's specialty drink before them: fresh limeade mixed with beer brewed in Las Casitas' own microbrewery. The ochre moon illuminated the sand and the waves. Anna could hear the distant strains of disco at the main pool, but down here at the Surf Shack, the only sounds were the swooping gulls and waves lapping the sand.

It was beautiful. Calming. Damn near perfect. The fact that she was experiencing this with a very cute guy who had just correctly used the word *onerous* made it even better.

As for Lloyd, he'd called her twice during the evening. One time to ask her to dinner, which she'd declined. The second time to inform her that tonight was disco night at Club Las Casitas next to the main pool, and since he could out-disco John Travolta circa *Saturday Night Fever,* they really should meet up. Anna

119

had allowed as how she hadn't come to Mexico for disco night, but she was certain that Lloyd could find plenty of girls who might appreciate his moves. Now she was wearing a cherry-pattern-on-white Miu Miu sundress she'd recently bought while shopping with Sam, sitting with a well-spoken surfer. And she was shocked at how comfortable she felt.

"Where in Australia did you grow up? Sydney?"

Kai looked impressed. "Good ear. Generally I get the British thing. Americans never guess Australia unless you talk about putting shrimp on the barbie."

Anna laughed. "You've been hanging out with the wrong Americans."

"Well, don't let it get round, but actually I'm a citizen of the good old U.S. of A. My mum is Hawaiian; my dad was stationed there in the service. We moved to Sydney when I was two. That accounts for the accent."

"How did you end up here in Mexico?"

Kai stretched his arms behind his head, revealing gleaming, golden muscles beneath a Fiji Surf Open 2004 T-shirt. "Ah, yes. My path to paradise. I was going to the University of Sydney. Supposed to be studying engineering. But the fact of the matter is, I was majoring in girls and surfing. Bloke I know got a summer gig here teaching tennis, told me they needed a surfing instructor. Didn't have to ask me twice. Within forty-eight hours I was hooked on the place. That was four years ago. He's gone on to a Club Med and I'm still here. Once you taste paradise, how do you settle for anything else?"

"I see your point." Anna took a sip of her drink as a light ocean breeze ruffled the hair from her neck. "Nothing feels real here. The problems and hassles of life . . . It all seems to just melt away."

"I'll drink to that," Kai said, hoisting his glass. "So, what about you, Anna Percy? What's your story? Of course, you can choose to invoke the Las Casitas paradise clause, which states that you can be anyone you want here. No past, no future."

"The Las Casitas paradise clause," she repeated. "That's tempting."

"It's tempted me for four years now. Ready for another?" He cocked his head toward her nearly empty glass.

"Sure."

Kai caught the eye of his buddy who ran the Surf Shack, and he immediately started mixing two more drinks.

"So what's your life like here, Kai?" Anna found it easy to keep the conversation going. "Beyond surfing, I mean."

"Beyond surfing is more surfing. It's addictive, like drugs or beautiful women—present company included. The waves here are some of the best on this side of the Pacific."

"That's it?" Anna asked.

He smiled at her. "That's it."

"That's enough?"

"Your problem is that you've spent too much time in civilization," Kai said lightly.

"And you never miss . . ." She searched for the right word. "More?"

"I did more, but that was long ago and far away. What can I tell you? I'm a happier bloke now by far." Kai's friend set the fresh drinks on their table and picked up the empties. "Joaquin, this is Anna. Anna, meet Joaquin. The second-best surfer at Las Casitas."

"Nice to meet you." The young man gave Anna a fabulous grin. Clearly Las Casitas picked its staff for looks at least as much as it did for skill. Joaquin was of medium height with a wrestler's build. His hair was bleached blond and spiky. "Kai treating you right?"

"Kai is treating me just fine," Anna assured him.

"Good. You two need anything, just let me know."

"Hey, how about you fire up the Julio?" Kai asked.

"You got it, man." Joaquin padded back through the sand to the Surf Shack. Moments later, the strains of Julio Iglesias and Willie Nelson singing, "To All the Girls I've Loved Before," filled the air.

Kai stood. "Dance?"

"To Julio Iglesias?" Anna asked archly.

"Hey, I like what I like." He reached for Anna's hand.

Anna was impressed by Kai's unabashed lack of pretension. Besides, what difference did the music make? It was still paradise.

"I'd love to."

Anna stood, took his hand, and went into his strong arms. It felt wonderful. Facts were facts: He was a party boy who'd dropped out of college to chase the perfect wave. But that didn't matter. She wasn't going to marry him or even have some big relationship with him. The paradise clause could work for her, too. Right?

With that thought, Anna lifted her lips to Kai's and kissed him.

It quickly became clear that Kai had other skills besides surfing. Anna lost herself in the moment. They swayed in the sand until she heard a familiar voice.

"Dancing on an uncertain surface is murder on the knees."

Kai and Anna broke apart to see Lloyd sitting on a stool by the Surf Shack. His silk shirt was open nearly to the waist, displaying far too much of his hirsute chest. But he wasn't alone. A cute brunette in a floral sarong and bra top sat next to him.

"This is Debbie; she's from Idaho." Lloyd introduced the girl at his side with a great deal of pride. Then he draped an arm around Debbie's neck. They were obviously on more than speaking terms.

"Indiana," Debbie corrected, but she kissed Lloyd's cheek nonetheless. Which had to mean their more-than-speaking terms encounter thus far had gone quite well.

Lloyd pulled Debbie closer. "Now, this girl can dance."

Debbie giggled. "I took lessons at Purdue."

"And I'm about to show her some new moves," Lloyd added with a wink. "All work and no play. But I wanted to see how you were, Anna. So, who's the lucky guy?"

Anna didn't want to introduce Kai. Yet she was thankful that Lloyd had found a new little playmate and would leave her alone.

"He doesn't speak English," Anna said quickly.

Lloyd wagged a finger at her. "You forget, Anna. I speak five languages."

"He doesn't speak yours, Lloyd," Anna said pointedly, as she felt Kai's hands go around her waist.

Lloyd nodded. "Got it. Well, it looks like you two speak the same language, anyway." He raised his glass in Anna's direction. "Carpe diem, then. Have a blast. See you later."

"Your escort who isn't your escort, right?" Kai guessed as Lloyd and Debbie headed back arm in arm up the path toward the pool area.

"Exactly."

"How bad can he be?" Kai teased. "He just encouraged you to seize the day."

So. Kai understood a bit of Latin, too. Impressive, for someone who hadn't finished college.

Then she realized what she was doing: assessing his intelligence, weighing whether or not he was educated enough, articulate enough, *suitable* enough for her to be with. Suitable enough. God, she was thinking like her mother.

Kai took her back into his arms. "Did I mention that you smell great?"

She snaked her arms around his neck and swayed with him to the music. "No."

"Well, you do. Particularly . . . . here."

He lightly kissed the side of her neck, just below her ear. Shivers ran down her body.

"Anywhere else?" Anna asked playfully.

He gently turned her around so that he was standing behind her. "Here." He lifted her hair and put his lips to the back of her neck.

Whoa. His arms went around her waist. They felt good. No. Great. Which meant she was as capable as anyone else of desiring a perfect stranger.

But should she? Could she?

He turned her back around and they were slow dancing again. "I'd love to be alone with you," he whispered into her hair.

She smiled up at him. "We *are* alone."

"Joaquin is my mate, but threesomes don't do it for me."

"Right. Joaquin. He makes a terrific—what do you call that drink again?"

"Paradise," Kai said.

Anna nodded. "Perfect."

"I totally agree." Kai kissed her. She kissed him back because she felt like it. The more she kissed him, the more she liked it. She felt his hand slide from her waist downward. . . .

The moment of truth.

One part of Anna was saying: "This is moving way too fast." But another part said: "Paradise clause, now!"

She could do it. She *would* do it.

She chucked her chin lightly in the direction of her casita. "Yes?" she asked.

"Definitely."

Fun

Kai looked around Anna's casita. "Wow, this place is huge."

"If that's supposed to make me think you've never been inside a casita, it's not working. Anyway, ultra-high-end resorts don't do ironic," Anna teased. She popped a Sheryl Crow CD into the player. "Is this okay?"

"Perfect." He put his arms around her, and they swayed to the music just as they had at the beach. Then he kissed her again. He really was a great kisser. Anna felt as if she was floating.

"Your hot tub?" Kai suggested with a whisper.

Hot tub. Anna couldn't decide if that would be sleazy. Clearly she was having trouble *committing* to the paradise clause.

No one's here to judge me.

Whatever happens between Kai and me will stay between Kai and me.

Right.

Exactly.

126

She willed her superego to take a big fat break. It did. Mostly.

"Hot tub," she repeated. "I have a bikini. But I don't have a suit for you. Can you get one—?"

"Anna . . ." he interrupted, then kissed her gently. "Why would we need suits?"

His hands went to the top of his jeans. Oh no. He was going to undress right in the middle of her living room, right this very moment. Well, it was her own fault. She had invited him here. What would he think she wanted to do?

Exactly what she was planning on doing, probably.

Still, as much as she told herself she wanted him, she blushed as he undid his top button. And looked everywhere except at his hands as they shimmied those jeans down, down . . . to reveal the surfer jams underneath.

Anna folded her arms, red-faced. "That was mean."

Kai hooted with laughter. "You should see yourself. You really thought I'd strip to nothing five minutes after you invite me to your casita? I'm pretty chill, Anna. We hook up, cool. We don't, that's cool, too."

He was just so sure of himself! How did people develop that quality? Maybe you just had to do it first and believe it later. So Anna pulled her sundress over her head and tossed it on the couch. She wore only the briefest pink Belgian lace bra and the tiniest of matching G-strings. Kai's jaw fell open. She tried for a look of total confidence and had no idea if she was pulling it off. But head held high, she headed for the hot tub and called nonchalantly back to him over her shoulder.

"You coming or not?"

Moments later, Anna had cranked up the tub's Jacuzzi jets and lowered herself into the steaming hot water. Her long blond hair floated around her. Oh, this was bliss, pure bliss. She felt every muscle in her body relax. Kai was across from her, underwater save for his head.

"This feels awesome," he declared.

Anna murmured in agreement. He floated over to her. Took her into his arms. And kissed her. It felt nice, so surreal. The next thing she knew, his hands were on the back clasp of her bra.

Red alert, red alert.

She politely backed out of his arms.

Kai held his palms up to her. "Whoa. We won't go there if you don't want to."

"I . . . I . . ."

Anna didn't know what to say. Did she want to? Or did she just *want* to want to? If she did it, would that be exploring new ground, opening herself up to new experiences? Or would that just be her trying to be someone she was not? How could she possibly tell the difference? Did she need a boy to fall for her, really care about her, before she'd have sex? And if so, was that more about her morals or her ego? To Kai, she was just another girl passing through paradise. So if she—

"I get the feeling your brain is working overtime," Kai guessed correctly.

"It's a character flaw," Anna admitted.

"Maybe it's a gift. I told you, Anna, I'm cool. How long are you staying at Las Casitas?"

"A few days."

"So no worries, then. Let's just see what happens."

Anna nodded. "I feel like an idiot, I should tell you."

"You're being way too hard on yourself. It's all supposed to be fun, you know?"

"I do," Anna said earnestly. "I really do."

"Then we're good." He kissed her lightly. "I can see myself out. Adios."

Then Kai stepped out of the tub, pulled on his pants, and drifted away into the night.

Time Sensitive

"Hey, Adam! Big guy, how're they hanging?"

Adam waved to Zack, one of his teammates on the basketball team as they passed each other on the main quad of Beverly Hills High School. It was Wednesday morning and the fashion show/gossip exchange/flirt fest known as changing classes was in full swing. A thousand students were going back and forth between the four main buildings that constituted Beverly Hills High, and Adam watched as Zack had to dodge his way through the human traffic to get to him. Adam held up a hand for Zack to high-five, and they did the requisite three slaps that were the unofficial greeting of the team. With Zack was a sophomore—Charlie Something-or-other—whom Adam didn't know well.

"Catch you at practice later," Adam told him.

"You got it, big guy. Bring the balls." Zack smirked. He elbowed Charlie, who guffawed.

"Uh, that's what we've got a team manager for," Adam replied.

"Yeah, right." Zack snickered. Laughing together, he and his friend loped away.

Okay, that was weird, Adam thought as he continued across the quad toward the science building—he had an AP biology class in five minutes. A few steps later, he encountered the team manager, a sophomore guy named Lawrence "Don't Call Me Larry" Rothstein. Lawrence loved basketball more than anything in the world and was a decent little player. But the emphasis was on *little* because Lawrence was barely five foot three. And he couldn't jump. So he'd asked the team coach if he could apprentice himself, because his ambition was to coach hoops in the NBA.

"Hey, point guard," Lawrence greeted him warmly. "Wazzup, Mr. Big?"

"Not much."

"Heard you had an awesome time last night."

"From who?"

Lawrence gestured in the direction of the gym. "You know. Around."

"Around *where?*"

"Oh, you know, man," Lawrence retorted evasively. "Listen, just between us—I'm asking this because it's my job, I swear I'm not prying—are you okay with that cup the trainer gave you? 'Cuz I thought maybe you felt *confined,* man."

Adam shook his head. "Nope. I'm just fine with my cup, Lawrence. Thanks for asking."

"Oh yeah, Mr. Modesty, I can dig it." Lawrence bobbed

his head up and down. "Well, if anything, you know, pops up . . ." He gave Adam a knowing look and ambled off.

"Look, there he is!"

Adam turned. Twyla Bonet was skittering toward him, dodging bodies, two of her skinny friends in tow. "Hey, why didn't you come to my birthday party last night?" she pouted, throwing her arms around Adam's neck.

"Uh, because I wasn't invited?"

She stepped back far enough that she could look into his eyes while keeping her fingers snaked around the back of his neck. "Of course you were invited!" She slipped her hand down and pinched his ass.

Adam jerked away from her. "What is going *on?*"

"Us, maybe," Twyla simpered. "Hey, I was thinking about going to the Playground tonight. Want to come?"

"At nine, nine-thirty, ten, ten-thirty," her look-alike friend added.

"Yo, what's up?" Parker Pinelli called to the girls as he loped over to them. "Killer party at Spider Club last night, Twyla."

"Hey, Parker," Adam greeted him. Parker was an actor wannabe who skated by on his incredible good looks. Lack of talent and IQ points didn't seem to prevent him from hooking up with some of the hottest girls in Beverly Hills. But Twyla and her friends barely registered Parker's appearance. They were too busy manhandling Adam. Which, from Adam's point of view, made zero sense. He knew he was supposed to like it, but he really wasn't attracted to Twyla. Frankly, he just found the attention peculiar.

"So Twyla, I got three extra passes to this private party at Deep tonight," Parker went on. "P. Diddy's shooting a video there. You fine ladies want to go?"

"That depends," Twyla answered coyly, accidentally-on-purpose brushing her left breast against Adam's arm. "Do *you* want to go?"

"Um, Parker said *three* passes, Twyla," Adam pointed out. "And I have a girlfriend."

"So?" She looped a playful finger through his belt. He stepped away from her.

"Okay, this is wack," Adam insisted. "Whatever you're on, go for a half tab next time."

He extricated himself from the girls just in time to see Cammie undulate in his direction. "Hey, handsome," she called.

God, she was something else. That voice. Just the sound of it could get him . . . Damn. He wished he could take her back to that beach. Right this very second.

She stood on tiptoe and brushed her lips against his. "Missed you."

"Missed you, too."

She edged up again to whisper in his ear. "Let's ditch school and go to my house. No one's there."

"I've got bio. And then a calc test."

"What's more important? Me or calc?"

"Let's just say the calc test is slightly more time-sensitive." He ran a hand down her back. "Can I take you up on that offer later?"

"Ooh, sounds fun, can I come, too?" Twyla asked.

Parker and Twyla's two friends had slipped away, but Twyla had hung around long enough to overhear what Cammie was saying.

"Sure. What say you mix drinks, turn down the bed, then back out of the room and close the door?" Cammie made a shooing gesture with her hand, and Twyla scooted away into the passing throng.

"Bizarre," Adam muttered. "I feel like I just walked into some surreal Charlie Kaufman flick, and I'm the only one who didn't get the script."

"The only movie I'm interested in has a cast of two." Cammie leaned into him.

"I second that emotion." He leaned in to kiss her. "I have zero interest in having Twyla give me a lap dance."

"A *what?*"

"She practically offered. Hey, it's not like I took her up on it."

"You're such a modest stud puppy," Cammie teased. "So, we on for later? I have to ditch early to go to Poppy's baby shower. But after that?"

"Absolutely."

The bell rang. All around them, kids hustled out of the quad and into the buildings. Meanwhile Cammie gave the finger to one of the ever-present security cameras mounted on posts in the quad.

"Testy, testy," Adam teased, wrapping his arms around her waist. "Actually, I've got a surprise for you. Later."

"Really?" She looked up at him. "Good surprise?"

"Hope so."

"Is it a *big* surprise?"

He laughed and swatted her butt. "I'm late for bio," he said, then veered off into the opposite hall. "I'll tell you later."

Three minutes later, he walked into his biology lab. "Adam, wow, you look so hot in those jeans," Krishna Kaplan remarked. She had an affinity for collagen and was known for having the puffiest lips at Beverly Hills High School. Now she gently bit her enormous bottom lip and then smiled.

Again, weird. Maybe he was dreaming that he was in some grade-C porn flick. If so, when Mr. Davis entered the classroom, he'd be clad in black leather and a dog collar, and built like Andy Roddick, and that new girl with the great ass would be sitting on his desk taking dictation.

Definitely no dream. Mr. Davis, whose massive stomach had obliterated his belt line late in the twentieth century, emerged in his usual khaki pants, blue polyester shirt, and lab coat stretched to the max. No leather. No dog collar.

Krishna, however, gave Adam a salacious wink.

Huh. Maybe all the flirting was because he and Cammie were now a couple. Mere mortal girls wanted whatever the goddess possessed, and the goddess of Beverly Hills High School was Cammie Sheppard.

Yeah. That had to be it.

Pink Rabbit Fur

Dee gazed around the ballroom at the Sharpe compound and broke into a broad smile. Everything was perfect. More than perfect.

There were fifteen round tables. At each table sat exactly twelve of the two hundred of Poppy's dearest friends and family who'd been invited to the baby shower. All female. And nearly every guest had obeyed the invitation's suggestion to wear either white or a shade of red.

Each table supported a statue of a naked Mayan fertility goddess, albeit with Poppy's profile—a trick she'd stolen from her own wedding, where there were ice sculptures of Aphrodite carved in her likeness. Red roses and honeysuckle sprigs surrounded the statue's base. From overhead, supported by strong monofilament line, hung jeweled mobiles of red pelicans carrying baby baskets. The name Ruby Hummingbird Sharpe was encrusted on each basket in Swarovski crystals.

Best of all, Dee had been seated at the main table right next to Poppy. The only other people there were Poppy's mother, grandmother, sisters, and her female cousins from Texas. There was a place set for Sam, but she was nowhere in sight.

Dee felt as if she had gotten a whole new family; the thought choked her up with happiness. Not that she didn't love her own family. But her father was the well-known and venerable rock-'n'-roll producer Graham Young. He'd been the go-to guy for a number of platinum-selling pop artists for two decades and was always busy in the studio or on the road with whatever diva was doing drugs and/or having a breakdown. As for her mother, she'd been one of the pioneers of the music video business—it was how she'd met Graham. But Karen had dropped out to raise Dee and run her husband's business from home. Now, with Dee a senior in high school, Karen had gone on a self-improvement kick that kept her almost as busy as Graham. She was either at the Century Club gym, taking history classes at Loyola-Marymount, or volunteering at the Los Angeles County Museum of Art. (Dee suspected her mom was doing one of the museum curators, judging by the amount of time she worked in his office.)

Dee was an only child. It didn't used to bother her—she and Sam and Cammie had been friends for so long that it seemed like they were sisters. But ever since Anna Percy had arrived from New York, there'd been tension in their trio. So to be in the bosom of Poppy's family was very precious. The more she thought about it, it was as if Poppy had been sent to her by divine ordination.

The proof of this was that Poppy had chosen *her* to

help with all the baby preparations. Poppy had even asked Dee to help choose her outfit: a custom-designed Carlos Miele red mohair pregnancy sweater with white satin cargo pants that exposed a bit of distended belly in all its glory to the world. Dee thought she had never seen anyone look more beautiful in her entire life.

It made her recall when she'd almost-sort-of thought that she herself was pregnant with Ben Birnbaum's baby. That would have been so cool. But Dee had learned her lesson: Don't hold onto something that isn't going to happen. She hadn't been pregnant, and she'd known it all the time in her heart of hearts, too. It had been a ploy for attention that she now knew was toxic thinking. Now, when something happened that made her feel bad, she'd replace it with something good and purchase herself a minibag by her favorite designer. Let go and let Gucci.

The waitstaff was all female, in button-down red shirts with white tuxedo pants. That had been Poppy's idea, as had the red-and-white color-themed menu: pomegranate, strawberry, and chestnut salad, followed by tomatoes au gratin and chicken in white sauce, finished with cherry sorbet and a strawberry-and-vanilla layer cake. There was also an Atkins alternative: thinly sliced, extremely rare roast beef.

Nor had Poppy and Dee forgotten the party favors. At each place setting was a gift bag, including a new shade of red lipstick MAC had created just for this occasion, called Ruby Hummingbird. There were also Francois Rose Parfum, a rose-toned BlackBerry, and a

Jules le Grat watch with loose faux rubies that floated over its oversized face.

The only male in the room was Yanni. He sat at a white grand piano, wearing a formal white suit and red tie, playing his compositions. These were melodious and serene, almost like the trance-inducing space music that Dee liked to play in her room before she went to sleep. In fact, Dee and Poppy had specifically requested that Yanni not play anything in a minor key, lest he upset the harmonic energy in the room. The musician had gladly acceded to the request.

"What's this thingie in the salad?" Poppy's oldest sister asked, pointing at a fruit she obviously didn't recognize.

"Pomegranate," Poppy piped up. "Flown in from Morocco. It's delicious and very good for you."

Her sister shrugged and forked up a slice of fruit. "I'm into iceberg lettuce and ranch dressing." Another sister nodded her agreement.

Culinary tastes aside, Dee noticed a striking resemblance among the Sinclair women. All of Poppy's relatives—grandmother, mother, sisters, and cousins—had wide blue eyes, thin lips, and high cheekbones. The only differences between them and Poppy were their exceptionally doughy noses and exceptionally minuscule cleavage. Poppy had taken care of both those problems her first month in Hollywood, though it had put her in credit card debt that had lingered until she met Jackson Sharpe.

After lunch, an army of international experts marched in and set up at stations around the ballroom: Russian nail techs from Galina's Nails in Bel Air, an army of masseuses with massage chairs from Fung Wu in Pacific Palisades, and the female stylists from Raymond's new salon on Canon Drive. Each guest could choose which type of pampering she preferred.

Finally, when every woman was well fed, gorgeous, and relaxed, Poppy went to sit in a throne-like red velvet chair that had been placed next to a large table brimming with wrapped gifts of every size and shape. Normally Jackson's assistant, Kiki, would have kept track of who gave what and then handwritten the thank-you notes for Poppy's signature. But Kiki was in Chicago with Jackson for a publicity blitz in advance of Jackson's newest movie, *Lucky Charmed* (a whimsical comedy in which Jackson played a forty-five-year-old American advertising executive who had run out of ideas but meets a leprechaun who saves his career—for a price). So Dee had been drafted for the job. She was more than happy to do it.

There'd been a big debate about how to do the presents. Normally they'd all be opened. Because there were so many guests, they'd decided to unwrap only a representative sampling.

Dee started things off by handing Poppy a large silver envelope. Poppy read it aloud and grinned from ear to ear. "This is the best! From Dr. and Mrs. Dan Birnbaum, a postpartum tummy tuck. Omigod, that is so thoughtful!"

Dee led the underwhelming round of applause. Dr.

Birnbaum—Ben's father—was a famous plastic surgeon. While a tummy tuck was a really useful present, it wasn't as if it had cost Janet Birnbaum a cent in time, money, or effort. Everyone knew it.

The gifts kept coming. An Ecco Baby Sling. A Baby Einstein Learning System. A Bebe Sounds sounds-and-movement monitor that raised an alarm if a baby stopped moving—even breathing—for more than twenty seconds, and a Sassy Deluxe Curved Back and Side Sleeper that was designed to help baby get a full night's sleep in her bassinet.

"Open mine," Cammie suggested, and passed a small square box to Poppy. It was wrapped in red leopard-print paper. Dee wasn't feeling any too thrilled with Cammie, who had showed up in a sky blue Dolce & Gabbana camisole and white jeans. She was the one guest who had eschewed red completely. But Poppy obliged, tearing off the wrapping paper and extracting a pink rabbit fur bra and thong set lined in red satin.

"Oh my gosh. Red fur! This is so wild! Wait until Jackson sees. It's a good thing we'll have two baby nurses so we can try these out! Thank you so much, Cammie."

The guests applauded enthusiastically for the outrageous gift. Dee had to admit it was just like Cammie to pull off something that no one else could. Like Sam always said—

Sam.

Wait a minute. Dee scanned the room. Where was Sam?

Cammie sidled over to Dee. "You did a great job on this shower, Dee. If I ever have a lapse in sanity and decide to breed, remind me not to have one of these. What you did here couldn't be topped."

Dee beamed. "Thanks, Cammie. That means a lot to me. Listen, have you seen Sam anywhere?"

"Last night. We went to Spider Club together," Cammie replied. "Why?"

"How about today?"

Cammie shook her curls off her face. "Now that you mention it, no."

"Isn't that strange? That she'd miss *this?*"

Cammie shrugged. "Not to me. Poppy makes Sam gag. So there is only one reasonable conclusion."

"What's that?" Dee asked.

"She had something better to do. Just like I do now. Enjoy the party. I'm off to enjoy Adam." With that, Cammie turned on her three-inch Kenneth Cole black patent leather pumps and strode away.

Setting the Mood

The bored bellhop whose nameplate said Peter opened the door to a suite at the Au Mer hotel in Santa Monica. Adam stepped inside. *Whoa. Impressive.*

"Our goal here at Au Mer is fun and luxury," Peter droned. "The rugs were woven in Turkey to match the earth tones of the George Smith custom furniture. In the bathroom, you'll notice that the nineteenth-century French washstand has been converted into a fully functional sink. The floors are parquet wood, the fireplace wood-burning, but don't even think about using it, because this a non-smoking room. The ocean can be reached from the elevator at the far end of the hall; it opens to our pool area and the beach. Happy?"

Adam could tell the bellhop was wary of a high school student who wanted to rent the suite for just one night. But Adam wasn't about to spend—*gulp*—three hundred of his hard-earned dollars unless he was sure the place would be perfect, the perfect place for him and Cammie to make love for the first time.

"Yeah, it's great," Adam replied. "Thanks."

Adam went back to the front desk, thanking his lucky stars that there'd been a last-minute cancellation that allowed him to book it at half price. He paid cash; it wasn't like he had a credit card. Counting out the crumpled twenties and watching them disappear into the cashier's drawer made his heart palpitate. How many lawns had he mowed, how many kids had he tutored to save up all that money? Now he was spending it on Cammie. But it was worth it, he vowed to himself. That's how much he valued what they were about to share.

As he waited for the front desk clerk to hand over the suite's key card, he thought back on the conversation he'd had with his dad. He couldn't believe that his father had asked him if he and Cammie were doing the horizontal. As close as he and his dad were, as much as they were able to talk about almost anything, there were still some things a person should keep private. Adam scratched his tattoo absentmindedly. If he were going to be completely honest with himself, he'd have to admit that what bothered him most was that he hadn't been able to tell his dad for sure that he loved Cammie. He definitely cared about her and felt like he knew her in a way that no one else did. He most definitely thought she was hot, and he loved how much she was into him.

So was that love? He had no clue. And he decided that was okay. He had deep feelings for Cammie. One part of his life was about to end and another part to begin. For now, that was enough.

When the desk clerk offered the key card, Adam

stuffed it into the back pocket of his jeans. Then he walked over to Main Street and ducked into a gift shop called Parsley Sage. Bells tinkled when he entered; space music and incense filled the air.

"Welcome to Parsley Sage. Can I be of assistance?" the proprietor asked. She was middle-aged and wore a brilliant flowing silk caftan. At least two dozen strings of beads hung around her neck, and her hands were covered in henna tattoos. She stood near a tiny indoor waterfall next to her cash register.

"Um, yes. Where are your candles?"

"Ah, candles," she intoned wistfully. "Sometimes I rue the invention of the electric light. Right this way." She led Adam to the back of her shop, where thousands of candles covered the rear shelves. They were every size, shape, and fragrance in the universe. "You have a preference? We have your votives, your scenteds, your tapered, your round, your exotics. . . ."

Adam wished the woman would go back to her waterfall so that he could shop for a candle in peace. "Wow. There's a lot of choices. Maybe you should give me a few minutes."

The proprietor didn't take the hint. "Perhaps if you describe the situation for which the candle is desired. I have a lot of experience in these matters."

"Uh . . . it's for my girlfriend," Adam said.

"Ah. Romance. Well, why didn't you just say so in the first place? I have the perfect thing." The owner made a beeline to the end of the shelf, uncovered a huge white candle in the shape of an entwined naked couple, and scurried back to Adam. "Scented with Grecian pheromones, guaranteed to induce passionate desire. I brought it back from Mykonos myself."

"How much is it?" he asked.

"It's a work of art, you know. One hundred and forty dollars."

For a *candle?*

"I was thinking about something more . . . modest. In price, I mean," Adam added.

She frowned. "Just how modest are we talking?"

Adam attempted a smile. "Um . . . ten bucks?"

The woman was crestfallen. "I'm so sorry."

"About what?"

"That you think this girl is only worth a ten-dollar candle. But if you insist, I have one or two under the register that might—"

"I could maybe go to twenty," Adam said, contemplating the few remaining bills in his wallet.

"Twenty dollars," she scoffed. "For anything special, you'll have to be willing invest fifty. . . ." Then she snapped her fingers and broke into a broad grin. "Oh no, wait. I know just the thing for a modest budget." She bent down to the bottom shelf and pulled out candle carton after candle carton until she found what she was looking for—a flower-shaped candle in swirling shades of purple. "Behold the gardenia. Just came in from Greece this morning. Smell."

Adam dutifully took a whiff. "Like flowers."

"Exactly. And I have the special elixir that accompanies it. Follow me." She went to another part of her store and found a flower-shaped bottle that matched the candle. "This special blend of body oils will send your woman to bliss."

Bliss, huh? Exactly what Adam wanted for Cammie. Not that he believed a word the woman was saying; he knew sales hype when he heard it. But on the other hand, to set the mood he wanted for her, it couldn't hurt.

"Okay, great, I'll take those."

The clerk reached for another bottle. "And the gardenia bubble bath, of course."

Adam ran his fingers through his cropped hair. "I don't know. . . ."

"Just imagine. The lights are low, the two of you, soaking in bubbles in the candlelight."

Adam nodded. He could picture it, he really could.

"Excellent! You're a bright young man." The clerk carried everything to her cash register and rang it up. "That will be one hundred and twelve dollars and forty-two cents. With tax."

Adam blanched. "But wait. I said I could only spend twenty dollars."

"On the candle. Which is thirty-two dollars—quite close to what you said you wanted to spend. Then there is the body oil and the bubble bath. The body oil alone is worth the price. These are not manufactured scents, I assure you, but the essence of actual flowers, specially grown in Chilean hothouses."

"But if the candle is from Greece, how can the scents be from—?"

The woman cut him off with a wave of her hand, then opened the body oil and inhaled. "Mmm. Irresistible. But if you want me to forget it . . ."

"No, no. Wait. Hold on a sec." Adam turned his back on the clerk and surreptitiously counted his crumpled bills. He could make this purchase. Barely. It would leave him with a net balance of zilch, but Cammie was worth it. "I'll take it."

"Wise decision," said the proprietor. "What's your name?"

"Adam."

"Adam, I like you. You remind me of my grandson. I want this to be special for you."

With that, she ducked under her counter, emerged with a huge handful of gardenia-scented votive-sized candles, and put them on the counter. Then she launched unbidden into a meticulous gift wrapping that involved boxing the main candle and shaping the ribbon around it into a Japanese crane. Then she lit a taper, dripped it on the box, and pressed a golden Parsley Sage seal into it. Finally she put everything in a green Parsley Sage bag.

"Voilà," she said, handing him his purchase fifteen minutes after she'd rung it up. "You're ready for adventure."

"Thanks."

Adam grabbed the bag and sprinted from the store, heading for the corner of Pier and Main. Just twenty-five minutes until Cammie was due at their rendezvous.

If he really hustled, he could shower, change, set up the suite, and still make it to where he said he'd meet—

"Adam Flood! Hi! Where are you running?"

Two girls he barely knew from school were at the corner, loaded down with shopping bags. Adam was surprised at their effusive greeting since he wasn't even sure of their names.

"Diva Dorfman?" the taller of the two reminded him. "I was in your lit class last year."

"Right. Diva. Hi." Adam recalled that Diva was short for the girl's real name, Devorah.

"And Blythe Medevoy?" the other girl said.

"Blythe. Of course," Adam agreed. "Nice to see you. But I'm kind of in a—"

"Just one sec. I just need your opinion on something, Adam," Diva said. She opened one of her bags and dug out a short, pale pink nightgown with a marabou-feathered neck and hemline and a matching marabou-feathered G-string. "Whaddaya think? Cute?"

Adam looked at his watch. Time was his enemy. And why the hell did she want his opinion? She hardly knew him.

"I guess it depends on your taste," he ventured.

She dangled the G-string very close to his face. "What's *your* taste?"

"You have to help her," Blythe chimed in. "It's a really *big* decision."

"It's . . . great, Diva. The lucky guy who gets to see you in that . . . wow."

"So, what'd you just buy?" Diva nudged her chin

toward the green Parsley Sage bag. "That's a great store."

"Something for Cammie," Adam said. He took out one of the gardenia-scented votive candles. "Does this get the female seal of approval?"

Diva sniffed. "Mmm. Try it, Blythe."

Blythe inhaled. "Adore it."

"Great. I did okay, I guess." He dropped the candle back into the bag.

"So Adam," Diva went on. "We're going to the Improv tonight. And then to Taboo in West Hollywood. Want to come along?"

"Got plans, but thanks. Gotta fly. Really." He saw he had a green light, so he jogged across the street toward the Au Mer. As he stepped up onto the opposite curb, he turned back to wave. The two girls were cracking up. Diva's package was at her feet, and she was holding her hands two feet apart. What was *that* about?

Well, whatever. All that really mattered was getting to the hotel, setting the mood, and letting it work its magic. And please God, letting that magic work on him, too.

Watch It, Miss Piggy

Cammie didn't feel like driving to the Santa Monica Pier—where Adam had asked her to meet him—since it would mean having to dodge the thousands of tourists that flocked to Ocean Avenue like seagulls to dead fish. So she called her father's driver to take her and made certain she was a perfect twenty-five minutes late. Half an hour would be pushing it. Sooner than that . . . well, wasn't she worth waiting for?

But now, as she walked onto the famous pier, her own heart was pounding. Oh, sure, she had acted all confident about Adam with Dee. But it wasn't the way she really felt at all.

"Hey, Cammie!"

There he was. He trotted over to her, one perfect red rose in his hand.

"Thanks."

Adam handed Cammie the rose. But as he did, an overweight tourist in a Green Bay Packers sweatshirt and golden polyester pants jostled Cammie as she walked by. A few bits of the cherry ice in her hand flew in Cammie's direction.

151

"Sorry, sorry!" the woman called, but didn't stop.

Cammie whirled on her. "Watch it, Miss Piggy!" she bellowed, then examined her top for any signs of cherry fallout. "That better not have landed on me."

"Let's put the bad twin back in her box, huh?" Adam gently asked. "She's not the girl I fell for."

Oh, God. Mean. But also honest. No one ever had the guts to be fully honest with Cammie.

"You're right," Cammie uttered. "Sorry."

He put an arm around her. "Cool. Let's get out of here."

He gently urged her away from the pier, then down to the beachfront heading south. They walked in silence for a few minutes.

"Where are we going?"

"It's a surprise. What did you and Sam end up doing last night?"

"We went dancing."

The corners of Adam's mouth tugged upward. "How many guys did you drive insane? Or can't you count that high?"

Instead of answering, Cammie gave him her most enigmatic look. Which quickly turned to surprise a few steps later when Adam turned up the path to the Au Mer hotel. "The Au Mer? This is where my father puts up his new clients. And then takes them to the bar when it's time to dump them."

"Forget that. We're not going to the bar."

Adam used his key card to open the ocean-side door,

and then led Cammie through the tasteful lobby to the elevators.

"You got us a room?" Cammie asked, hope bubbling up inside her.

"You could say that."

They took the elevator to the seventh floor, where Adam led the way to suite 705. And opened it.

Cammie's quick intake of breath was audible. Adam had strewn the entire suite with white rose petals. She drifted toward the bedroom; a bottle of champagne was nestled in an ice bucket next to the king-size bed, with two crystal flutes nearby. The suite itself was alight with votive candles. On the nightstand, there was a large floral-shaped one; next to it, a purple bottle of massage oil.

He had done all this for her, planned and paid and primped and . . .

Cammie exhaled slowly; she felt a strange ache behind her eyes. She was, by conscious decision, of the love-'em-and-leave-'em variety. The only boy who had ever dumped her was Ben Birnbaum, and that experience had shaken her more than she would ever admit to anyone. When she was sober, she didn't usually admit it herself.

Male attention was something she took absolutely for granted. But even though men and boys alike panted after her on a regular basis, none of them knew her. None of them really cared about her. There'd been plenty of sex. She'd had it on the rooftop pool of Le Parc Central hotel in West Hollywood. She'd had it on the roof the Beverly Center and in the basement of the

Leopard Lounge. She'd had sex in planes, trains, and automobiles. And yes, even in the occasional bed.

But no guy had ever gone to this kind of trouble for her before. No guy had cared enough.

"What?" Adam asked, concern in his eyes. "You look upset."

She shook her head.

He made a sweeping gesture. "It's all for you, Cam. The candles, massage oil. There's even gardenia bubble bath."

Cammie didn't trust herself to speak, so she just nodded again.

"I ran into Diva Dorfman," Adam went on. He sounded more nervous now. "She approved the candles."

Hearing about Diva Dorfman brought back Cammie's sense of the absurd. "Diva? She would know. She's done everything at Beverly Hills High that zips at the crotch."

"Except me," Adam pointed out. "But she did invite me to hang out tonight—that was strange. And she showed me this sheer nightie thing she bought."

Cammie smiled. She'd changed before she came to meet Adam, so she could do what she did next: unbutton the top button of her Anna Sui orange sleeveless top. "She was flirting with you, Adam. Kind of like this."

"Why would she flirt with me?"

"Because you're hot." She undid another button, then leaned over and kissed him lightly. "Besides, I may have been singing your praises."

"Singing my—" He stopped. "Holy shit. That's why I got the stupid cup-size jokes. And why Twyla was all over me. And Diva. You told people I was . . . ?"

Cammie nodded. A second later, the blouse was off, exposing her Tres Gazelle peach silk bra. She reached over to unbutton Adam's shirt.

He caught her wrist. "Cammie, for one thing, you don't even know if it's true. And for another, that kinda thing should stay between us."

"Oh, come on. Of course it's true. Look at the size of your feet. Besides, I just raised your stock," she said lightly. "Now you get a chance to prove me right." She took his hand and led him into the palatial marble bathroom. He'd lit small candles all around the sunken bathtub. She slipped off her Chloé silk capris and stretched in her lingerie, knowing how terrific she looked.

He unbuttoned his own shirt and pulled it off. Tugged his T-shirt over his head. Then he sat on the edge of the tub, poured in a generous dollop of gardenia bubble bath, and began to fill the tub with water.

"Make it really, really hot," Cammie whispered in his ear as they watched the bubbles froth.

"You got it." Adam cranked the hot water tap all the way to the right. Between the candles and the steam rising from the tub, the room was delightfully toasty.

Cammie smiled. "It's getting so warm, I really think I should take off my—"

Suddenly an earsplitting buzzer as loud as a retro air raid siren sounded in the suite. The horrible noise was everywhere—the bathroom, the sitting room, the bedroom. Adam ran out into the main suite, looking for a way to shut it off. As he did, icy water began to spray from the ceiling fire sprinkler system.

"Damn!" Cammie screamed as water cascaded over her.

"The candles and bath must have set off the automatic sprinkler system!" she heard Adam yell. "I can't turn the damn thing off!"

A moment later, there was loud pounding on the suite front door. "Hotel security!" a voice boomed. "Open up!

"Shit!" She grabbed the complimentary Au Mer silk robe that hung on the back of the bathroom door and ran into the bedroom, toes squishing into the soaked carpet, as water continued to rain down from the ceiling sprinklers. Meanwhile Adam opened the door to two security guards and a manager. The manager had the face of a hawk and the body of a linebacker; the security guards in blue rent-a-cop uniforms looked as if they'd been plucked from *The Sopranos*.

"Fire in here?" the manager demanded.

"No fire," Adam replied.

Scowling, the manager strode into the suite and was instantly doused. But he went to a wall panel near the television, removed the cover, and punched some kind of a code into a keypad. Instantly the water and the alarm both stopped. Then he whirled on Adam. "Were you smoking?" he thundered, getting so close to Adam that he was practically spitting.

Adam took a small step backward. "No, sir. Maybe it was . . . the candles?"

The manager looked as if he was about to bust a blood vessel. *"You were burning candles in here?"*

"A few," Adam admitted.

"Weren't you informed this was a non-smoking suite?"

"We weren't smoking. We really are terribly sorry, sir."

"What do you think multiple candles emit into the air? Cat piss?" The manager seethed.

Oh, please, enough of this shit, Cammie thought. Who did this little hospitality industry nobody think he was? Where did he get off humiliating Adam?

She gritted her teeth and stepped forward. "Excuse me, what did you say your name was?"

"Bruce Sullivan." The manager glared at Cammie. "Night manager. And who are you?"

"Cammie Sheppard. My father is Clark Sheppard. He gives you about two hundred thousand grand's worth of business a year. Maybe you've heard of him."

"Maybe," Bruce allowed.

Cammie didn't give an inch. "Think about it, Bruce. People light candles in hotel suites all the time, and it doesn't unleash Niagara Falls. What the hell is wrong with your sprinkler system? Excuse me."

Cammie went to the closet where she stowed her purse, extracted it, then found a credit card in her wallet and tossed it to him. "So let's skip your little temper tantrum and call it a day. Put the damages on my Visa. And get us a dry suite."

Bruce shook his head. "I'll run this card. But you are not welcome at this hotel."

"It doesn't matter; your suites suck," Cammie commented. "Anyway, I'll be sure to tell my dad and the rest of the agents at Apex to take their business to the Hotel Bel Air."

Mr. Night Manager ignored the threat; he and his sidekicks strode out of the room. Adam shut the door behind them and turned to Cammie. "Well, mission not accomplished. That wasn't exactly the way I was planning to get screwed," he managed ruefully, trying for a joke.

How could she not love this guy? She wrapped her arms around him and kissed him.

"I'll pay you back for whatever this costs," he told her.

"Believe me, my father will have his attorneys handle this; it won't cost us anything. They'll probably give him a two-week voucher for a better suite than this one."

He smiled down at her. "You are something else, Cam."

She kissed him again. "All of this . . . what you planned for us . . . it was so sweet. It really would have been 'it' this time."

"Definitely," he agreed.

She gazed up at him. "You know what? I'd rather be right here, right now, like this, with you, than having wild sex with anyone else."

Cammie knew herself to be capable of saying pretty much anything to anyone to achieve whatever it was she wanted to achieve. So the fact that she said this to Adam wasn't bizarre. What *was* bizarre was that she meant it.

A Moratorium

Anna dragged her board out of the briny water and dug its end into the sand. "I'm sorry, Kai, it's hopeless."

She'd scheduled a two-hour private surfing lesson with him, vowing that she'd master the damn thing once and for all or at least get one ride on a wave. Kai had been patient and supportive. And this time, there was no need for a wet suit—the ocean had warmed to eighty-one degrees Fahrenheit; practically a bath temperature. Plus the late afternoon had been beautiful—the air temperature as balmy as the water, the sun bright. Anna had been amazed at the clarity of the light closer to the equator and far from the smog of Los Angeles. The surf had been cooperative, too—three-foot swells, with eleven-second intervals between sets. Kai had pronounced the conditions absolutely perfect.

But Anna still couldn't surf. Try as she might, every time she got to her feet on the board, she lost her balance and flipped it over. She spent more time in the water by her board than on it. It irked her. For one thing, she hated to fail. For another thing, there was nothing wrong with her balance; years of ballet had proved that.

"Maybe you ought to try waterskiing," Kai suggested.

"No. I want to surf," Anna said stubbornly.

Kai dug his own board into the sand next to Anna's. "You always get what you want?"

"No," Anna said, but there was a pause in her voice.

"Usually, though," Kai surmised. "That's how you think life should be, right?"

Anna brushed the hanks of wet hair back off her face. "If I work hard at something? Yes."

"So all the people with crappy jobs and crappy lives just don't work hard enough?" Kai mused. "That's your life philosophy?"

"That's not fair. You're putting words in my mouth."

"Not really," Kai said. "I'm reading between the lines."

Did she detect an edge to his voice? They hadn't yet discussed last night. Anna had been raised by a woman who could carry on a pleasant conversation about the weather while watching pachyderms mate, the old "if you don't acknowledge something, it doesn't exist" philosophy. So Anna's instinct had been to just pretend that last night hadn't happened. But now she realized that that was exactly what her mother would have done. She forced herself not to do it the Jane Percy way.

"I just want to say that I probably should have thought things through before inviting you to my suite

last night," Anna began. "I thought I was ready for . . .
something . . . I wasn't ready for."

It wasn't exactly direct. But it was the best she could
do at the moment. And it was the total truth.

"It's a sheila's prerogative to change her mind," Kai said.
"A sheila?"

Kai laughed. "Aussie slang. A female, I mean. Anyway,
no worries. Really."

He really was being nice about it. One tiny part of
Anna was grateful. Another part was tweaked that he
wasn't more upset by her rejection of him; ridiculous,
she knew, when all she'd ostensibly wanted was a fling.

"Drink?" he asked. "Joaquin's on duty. He makes a
killer margarita."

"Just some lemonade, if he's got it."

"This is Las Casitas. We've got it." They went to the
Surf Shack bar and perched on a couple of bar stools
next to an elderly, distinguished-looking couple who
were deep in conversation in Italian. Joaquin poured
them two glassfuls of icy lemonade, then brought them
a plate of fresh-baked Mexican poppy-seed pastries
from the Las Casitas bakery.

"Bottoms up," Kai toasted. "Life is too short to
stress out; that's my motto."

"You're one of those people who lives only in the
present, aren't you?" Anna pondered as Joaquin refilled
her glass without her having to ask. "And you just
accept whatever happens?"

"Pretty much," Kai agreed.

"No ego involvement?" Anna asked. "No wants? No mountains to climb?"

"Definitely no mountains to climb," Kai decreed. "That's me."

It's definitely the opposite of me, Anna thought. *Not that my approach has worked out so well.*

"You know, I can almost see your brain synapses firing overtime," Kai went on.

"I know," Anna admitted. "It's like I can't turn it off. I'm starting to think it's congenital."

Kai leaned back in his chair. "That's why you can't surf, you know. You have to turn off your brain and just be in your body. Be the wave."

"Be the wave?" Anna echoed dubiously. "How Zen."

"It is. Nothing to it but to do it." He grinned. "You know, I'd love to kiss you right now."

Anna was surprised and flattered. "After what I pulled last night, you still want to kiss me?"

"Not on the job, though," Kai teased. "But after six . . ."

Anna felt much better. Now she knew for sure that he wasn't mad. She might not understand him—his life view was so foreign to her—but she definitely liked him. "After six. Are you sure you want to plan so far in adva—" Anna broke off, mid-word, squinting past Kai at someone heading their way across the sand.

Kai turned. "What's up?"

"Unless I'm delusional, that's—"

"Anna!"

It was Sam Sharpe, clad in L.A.M.B. black capris and

a Bebe yellow halter top, jogging the last hundred feet toward her.

Anna jumped up, met her halfway, and gave her friend a huge hug. "Sam! What are you doing here?"

Sam laughed. "Slumming!"

Kai trotted over. "Hi. I'm Kai. I teach surfing here." He shook Sam's hand. "You're a friend of Anna's?"

Sam nodded and pointed to the surfboards. "Never would have guessed. I'm Mary Poppins. At least that's the name I used to register."

"A pleasure to meet you, Ms. Poppins. This is the most discreet place on the planet, Ms. Poppins. You'll love it here, Ms. Poppins," Kai assured her. "I'll let you guys catch up. Anna, if you're up for another lesson or anything . . ." He let the "anything" hang in the air—the intent was clear. "You know where to find me,"

"Tasty," Sam commented, checking out the rear view with approval as Kai went inside the Surf Shack. "You don't waste any time."

"He's teaching me to surf. Well, trying to, anyway." She punched Sam playfully on the arm. "Now shut up and explain."

Sam shrugged. "Remembered you were here, got bored with Beverly Hills, planes, trains, automobiles, roll the credits. I hope you're glad to see me."

"Yes, of course," Anna assured her.

Sam grinned. "Good. I'm starved. Do you have any idea what living on a thousand calories a day does to a person? It's not pretty."

Anna laughed. "Let's go eat—the food is fantastic, you can get anything you want whenever you want—and you can fill me in on everything."

"So long as you fill me in on surfer boy," Sam allowed. "He was looking at you like you were a cold drink and he was a hot day."

Anna didn't feel ready to tell Sam about the seduction that wasn't of the night before, so she deftly deflected the hint. "I *will* learn to surf by the time I leave here."

Sam slung an arm around Anna. "Who knows, maybe I will, too."

"I mean, do I set myself up for this shit?" Sam mused in between bites of her fried soft-shell crabs. She stopped for a moment to savor the food. "You have no idea how good this is until you've starved yourself for a few weeks."

Anna knew that was true. "I guess that's one argument for starving yourself."

"Oh, stop flaunting the fact that you've never had to diet, Anna." Sam blew her a kiss. "Anyway, the question is, how could I possibly have thought that clubbing with Cammie would make me feel anything other than awful? The only hot guy who came on to me was some asshole actor who wanted to get to my dad. I swear, if I'd told him he could read for my father's next movie, he'd have jumped me on the dance floor, fat thighs and all." She took a long sip of her Diet Coke.

Anna had been through variations on this conversation

with Sam many times. But hey, that's what friends were for. "You're not fat, Sam."

Sam licked some crab off her pinkie. "Oh, please do not start with that, Anna."

"But you're not. Okay, you're not as skinny as Cammie, maybe—"

"Or Dee, or you."

"But so what? Dee's not as smart, and Cammie's not as talented."

"Gee, that makes me and my cellulite feel ever so much better."

Supportive having failed, Anna decided to go for blunt. Sam was a tough girl; she could handle it. "Sam, I have only one thing to say: Get over it."

"Excuse me?"

Anna swept her arm out. "You're a beautiful girl. You've got that beautiful brown wavy hair and those deep brown eyes. And besides, look around. We're in paradise! How can you obsess about your thighs in paradise?"

"Because I just ate my weight in soft-shell crabs and all I can think about is dessert." Sam peered ruefully down at her stomach.

"So go for the sugar rush!" Anna exclaimed. "Seriously, Sam. Why wreck the experience of being here?"

A slow grin spread over Sam's face. She took in the scenery—they were eating at the outdoor buffet. It was served in a pavilion that had been built with three sides in open air and one side facing the ocean. But save for her and Anna, the pavilion was completely deserted. To their left and right, though, hovered waiters and bus-boys and a sommelier, in case they wanted to select a perfect bottle of wine to accompany their meal. It was as if the resort were there for their enjoyment alone.

"You're right," she declared. "I totally suck. This place is unbelievable. Some people come to Los Angeles because they think it's heaven. But heaven is actually Las Casitas. And not just because their chef made the best fried soft-shell crabs I've ever tasted or because I've consumed more calories in the last hour than in the last two weeks put together."

"Now you're talking. And I'm really glad you're here. But let's have fun, okay?"

"I was obsessing, wasn't I?"

Anna nodded. "Kind of."

"God, I *hate* girls who do that. Okay. You're right. I hereby declare a moratorium on all things in the real world." Sam looked around. "Where's the dessert table? I have a craving for Dutch chocolate cake with a scoop of mint-chip ice—"

"Well, hello there."

Oh no. Anna almost groaned out loud. It was the one and only Lloyd. He leered down at her and Sam with new arm candy. His girl of the moment was a very tall, very slender brunette in a white bikini. Her long dark hair was done in tiny braids all over her head, and she had a small piercing in her navel. Lloyd wore an open Hawaiian shirt and orange surfer jams. His hairy toes were still on display in the same water buffalo moccasins.

"Hello, Lloyd," Anna greeted him with exaggerated politeness, then cocked her chin at Sam. "This is Mary Poppins. She just arrived today."

The girl with Lloyd giggled. "How could your parents name you Mary when your last name is—I hope I'm not offending you," she added hastily.

Lloyd pointed to the girl on his arm. "This is Jennifer from Wisconsin."

"Washington," Jennifer corrected.

"Right." Lloyd patted her hand, then turned back to Anna and Sam. "Mind?"

Without waiting for their answer, he pulled two wrought-iron chairs over to their table and motioned for Jennifer to sit in one of them. She did, and then he slid in next to her.

"Lloyd works for my father," Anna explained to Sam. "Nice to see you, Lloyd, but we were in the middle of a private conversation."

"Hey, way too serious," Lloyd insisted. He draped an arm around Jennifer and regarded Sam. "I'm down here to do some business."

"You should see the dining room table in his casita. It's covered in a sea of paper. And there's a laptop!" Jennifer put in, as if Lloyd were working for the CIA.

"But we don't need to talk about business." Anna tried to redirect the conversation. She didn't think her father would want it to be common knowledge that Lloyd was there to check the place over for a possible syndication buyout.

"You're making some good sense there, Anna," Lloyd said, giving Anna a quick wink okay. "Got it."

"So, what do you do in Washington?" Sam asked Jennifer.

"I don't spend much time there. I'm mostly in Europe. I'm a model."

"Who would have guessed?" Sam quipped.

Lloyd turned to Sam. "So, Miss Poppins. Enjoying your identity?"

"Sure. I just flew in on my parrot-handle umbrella."

Lloyd winked again. "I assure you I'm the soul of discretion, *Mary,* although from a psychological point of view you might want to consider why you selected a pseudonym that is so obviously a pseudonym. It betrays a certain ambivalence; that you need the cachet of being someone I should know while at the same time you resent it."

"Gee, let me write that down," Sam deadpanned.

"Also," Lloyd continued, "if we look at it from the standpoint of the laws of probability—the class of people here, et cetera, et cetera—the odds of being recognized are high. But if the secretary general of the UN and Sting are happy to vacation here under their own names, I don't see what you're afraid of."

"Know what, Lloyd? I've got a great idea. How about we pretend that we haven't met?" She stood. "We leaving, Anna?"

"We are." Anna rose, too.

"Regarding you and the surfing teacher," Lloyd called

after Anna. "You might want to watch that fraternizing-with-the-employees thing. It might cloud your judgment."

Sam shook her head as she walked away. "What an asshole."

"No kidding," Anna agreed. "The trip down here was hell on wheels."

"You mean you drove here with him?"

Anna waved a dismissive hand. "It's a long story that you don't want to hear. But trust me, he is truly as loathsome as he seems."

"Well, then, we'll just have to ignore the hairy toad," Sam decreed. "Or is it hairy *toed*?" She pointed toward her feet.

Anna cracked up. "You noticed his toes! Aren't they vile?"

Sam made a face. "*Beyond* vile." She looped an arm around Anna's waist. "So what's next on our agenda?"

"There's a street dance in the 'village' tonight," Anna said. "Kai told me it's amazing. We could check that out."

"Excellent," Sam agreed. "Because personally, I am up for anything." She paused. "Except Lloyd."

Platform Goth Queen Boots

Cammie couldn't quite figure out how she'd gotten where she was: driving her own car, with Adam in the passenger seat, on her way to the winter Coachella, an outdoor music festival in the desert.

After the sprinkler debacle at Au Mer, they'd walked down to Breakers on the Beach—another elegant Santa Monica beachfront hotel—and stopped in the lobby bar for coffee. Then, out of the blue, Adam's cell had rung. After a lot of "uh-huh's" and a few "sweet's" he'd hung up, eyes shining.

It had been one of his basketball buds. The guy had two tickets to that night's concert in Coachella, but his girlfriend had suddenly come down with strep. Did Adam want the ducats? All he had to do was pick them up at will call.

Cammie had vaguely heard of Coachella, just like she'd vaguely heard of the concerts at Woodstock. And wasn't there some other feminist music festival thing where a lot of ugly hairy women who didn't wax sang plaintive songs about being ugly and hairy? She wasn't much of a festivalgoer. Why should she be, when she could get into the hippest, most exclusive clubs in Los Angeles, to see the top name artists? When she could hear U2 at a private party at House of Blues or Usher at a friend's birthday party? Why would anyone mingle with the unwashed masses unless they didn't have an option?

So she feigned enthusiasm when Adam raved that his favorite band, the Donnas, would be performing. Really, though, she wondered why he preferred a two-hour-plus schlep to the desert to hear bands she rarely listened to over reconvening at an alternate location to consummate the unconsummated.

God, love sucked so hard. She would have done almost anything for Adam, including things he'd probably only read about on the Internet. Hell, if he'd invited her to Daytona Beach to see a NASCAR race, she would have said yes . . . and she didn't even know exactly what NASCAR was.

Coachella. The Donnas. This was definitely not her life. But if it made Adam happy, she was ready to give it a one hundred percent Cammie Sheppard effort.

They stopped at her house so she could change clothes. When he waited downstairs, she did a quick computer search on the Donnas. Up came their photo: four punk girls with long straight hair, wearing Levi's, sneakers, little T-shirts, and attitude. Ugh. So not her style.

First stop: the world's fastest flat-ironing job on her hair. Second stop: her stepsister Mia's closet, which she raided for a pair of Levi's, a Chaminade High School sweatshirt, and a down vest. Double ugh. But it did look vaguely Donnas-esque, plus she'd be warm. February nights in the desert got very chilly.

She drew the line at sneakers, though, going instead with her retro Moschino orange velvet lace-up boots with the three-inch stiletto heels. They'd look hot with anything, even the horror of an outfit she was wearing.

Adam reached across from the passenger seat and squeezed her knee. "You look really cute, did I tell you that?"

"Thanks."

He took a CD out of his jacket pocket. "I'm gonna play the Donnas. Like a warm-up. Okay?"

"Great." Cammie opened the CD player; Adam popped in the disc, and they were serenaded all the way to Palm Springs with tunes about sex, drugs, and rock 'n' roll. Screwing a stranger in a car, like that. But Cammie wasn't in a screwing-a-stranger frame of mind. There was only one person she wanted to screw. He was no stranger. Except maybe to screwing.

"The Donnas are so amazing," Adam was saying. "Really assertive girls who go after what they want."

"Maybe they just write really assertive lyrics and pose a lot." Cammie gave him an arch look.

"Well, it's not like I know them personally," Adam conceded.

"But you'd like to."

"Hell, yeah," he admitted.

Maybe he'd like to have sex with each and every one

of them, too, Cammie thought. Maybe if one of them were his girlfriend, they'd be rolling around in the silk sheets that very minute. How depressing was that? She, Cammie Sheppard, the girl every guy wanted, was stressing that the boy *she* wanted was hotter for some pasty-faced, stringy-haired girls in an overrated band than he was for her. Talk about your alternate universe.

Another half hour brought them through Palm Springs to Indio, site of the Coachella concert, which was held at a polo field. The parking lot was jammed—there were plenty of people hanging around, throwing Frisbees and partying to the music that poured into the night from inside the gates. The promoters were expecting more than twenty thousand people, but since Cammie and Adam were arriving so late, they managed to find a parking spot that someone had already vacated quite close to the small stadium. From there it was a short walk to the will-call booth. Cammie could see how excited Adam was to be at the festival: If she hadn't taken his arm, he might have jogged over to pick up their tickets.

They got their tickets, then had to walk several hundred feet to the entry gate. The walk took them past an extensive display of massive art installations and abstract sculptures as well as booths hawking various left-wing political literature and save-the-earth info. But the area was deserted—everyone was inside.

Moments later, they cleared security and were listening as a new band started to play.

"Radiohead," Adam and Cammie said at the same moment, then looked at each other and laughed.

The place was rocking—body heat alone from the twenty thousand concertgoers raised the temperature by at least ten degrees. Some people were sitting in the bleachers, but the vast majority were down on the field, dancing, singing, moshing. Adam didn't hesitate; he took Cammie by the hand and led her into the middle of the undulating sea of flesh as Radiohead jammed away.

"This is so cool, isn't it?" Adam shouted. "I knew Radiohead was playing, but I was sure we'd get here too late!"

"It's great!" Cammie said, lying through her perfect teeth. Not that Coachella was bad or anything. Just . . . primitive. She looked around her—everyone was as poorly dressed as she'd expected. Then she looked at her own borrowed clothes. Including herself.

"We got here just in time. The Donnas are on next!"

"Lucky us!"

"Come on!" Adam tugged Cammie forward. "Let's see if we can get closer to the stage."

Fine, whatever. She allowed Adam to lead her deeper into the crowd until they were less than a hundred feet from the stage. Then the spike heel of her left boot hit something hard, and her ankle turned abruptly.

"Aghh!" she sputtered as she stumbled into a couple who sported his-and-hers dog collars that were chained together by a steel leash.

"Watch it!" the female half of the canine duo barked.

"Sorry," Cammie mumbled, righting herself. As she did, she felt the same heel sink into something soft.

"Shit! You just impaled my fucking foot!" A pony-tailed guy in hippie garb pushed her away, then bent to examine his sandaled left foot for damage. Cammie noticed that he wore white socks under those sandals, grounds for arrest by the Beverly Hills fashion police.

"You okay?" Adam asked.

"Sure, fine," she told him, despite the fact that her boots were wreaking carnage right and left. She wondered if he thought she was an idiot for wearing them to a crowded outdoor concert but was too sweet to say anything.

They got close to the wide stage—close enough for Cammie to catch an occasional glimpse of the Radiohead bass guitarist and drummer through the crowd. The lights were bright; the music was pounding. Cammie could feel the strum of the bass in the pit of her stomach. She got pushed from the back by a dancing girl and from the side by another couple. For a moment, she felt a wave of claustrophobia—why wouldn't these fucking people just mind their space? Then a couple in deep make-out mode bumped her from behind. She sighed and edged forward. She could handle this. Especially when she looked at Adam's face and saw it shining.

Radiohead finished their set to massive applause. Then someone came onstage and read bad poetry while the roadies did a quick changeover for the Donnas.

"Oh, man, this is gonna be so sweet."

Cammie turned and saw a short guy to her left; he couldn't have been more than five-foot two, with stringy dark hair and a rodent-like overbite that screamed for an orthodontist's intervention. Cammie towered over him, even more so because of her high-heel boots.

"I love the Donnas," the guy told Cammie. "They're so bitchin'. You?"

Cammie shrugged. "My boyfriend's a big fan."

"Oh yeah. Big fan," Adam repeated back, joining the conversation.

"My man." The short guy shared a fist bump with Adam. "I dream about those chicks for real. I figured this might be my only chance to see them, but how the hell was I gonna see 'em over the crowd, you know? My friend offered to lend me these platform goth queen boots, but I don't see how you chicks walk in those puppies."

The guy reeled slightly; Cammie could see his red-rimmed eyes. Clearly he was stoned out of his mind.

"Been hitting the Thai stick, dude?" Cammie asked smoothly.

He shook his head. "Nah. White Russian bongs before the show with some of Mendocino's finest. Bitchin'."

Bitchin'? Cammie thought. No one said "bitchin'" anymore. In fact, no one did White Russian bongs anymore. They weren't old enough to be retro or new enough to be hip. Everyone she knew in Beverly Hills had taken up old-fashioned hookahs. Like fashion, illegal drug consumption had a shelf life. Whatever. She'd just ignore the little weasel.

"Ladies and gentlemen," a guy onstage bellowed into the microphone. "Put your hands together for . . . the Donnas!"

The crowd roared; Cammie edged to her left in an effort to see the girls as they strutted onto the stage. They looked just like the picture that Cammie had seen on the Internet. In fact, they were wearing the exact same clothes: four girls in their early twenties with long straight hair, doing variations on the Avril Lavigne theme.

Meanwhile Cammie saw Rodent Boy pull something out of his pocket. A folded paper, which he hastily unfolded. What was it? Some Medocino green he'd saved for the occasion? A couple of tabs of E? She leaned over to check it out. None of the above. In fact, it was an eight-by-ten publicity photograph of the Donnas.

Cammie cracked up as she figured it out. The short guy had accurately anticipated being dwarfed by the crowd, so he'd brought a photograph of the band so he could pretend he was watching them while they played. Cammie nudged Adam so that he'd take in the guy and his photo.

"Great, man," Adam told the short guy, chucking him on the shoulder. "Way to plan ahead."

"I fucking love you girls!" Rodent Boy yelled, never once looking up from the photo.

Adam and Cammie cracked up. As different as they were, they shared a sense of humor and an acknowledgment of the absurdity of life. Knowing that made Cammie fall for him all over again. He stood behind her, arms around her waist, and they shimmied to the music together. The truly weird thing was, the more Cammie heard, the better it sounded. Those girls could really rock. It wasn't that she was ready to run out and buy their CD. No goddamn way. But that Adam had introduced her to their music and to an experience like this and that she wasn't ready to insist they leave immediately . . . Well, it was something.

After the Donnas came the Flaming Lips and then the Foo Fighters, both bands Cammie actually knew. She was enjoying herself, getting into the vibe of being part of a mass of people that had a power and an energy of its own. It wasn't as good as sitting at a table twenty feet from Jakob Dylan and sipping a bourbon Manhattan straight up, but it was still fun in its own proletarian way.

Cammie wound her arms around Adam's neck during a break in the music and kissed him softly. "Thanks for bringing me. This is great."

"You're welcome." He kissed her back. The kiss escalated until they couldn't keep their hands off each other.

"We have such sucky timing," Adam joked, leaning his forehead against Cammie's.

"Why isn't there a bedroom here?" Cammie asked.

But there wasn't. All they could do was enjoy the concert. Which they did, until the Cure closed the show sometime after midnight.

Tired but exhilarated, they straggled out of the stadium with everyone else as the sound system played some old Mothers of Invention songs and found their car in the lot. With five thoroughly drunk guys partying on it and around it. One stood on the hood, unzipping to pee.

"Get off, man," Adam ordered.

"Hey, man, your girlfriend is fucking Paris Hilton!" The guy pointed at Cammie.

Cammie rolled her eyes. Men could be so blind. She'd occasionally heard the comparison before when she'd flat-ironed her hair. But everyone knew that Cammie was better looking. For one thing, Paris was built like a boy. Once upon a time, Cammie's bounty had been less than overflowing, too. But that was before she purchased a perfect, perky pair of D-cup implants on her fifteen birthday.

"Hey, dudes!" The pisser called to his friends. "Fucking Paris Hilton!"

"Wow, you recognized me," Cammie replied. "Cool."

"Yo, where's Tinkerbell? That rat dog of yours?" jeered another drunken guy.

"Please don't let this get around," Cammie told them, lowering her voice confidentially. "But I just went on the South Beach Diet and ate him for dinner. Fried."

"Righteous, man!" The pisser jumped off the hood and weaved away with his friends, leaving Adam and Cammie grinning at each other.

She slid into Adam's arms, pressed against the steady beating of his heart. She felt safe there, so calm and happy. The moment of lust they'd shared inside the stadium had passed, but she didn't care. Nor did the prospect of the long drive back to Los Angeles faze her. When Adam kissed her temple and tenderly stroked her hair, Cammie decided this was the best kind of bliss. Because while she'd known the sexual kind many times, she had never really known the tender kind.

Perfection

S am twirled in front of the floor-length mirror. "Okay, am I insane or does this actually look cute on me?"

She and Anna were visiting one of the boutiques in the Mexican village at Las Casitas, a shop that had stayed open late so that guests could wear authentic Mexican clothes to the street party that night. There was one rack of colorful hand-embroidered dresses, another of brightly colored peasant blouses and full skirts. Mexican jewelry in heavy turquoise and silver lay on black velvet in a glass display case. Sam had selected a heavily embroidered white off-the-shoulder peasant blouse and a wide black skirt that fell to her calves. She'd traded in her usual designer heels for hand-tooled Mexican sandals.

Anna, meanwhile, had purchased sandals that laced around her ankles, along with a yellow embroidered shift that brought out the golden blond in her hair.

"Muy bonita," the lovely woman behind the counter told Sam. Then she handed each girl a passion flower.

"You put this behind your right ear if you are single and your left ear if you are taken."

Sam and Anna looked at each other. "Right ear!" they declared at the same moment, then signed their sales slips and skipped out the door.

The street party was already in full swing at the Las Casitas authentic village, at the east end of the resort, about ten minutes' walk from the main pool. More Disneyland than authentic, it was still charming. Two cobblestone streets crossed at a town square that was circled by craftspeople. They wove baskets, made jewelry, and cooked mouthwatering food on open-air grills. It seemed like every guest at Las Casitas was there, too—the spacious resort, which seemed so empty so much of the time, was rollicking. Waiters passed through the crowd carrying empty salt-rimmed glasses. Hosts directed the guests to a fountain in the center of the town square that sprayed mixed margaritas instead of water. Right by the fountain, a mariachi band played traditional Mexican music.

Sam and Anna worked their way to the one end of the square, where a drop-dead handsome man in his late twenties was teaching the crowd to cha-cha in preparation for a dance contest. As he ran through his lesson, the mariachi band quit, and the resort house band tuned up behind him.

"We should learn," Sam said, following the man's feet as he demonstrated the steps. "I've always wanted to."

"I know how," Anna replied. "It's fun."

Sam shot her a look. "Who taught you?"

"In fourth and fifth grade, I was sent to Cotillion."

"What the hell is Cotillion?"

"Essentially, it's training in how to be polite, know all the basic dance steps, the proper way to bow to royalty—"

"Wait. You're trained in how to bow to royalty?" Sam repeated. "And you're telling me this with a straight face?"

"Believe it or not, the knowledge has come in handy."

"Jeez. The only kings we have in Hollywood are named Weinstein and Spielberg." Sam moved her feet in imitation of the dance instructor's steps. "Step-step cha-cha-cha," she muttered. "This isn't so hard."

The band started to play, and the resort's evening social motivators—employees whose only job was to start the party and keep it going—moved among the guests, teasing and cajoling people to dance, introducing them to one another. One of them, a beautiful guy with a waterfall of inky hair, urged Sam toward a pot-bellied thirtyish guy in a Mexican wedding shirt and thoroughly American golf shorts. When he saw Sam, he reached out a beefy hand.

"Cliff Reese. Grand Rapids, Michigan. I won a sales contest, and they sent me here. Can you believe it?" If he hadn't told Sam he was in sales, the strength of his grip would have.

"Mary Poppins. London, England," Sam replied. She glanced over her shoulder and saw Anna being paired up with a skinny man who was old enough to be her father. The man wore a gaudy Hawaiian shirt.

"Did you say Mary Poppins?" Cliff asked. "That's not your real name, right?"

Sam lowered her voice. "Don't let it get around, but it used to be Poopins. After my parents passed away, I changed it."

Cliff furrowed his brow.

"Okay, Cliff, ya got me," Sam went on, making it up as she went along. "My great-grandfather's last name was Popinakov, but they changed it at Ellis Island to Poopins. Then my grandfather stayed in London after the war, but my dad came to America when I was three. That's why I don't have an accent. But I still have a British passport. Tallyho."

"Okay, men, take your partners in your arms!" the dance instructor called. Cliff's arm slid around Sam's waist.

"I'm kind of new at this," Sam explained.

"No prob," Cliff replied.

The music began in earnest. It turned out that Cliff was an excellent dancer. He made the cha-cha easy, and soon Sam was weaving and twirling with the best of them, a huge smile plastered on her face as her feet flew over the cobblestone street, skirt twirling around her as she spun. Sam wondered if maybe she should go on being Mary Poppins. Because Mary was a happier girl than Sam Sharpe had ever been.

"Here." Anna grinned, handing Sam a mud slide. "You look like you could use this."

"Definitely," Sam agreed, taking the drink and draining

it. "That schmuck was such a good dancer. Then he had to try to stick his tongue down my throat."

"Bad manners," Anna joked. "Evidently his parents didn't make him go to Cotillion."

"Ha." Sam blotted her lips with a napkin. "Much better."

It was an hour later. The street party was in full swing, but Anna and Sam had escaped to one of the open-air cafés and were watching the action from a couple of wicker chairs that faced the square.

"God, why couldn't that social director have paired us up with two cute guys?" Sam asked.

"Cute" made Anna think of Ben.

"And one of them would look like, say, Ben Birnbaum." For once, she didn't edit her thoughts.

Sam looked surprised. "I thought you guys were history."

"I don't know what we are." Anna took a sip of her drink—a coconut-and-rum concoction that was a Las Casitas specialty. "I still think about him, Sam. I know he thinks about me, too, because he called and left this long message."

Sam raised a hand to shut Anna up. "Stop right there. This is a no-Ben zone," she decreed. "Besides, aren't you hooking up with that surfer guy?"

"Kai? We didn't make plans." She gazed around. "I don't see him out there."

"Do you care?"

Anna shrugged. "I do like him, but . . . I'm making a

concerted effort to live in the moment. And evidently, this is a moment he's not in."

The band on the square stopped playing. But off in the distance, they heard a pounding bass line.

"Where's that coming from?" Sam asked. "I thought we were the only party in town."

"I don't know. . . . Oh yes, I do." Anna recalled Kai's very thorough tour of the grounds her first day at Las Casitas and grinned. "At least I *think* I know. Follow me."

Five minutes' walk past the spa and gym brought them to a sloping path, where the music they'd heard in the distance grew louder.

"Let me guess," Sam ventured. "It's a special party for people who hate mariachi and cha-cha and can't stand Mexican food."

"Not exactly." They reached an illuminated white sign in English, Spanish, and French. Literally. Anna gestured to it. "Behold."

LAS CASITAS AU NATUREL.
ROPAS OPTIONAL.
AGE EIGHTEEN AND ABOVE, *SOLAMENTE!*

"Get out!" Sam laughed. "Does '*ropas* optional' mean 'Chubbies are invited to keep their clothes on'?"

"Stop," Anna chided her. "Anyway, neither of us is eighteen."

"Like anyone cares," Sam scoffed. "Let's go. We can keep our clothes on and ogle."

Beyond a copse of trees, the path opened up into a swimming area; instead of a concrete pool, it was an artificial lagoon lit by giant torches. Naked people of every size and shape—a few of them in swimsuits, most without—cavorted in the water or hung out on chaise lounges. The lagoon-side bar was just as crowded, with people boogeying to a DJ's music on a jammed dance floor. There was a one guy in particular they couldn't miss, dancing with manic energy at their end of the dance floor, doing his best imitation of a dying gyroscope.

Lloyd. Naked Lloyd. His Hirsuteness.

Anna winced. "Oh no! Let's see if we can slip by before he—"

Too late. He spotted them and waved manically. "Anna! Mary!"

"Pretend we've gone deaf," Sam suggested.

Lloyd came trotting in their direction. Anna couldn't help looking at . . . everything. And everything didn't exactly . . . measure up.

"Someone's showing off his shortcomings," Anna whispered to Sam, which made Sam guffaw.

"Hey, lovely ladies," Lloyd greeted them. He'd picked up an exotic cranberry-based cocktail on the way over. "Why not take it all off and join the party?"

"We're just . . . passing through," Anna said, fixing her gaze on his face.

"You know, you'd be a happier and more fulfilled

woman if you loosened up a little, Anna," Lloyd shot back. "Just an observation."

"Observe this," Sam said, and gave him the finger. Then she looked down at his crotch. "Oh, wait, you already have one of those. And it's just about exactly the same size!"

Anna bit her lip to keep from laughing, and Lloyd turned the color of whatever fruit-punch-based exotic drink he was sipping

But his voice stayed absolutely cool as he gazed pointedly at Sam's thighs. "Yeah, let out that hostility, Mary. Remember, it's not what you're eating, it's what's eating you." Then he and his body hair boogied back to the dance floor.

Sam's jaw dropped. "He's good. He's an asshole, but he's *good.*"

"I see why my dad hired him," Anna commented. "Anyway, let's go."

"Where?" Sam asked.

"Anyplace that we can't see him."

They continued through the clothing-optional section, past its rows of casitas and toward a gaslit path that led down to the au naturel beach. They were far enough away now from the lagoon for the music to fade to near nothingness. The beach itself was deserted; no sound but the gentle waves and a lone tropical night bird calling to the moon. By wordless agreement, they kicked off their sandals, left them under a wooden chaise longue, and walked for another five hundred yards.

They were past the resort boundary but didn't care.

"This is bliss," Sam said softly.

"I know. Your dad wasn't upset that you wanted to come to Mexico by yourself?"

"Please." Sam snorted. "He never knows where I am, and he could care less. None of them give a shit. The Poppy-Dee love fest thing has become nauseating."

Anna paused. "Wait. Wasn't Poppy's baby shower today?"

"Yeah. So?"

"You didn't go."

Sam shook her head and splashed ankle deep into the warm Pacific. "Nope. And I'm a better woman for it. Poppy loathes me. She wishes I'd go off to college already, preferably someplace in Antarctica. And I loathe her. She has no boundaries, no sense that she's coming into a family. She talks *baby talk* to my father. Was I supposed to go to her baby shower and gush over a little sister that I wish I'd never have?"

"I see your points." Anna nodded.

"Plus she's made Dee her new surrogate daughter. Believe me, no one at that shower even realized I was gone." Sam raised her arms to the sky. "As a choice between that hell and this paradise . . . there is no comparison. I could stay here forever."

Anna smiled. "'Nothing gold can stay.'"

"We're quoting Robert Frost?" Sam teased. "That's the first poem I ever memorized."

"I love it," Anna said softly. "I guess because I'm a

perfectionist. And perfection is, by definition, always transitory." She bent down, picked up a flat stone, and skimmed it into an oncoming wave. It bounced five times in the moonlight before disappearing beneath the water.

"Okay. Now that you've sufficiently depressed me—"

Anna searched for another skimming stone. "I just meant that if this were forever, it wouldn't be perfection anymore."

"Yeah, yeah, I got it. But what's the point of anything, then? What's even the point of falling in love if it's only going to end?"

"To be happy while it's happening, I guess," Anna mused. She found another good one. This one took a single hop when she skimmed it and then was gone. "But I'm hardly the oracle. Look what happened between me and Ben."

"Him again." Sam sighed. "Why don't you just fly to New Jersey, bone his brains out, and see if the magic is still there?"

"If I 'bone his brains out,' as you so delicately put it, we'll want each other all over again."

"Big deal. Are you still in love with him?"

"Sometimes I think so. Other times, I think I just lusted after him and talked myself into believing it was love because that's what I wanted it to be."

"Enough. You sound like a bad episode of *Hermosa Beach*." Sam reached down and splashed Anna. Anna splashed her back. Sam danced around, shimmying her Mexican shirt up and over her head and then flung it at the beach. "Oh, Lloyd? Come here, lover boy!"

"Great idea." Anna laughed, stepping out of her own dress. "Want to go skinny dipping?"

"Sure. Why not?" Sam agreed as the moon cooperated for her by ducking behind a cloud. "Using the term loosely, of course."

Both girls scampered onto the sand, where they pulled off the rest of their clothes. Then, with a whooping cry, Sam ran into the ocean. "Oh my God, this is fantastic!"

Anna waded in after her. "The water's so warm."

"I l-o-o-o-ve it here!" Sam shouted, and then flipped onto her back to gaze at the stars.

"I love it, too!" It was a male voice, from out of the murky darkness of the ocean.

Startled and a bit frightened, Sam whirled to find the source of the voice. There it was—about thirty feet away, a small wooden panga boat. Though she couldn't see the boat's pilot—probably a British fisherman, she reasoned—he was most definitely male. And she was most definitely naked.

"Get away from here, you pervert!" She dropped down into the water until it covered her to her chin as her mind raced. He was probably some guy who worked at the resort and cruised out at night. He probably had infrared goggles. What a sleazoid. Had he seen her naked? Probably.

"I mean it, dickweed! Fuck off!"

She watched the small rowboat move out to sea; she and Anna were alone once more. But the magic of the moment was gone. Just like that, paradise found was paradise lost.

Drop the Phony Accent

Sam and Anna were at the Surf Shack, trying to enjoy the huevos rancheros they'd ordered for breakfast. But the woman of a certain age with bleached blond hair and an extraordinarily professional face-lift at the next table was making it difficult. She'd been on her cell phone for the past twenty minutes, discussing a Miami Beach real estate deal at earsplitting volume.

"She should turn the fucking thing off," Sam muttered darkly. "She's on vacation."

"I totally agree," Anna said despairingly.

"So, Anna!" Sam raised her voice, hoping the woman would get a clue. "You have another surfing lesson with Kai this afternoon while I hit with the tennis pro. *Right?*" She cut her eyes to the woman on the cell phone, who was touching a spot behind her right ear, most likely feeling for her recent surgery scars. She was still utterly oblivious to how obnoxious she was and prattled on about points and mortgage brokers and how she had to take possession by the end of the month or else the agent's head would roll.

Sam leaned closer to her and practically shouted in

her direction. "And then we're going shopping at La Trinidad afterward, *right?*"

The woman finally looked at Sam. "Could you hold it down? You're very rude."

"You *must* be kidding," Sam told her. "You don't need the phone; they can hear you just fine in Florida."

"Bitch." The woman strode away, still yammering into her cell.

"I've got an idea." Anna's face lit up.

"Hook her up with Lloyd?"

"Better." Anna reached into her purse, took out her cell, and clicked it off. "Voilà."

"You're absolutely right. It's a disgusting habit." Sam found her own phone and did the same thing. Never mind the fact that she was supposed to go out with her dad and Poppy tonight. Or that Jackson would be calling any minute now to find out when the hell Sam planned on coming home. Probably because of it. "You know, I don't think I've turned my cell off since 2002. I suddenly feel *much* better."

"I don't even bring mine to this place," said a male British voice. "Hello."

Sam looked up. And froze as she put two and two together. She recognized the profile of the guy and thought she recognized the voice, too. It was the man from the boat last night. The one who had seen her naked during her not-so-skinny-dipping expedition. He was tall and dark, with high cheekbones and a grin that showed off twin dimples.

Shit. Like last night's in-the-dark humiliation wasn't enough; now she had to face the asshole in broad daylight and see that he was good-looking, too. More Latin than London, but still.

"Well, well, if it isn't Peeping Thomas," Sam singsonged to him. "If I have to tell hotel security that you're stalking me, I will."

The guy smiled courteously. "I certainly apologize if you experience 'hello' as harassment. You've got to admire the audacity of the American legal system. You are Americans, correct?"

Sam folded her arms. Okay, so he was cute—copper skin, snapping dark eyes, wavy dark hair, and a perfectly chiseled jawline—a Gael García Bernal type, with an upper-crust British accent. He wore a white Irish linen shirt with the sleeves rolled up above his elbows and classic Levi's 505s that were neither too tight nor too baggy. But whatever. He'd still seen her naked.

He took a step toward the table and extended his hand to Sam. "I am Eduardo Muñoz. A guest at this hotel."

Sam reluctantly shook it. "Mary Poppins. And my friend—"

"I'm Anna Percy," Anna filled in, much too friendly for Sam's taste. "Would you like to join us?"

Sam shot Anna a dirty look, but Anna shrugged as Eduardo pulled a chair up to their table. All Sam could think about was last night. Truth was, no guy she'd ever fooled around with had seen her naked. She always managed to either get the lights out and her body under the comforter in advance of the main event or keep on some strategic bits of clothing.

"Have you been here before, Mary?" he asked. "I don't recall ever seeing you."

Sam shook her head. She couldn't figure out why he was hanging around to make nice. It had to be for Anna. Yep, that was it. He was pretending to chat her up so that he could move in on Anna.

"I try to come at least once a year. This is the best season."

"Great," Sam replied tersely.

"You're a mistress of understatement, Miss Poppins," Eduardo teased. "Do you have plans later? I thought perhaps you'd like to go sailing with me. On one of the resort catamarans?"

Jeez, if he was about to make a play for Anna, why didn't he just do it directly? She was not up for playing intermediary.

"Sorry, I've got plans." Sam checked her Cartier tank watch. "In fact, I'm already late. Have a pleasant life, Eduardo."

As she pushed away from the table, she saw Anna's eyebrows rise in surprise. But Sam had been through variations on this routine too many times. Whoever this guy was, however it was that he could afford to stay at Las Casitas, he wasn't real. Even if he wasn't interested in Anna, she knew how the second and third acts of this screenplay would go. He'd probably found out exactly who Sam was from some friend in the Las Casitas office. He'd tell her how beautiful and fascinating she was. Then he'd suddenly drop the phony accent, claim how it proved he was a great actor, and ask her to introduce him to her dad.

Screw him, Sam thought, hurrying away from the table. Screw his phony attention. And double-screw him for having seen her naked.

Anna was left at the table with Eduardo.

She felt a little ridiculous. "I apologize for my friend. She . . . has some things on her mind."

"Perhaps I was a bit too abrupt," he mused. "I didn't mean to offend."

"No offense taken." He was sweet and so cute. Even given her embarrassment of the night before, Anna wondered why Sam had run from him like he had the plague.

She started to get up. "I hate to leave like this, but I've got a surfing lesson in ten minutes."

"Does your friend surf?" Eduardo asked hopefully.

"No."

"What's her name? It surely isn't Mary Poppins."

Anna debated what to say and finally told half the truth. "Sam. Short for Samantha."

Eduardo smiled. "Samantha. Beautiful. *Muy linda.* A beautiful name for a beautiful girl."

Jackson Sharpe always appreciated returning to his Bel Air estate after time away. It reassured him of how rich and successful he was; this villa, with its tennis court, pool, three guesthouses, formal gardens, and ten thousand square feet of living space was tangible proof. He knew that Hollywood was a hornet's nest; he couldn't ignore the recent whispers that he was past his prime—that just like Harrison Ford and Robert Redford before him, he was already on the downward slope of stardom. Though it was a Hollywood blood sport to take shots at the person on top of the heap and knock them off just for kicks, Jackson knew that all he could do was to stave off the inevitable before he joined Ford and Redford and even Eastwood in the land of the weren't-they-once-handsome-and-somebody?

That day, he hoped, was years away. Right now he could still open a movie, no matter how dreadful. Not only in Los Angeles, but in France and Mexico and Tel Aviv and Bombay, thus making a bargain the twenty-plus million dollars that was his current quote.

He worked hard. Not just when he was on the set, but with publicity. It was why he went to Chicago to do *Oprah* and why he was going on *Jay Leno* that night. His appearance was being promoted heavily, and Leno, a personal friend—they loved to compare their car collections—had made the rare gesture of inviting pregnant Poppy and Sam to join Jackson on his show.

"Hello!" Jackson called as he entered the massive double oak doors that led to the marble lobby of his castle. "Who's home?"

"Meester Jackson! Welcome home!" Svetlana, the

maid, skittered into the lobby, smiling. "You have luggage, sir?"

"Outside," he said easily. "Where's my girl?"

"Mees Poppy is upstairs in suite, sir. Baby shower yesterday was beeg success."

"Glad to hear it. I'll just head up and see her. Thanks, Svetlana."

"You are most welcome." The maid beamed her appreciation that her boss remembered her name.

Jackson bounded the wide stairs two at a time. He was anxious to see his bride of six weeks. No need to worry about his luggage. The help would bring it in, unpack it, sort his clothes, have them laundered, and put them away.

He passed through the master suite sitting room—as big as the living room in the modest Ohio wood frame house where he'd spent his youth—where a fire burned cozily in the fireplace. And then into the master bedroom, where he found Poppy on the mahogany-and-red-velvet chaise that Harry Schnaper had shipped in from Milan.

A wet washcloth covered her forehead. Sitting next to her on the chaise was Dee. He'd known Dee since she and Sam had gone to preschool together in Brentwood.

"Oh, Jackson." Poppy roused herself enough to offer a wan smile and a limp hand.

"My God, what's wrong?" Jackson cried, hurrying to her side.

"Nothing, sweetie, just a headache. I missed you so much."

"I missed you, too." She made space for him on the chaise. He sat beside her, moved the washcloth, and kissed her damp forehead. "How bad is the headache? Do you need to see a doctor? And Dee, don't you belong in school? Are you waiting for Sam?"

Jackson saw Poppy and Dee exchange an unreadable look. "Poppy asked me to stay with her," Dee explained. "I made some chamomile tea. Ming Tsu is coming from the Alternative Medicine Center in Malibu to do reflexology. I'm sure that's all that Poppy needs."

Jackson took Poppy's hand. "That's good. You remember we're doing *Leno* tonight."

"Of course," Poppy replied. "Roberto Cavalli designed the most fabulous maternity dress for me. I just hope Alber Elbaz at Lanvin doesn't get pissed because I asked him first, but his idea was just so—"

"I'm sure it will be fine," Jackson interrupted. He cared very much that the women in his family looked good, but he also had no patience for fashionista drivel. "And Sam's ready, too?"

Poppy and Dee traded another look.

"What?" Jackson asked. "Don't tell me—she's planning on wearing leather chaps?"

Poppy bit her lower lip. "Um, I don't know, exactly."

"Then find out."

"There's a teensy little problem," Dee chimed in.

"Which is?"

Dee shrugged a helpless-little-girl shrug. "Sam isn't here."

Jackson didn't understand. "Well, then call her."

"We did," Poppy said. "A bunch of times. But it goes right through to voice mail. We left a million messages."

Jackson looked disgruntled. "So where is she?"

Poppy bit her lower lip. "That's the problem, sweetie. She wasn't at the baby shower. We haven't seen her at all. The Jeep is gone, too."

"How can she not have been at the baby shower?" Jackson asked, incredulous.

"*You* know Sam," Dee said. "She probably tried on a million outfits and decided she looked awful in all of them, due to her low self-esteem. So she didn't show up. I feel terrible about this."

"It's not your fault." Jackson rubbed his chin. His first thought was the family's appearance on Jay Leno's show that night. *Dammit, Sam better not fuck it up.*

"Are you saying she didn't come home last night at all?"

"No," Dee replied. "I kept checking her room."

"But she's stayed out all night before, sweetie," Poppy reminded Jackson. "Like if she's with Cammie or something."

This was true, he realized. Dee and Poppy were probably right: Sam had tried on a million outfits for the shower yesterday, decided she was fat, and blown it off. Then she'd spent the night drinking in one of the clubs she went to all the time. Maybe she hadn't made it back to the main house after that.

"Have you checked the guest houses?"

Dee nodded. "Empty."

"How about Cammie?"

"She wasn't there, either," Dee reported.

Shit. There went his second option.

Jackson rose. "Track her down for me, okay, Dee? You know who her friends are."

Dee nodded.

"Because we're live at eight-thirty at NBC in Burbank. She *has* to be there."

"Don't worry, sweetie," Poppy assured him, reaching for his hand. "She couldn't possibly forget. I don't think."

"Find her, Dee," Jackson repeated.

He was already thinking of the jokes that Jay would make if he and Poppy showed up at the studio without Sam. Hell, Leno could do his whole monologue at their expense. It didn't matter that they were friends—it was Leno's job to be funny.

Jackson kissed Poppy's hand by way of disengaging and strode from the room. Why couldn't a man come home to the bosom of his family and just relax for once, goddammit. But no. It was always something. Where the hell was his daughter?

A Date

C ammie had plans.

The night before, she and Adam had come home from Coachella too tired and grungy to think about fooling around. But when Adam rang her doorbell before school the next morning and Cammie answered, her father had already left for work. Her stepsister, Mia, was off to her school in the valley; her stepmother, Patrice, was at an early morning shoot for an indie film in which she'd agreed to play a cameo; and the staff didn't arrive for another hour.

The house was empty. She couldn't have planned it better herself.

"Interesting outfit for school," Adam observed, taking in her red silk kimono.

She put a finger through his belt loop. "How about a shower?"

"How about school?"

Cammie smiled knowingly. "College tour. We went to the Claremont Colleges and got back late."

"Ah, yes, the official Beverly Hills High School

second-semester-senior-year skip-your-classes mantra,"
Adam said, laughing. "Repeat after me. College tour.
College tour."

"Exactly." Cammie coaxed him inside. "If you don't
use it at least once every two weeks, the guidance coun-
selor calls your house."

"Anyone else here?"

Cammie shook her head.

Adam grinned. "God, I love being a senior."

"I know something you're going to love even more."
She led him upstairs to her pink-and-white splendifer-
ous bedroom and then into the gold-and-marble bathroom with a heated floor for chilly mornings. She
turned on the two-spigot shower, then took off his
shirt and then his undershirt. As steam filled the bathroom, he dropped his jeans.

"You don't have a sprinkler system in here, I hope,"
he teased.

"Nope," Cammie said. "We can make it as hot as we
want."

Down went his boxers. Off went her kimono.
Then once they were inside the glass door, they
kissed under the pulsing water until they were both
breathless.

What was that thing they played whenever the president of the United States walked into a room or something? "Hail to the Chief"? Cammie felt like singing it
at the top of her lungs. Because he was definitely standing at attention. Then they were out of the shower,

down on the thick rug outside the stall, and—finally!—
they were going to—

"Cammie? Cammie!"

Shit, shit, shit.

Cammie recognized the voice. The bathroom door
swung open.

"Oops," Dee squeaked, staring down at them with
either complete embarrassment or intense interest,
Cammie couldn't tell which.

"Don't say oops, Dee. Say good-bye," Cammie
ordered as Adam scrambled to toss her a fluffy gold
bath towel.

"But it's important," Dee insisted. She sneaked a
quick look at Adam, who was fastening a matching
towel around his waist. "I swear, I'll only look at you
guys from the neck up."

"Your timing sucks," Cammie declared.

Dee shrugged. "I'm really sorry. But honest to God,
it's a crisis."

"Couldn't you have called?"

"No one answered. Has either of you seen Sam?"

Adam shook his head as Cammie glared at her.
"That's the crisis? You want to know if we've seen Sam?
Wait downstairs. We're busy. We'll be down in . . . an
hour."

Cammie knew that if Adam was truly a virgin, she
was being optimistic, but what the hell.

"No, you don't understand," Dee pleaded, her
saucer eyes growing luminous. She sat on a brocade

stool in the corner of the bathroom. "Remember when Sam didn't show up for Poppy's shower? Well, no one has seen or heard from her since before then."

"Did you call Anna?" Adam asked.

Dee nodded. "Her cell, like a zillion times. And we've tried Sam's cell a zillion times, too. No answer."

"Well, if neither of them answers, it's a good sign. They're probably together with their cells off," Cammie declared. "That's not exactly rocket science."

"Okay, maybe," Dee responded. "But where? Jackson and Poppy and Sam are supposed to be on *Leno* tonight. Poppy's a wreck. It could be bad for the baby."

"If Poppy's a wreck, it's only because she thinks it could make her look bad on national TV." Cammie dropped the towel to the floor, found her kimono, and slipped it back on. "Same goes for Jackson."

"Well, it doesn't go for me," Dee insisted. "You and Sam are my best friends. Other than Poppy."

Cammie could see that Dee was genuinely worried. She decided to take some of the sting out of her voice. "I'm sure they're fine, Dee, really. My guess is they're off having a blast somewhere and they just don't want anyone bothering them."

Dee nibbled on her lower lip. "Maybe."

"Can't say I blame them," Adam added pointedly.

"Well, if you hear—" Dee began.

"You'll be the first to know," Cammie promised.

"'Kay, thanks." Dee hugged Cammie. Then she hugged Adam, too—for a little too long, Cammie thought—and scampered out.

Cammie turned to Adam and started to shed her kimono. "Where were we?"

"*¡Hola, Señorita Cammie! Usted está en casa?*"

Cammie gritted her teeth in frustration and tied her kimono again. "Crap. It's the housekeeper. Here early."

"Um . . . all good things come to those who wait?" Adam asked, trying to lighten the mood.

"I was thinking more: The early bird gets the worm," Cammie said, giggling at her own twisted humor. When Adam laughed with her, she gave him a big hug. "How can I not be into a guy who laughs at a line that gross?"

He tilted her chin up to him. "Did I tell you yet today how great you are?"

She smiled up at him. "You just did."

Sam hated how she looked in her tennis dress, even if it was Lilly Pulitzer. But she vowed not to dwell on the negative. She was still in Las Casitas paradise. She wasn't going to bring herself down with Beverly Hills–think.

When she got to the resort tennis shop, she was told the head pro—a former ranked player from England—would be back shortly. Would she like to select a racket, perhaps a Wilson H6 Hammer, the same model Serena

Williams used? Sam nodded. If it was good enough for Serena, it was good enough for her.

"Hello, Samantha. Ready to hit?"

Sam turned toward the voice that came from the doorway. Only it wasn't the pro, despite his British accent. It was the guy who had joined them at breakfast this morning, the same guy who'd seen her naked on the beach the night before. What was his name again? Sam didn't recall. But whatever it was, decked out for tennis and carrying several rackets in a Yamaha tennis bag, he looked positively sizzling.

"You're not the real pro," Sam said accusingly. "And where'd you find out my real name? A friend in the office?"

"Your friend, Anna. I'm Eduardo, if you forgot. You must have known I wouldn't believe you are really Mary Pop—"

"And you must have figured out if I told you I was Mary Poppins, there was a good reason," Sam shot back. She knew she was being overly bitchy. But she also knew that a guy this fine who'd already seen her in her birthday suit could not possibly be interested in her. There had to be an ulterior motive.

"The pro's been detained," Eduardo explained. "Can I warm you up?"

Sam frowned. "How do you know that the pro's been detained?"

"I asked."

Sam put her hands on her hips. "You asked?"

"Correct."

As Sam considered, Eduardo held open the door to the pro shop. Well, why not? A few minutes of warm-up with this guy and hopefully he'd blow his cover. Though when she gave him a nod, his smile did light up the shop. Maybe he was being genuine with her. He'd have to be a pretty amazing actor to fake that kind of joy.

Sam followed him out to one of the resort's immaculate grass courts, picked up some new balls from an instructor's basket near the net, and went back to the baseline.

Though she liked the game, had taken a lot of lessons when she was younger, and had a private hard court out behind her father's mansion, Sam didn't play much tennis. She'd never been particularly good at it. So it seemed a miracle that she was able to return nearly all of Eduardo's balls, on both the forehand and backhand sides. It felt great, running around the court, smacking her shots with confidence, inhaling fresh ocean air instead of the polluted Los Angeles variety. She didn't realize until she was ready to quit that the pro hadn't showed up at all.

"Let's call it," she said to Eduardo after she'd ripped a dazzling forehand past him at the net.

"Good idea." Eduardo flipped the two balls in his pocket toward the rear fence and wiped his brow with the bottom of his shirt. Sam was charmed by this earthy gesture. "You gave me a workout."

"Where'd you learn to play like that?" she asked, realizing that he'd barely made an unforced error during their time on the court.

"Lima." He opened the door in the chain-link fence and ushered her off the court.

"Lima?" she echoed. "As in Peru?"

"Exactly. Are you in a hurry?"

She and Anna were still going shopping in La Trinidad. But that was two hours from now. "Not really," she admitted.

Eduardo smiled. "I was hoping that would be your answer. Do you like surprises?"

"Depends."

The snort of a horse—no, two horses—from behind the tennis pro shop got Sam's attention. Then a young man who worked for the resort came into view, leading two gorgeous bay horses, saddled up.

"Do you ride?" Eduardo asked.

Sam nodded, her eyes still on the horses. "Sleep-away camp in Maine when I was twelve. I had a crush on the equestrian—wait. Why am I telling you that? What are these horses doing here?"

"I thought perhaps you'd enjoy a trot down the beach."

Sam was trying to let this sink in. "You had them bring horses."

"Precisely. There's something I'd like to show you. All right?" He held a hand out to her.

She didn't know what his game was, but he was

gorgeous, the horses were gorgeous, and this day in paradise was gorgeous.

What the hell, she figured, and took his hand. Let's go for a ride.

A fifteen-minute gentle canter north on the beach from the resort brought them to an unspoiled expanse of palm trees and brilliant white sand. Sam thought that Eduardo had wanted to show her a glorious deserted beach. Fair enough. But instead of stopping, Eduardo urged his horse into the ocean—it splashed through the calm, foot-deep brine toward a small island a few hundred yards away. Before Sam could say anything or do anything, her horse plunged into the warm water, too.

A minute or two later, they were ashore; Eduardo led the way through the underbrush to a hoof-beaten trail and then to a clearing. Sam's mouth dropped open when she saw what was in the center of the clearing: a linen-covered table for two, with wicker chairs and a beach umbrella shielding it all from the sun. On the table was a pitcher each of iced margaritas and lemonade, tostadas, fresh oysters on the half shell, a basket of baked rolls, right out of the oven—the wonderful odor wafted through the air—and giant, succulent strawberries.

"Um, do you have a hidden love for romance novels?" Sam marveled, eyeing the lavish spread.

Eduardo chuckled and dismounted his horse, hitching

the animal to a tree. Then he held out a hand so Sam could dismount; he secured her horse, too, before holding a chair out for her. "Sit, please. I will tell you the whole story."

She sat, still in a state of shock. "When did you arrange all this?"

"I told you, I've been to Las Casitas many times. It's a wonderful resort. The staff can accommodate almost any request, as long as it is reasonable."

"And apparently at Las Casitas a beach-side smorgasbord for two complete with horses is reasonable." Even Sam was disarmed by the opulence. He nodded.

Sam cocked one eye at him. "What if I'd said no?"

Eduardo shrugged. "Brunch for one, I guess, alone on this beautiful island. It wouldn't have been bad. But here we are. Two of us. Much better. Please."

He gestured toward the food. As in: Please eat. This was getting more surreal by the minute. Boys in Beverly Hills *never* told her to eat.

Sam reached for a crusty roll. "It's still hot."

Eduardo smiled. "As requested. The catering staff is very thorough."

Uh-huh. Sam figured she was dreaming, because things like this just didn't happen in real life. But as long as she was in this fantasy, she might as well enjoy it. She buttered the roll, took a bite, then slipped an icy fresh oyster into her mouth. Fabulous.

As they ate, Eduardo told her about himself. He was the eldest son of a prominent Peruvian politician. He came from a large family that lived in a huge villa outside of Lima; he had been educated at Andover in Massachusetts, then at boarding school, and at Oxford in England. Now he was studying art at the Sorbonne in Paris.

"Basically, you're from a royal Peruvian family," Sam summed up, biting into a strawberry.

"Peru has changed. It's a democracy now," Eduardo told her. "But close enough. Some say my father will be the next president. So tell me about you, Mary Poppins."

"Let's stay with you for the time being." Sam swallowed the strawberry and reached for another. "And let's drop the bullshit, though I must admit that it is clever bullshit. Here's my version. You're a screenwriter wannabe from God knows where. Any moment now, you're going to reach in your tennis bag for the spec you always carry, the one you think should star my father. In fact, no one could play the role *but* my father. How am I doing?"

Eduardo reached for an oyster and motioned for Sam to open her mouth. Why she did it, she didn't know. He slid the oyster down her throat. "What are you talking about?" he asked while she chewed it.

Sam licked oyster juice from her lips. "You expect me to believe that you don't know who I am?"

Eduardo shrugged. "A girl named Samantha who is very suspicious of me for reasons I cannot quite fathom."

Jeez . . . he was really clinging to his story. On the

off chance that he was telling the truth, Sam cautiously began to offer some truth of her own. That she was the daughter of the great Jackson Sharpe. "But you already knew that," she concluded.

"No, I didn't." Again he looked utterly guileless. "Of course, I've heard of your father. Being his daughter must be troublesome, from time to time."

"Yes," Sam admitted honestly. "It is. I'm a suck-up magnet."

"I have the same issue in Lima. Anyone who wants a favor from the government wants to be my friend. That's why I never minded being sent away to school. Are you still angry that your friend shared your name with me?"

"No," she decided. "I'm not."

How could she stay mad at him? He seemed so nice. And interesting. And thoughtful. And hot.

Sam spread her arm wide. "I still can't believe you planned all this. Did you buy off the tennis pro, too?"

Eduardo looked sheepish. "Let's just say I arranged for him to be unavoidably detained. I couldn't figure out another way to spend time with you."

"It worked."

"Good. The only thing is, I wish we had met earlier, Sam. Tomorrow I must return to Paris."

She was amazed at how awful that made her feel. It wasn't like she knew him.

"Oh, well," she finally said, reaching for the last strawberry. "This was fun."

"Actually I was hoping that you'd have dinner with me tonight. At the French restaurant? They make a wonderful *epaule d'agneau.*"

"Translation?"

"Braised mutton shoulder. With a wine list that's unparalleled."

Sam made a face. "I'll skip the mutton. But, yes, it sounds great." She felt shy . . . even more shy than she'd been in the water last night.

"Wonderful." Eduardo beamed at her. "Then it's a date."

Sam couldn't believe what was happening; that this incredible guy had taken one look at her—a naked her—and had decided to pursue her. She made one last stabbing test at his sincerity.

"You know, my friend Anna speaks fluent French," Sam commented. "I guarantee she knows what wine goes with what dish. She probably studied it. Maybe we should invite her, too."

Eduardo shook his head emphatically. "I'd prefer to have you all to myself."

"Oh."

Oh? That was the best she could come up with? *Oh?*

"I mean, it's a date," she added. "Anna and I are going to La Trinidad to shop. The hotel van is bringing us back to the resort at five-thirty."

"Excellent. I'll meet you up at your casita at seven. All right? Enough time to get ready?"

"Perfect," Sam agreed. And it really was perfect, like some fairy tale she had dreamed up. But no alcohol or

hallucinogens were involved—this was real life; it really
was happening.

Then Eduardo leaned across the table, took her
hand, and kissed it. It wasn't lame or corny at all. It was
sweet and sincere and, from Sam's point of view,
absolutely amazing. But even more amazing was what
he said when he moved her hand from his warm lips.

"Sam, may I say one more thing to you?"

She nodded.

"Just this." He gazed into her eyes. "You are very
beautiful."

Moth Larvae

Anna and Sam studied the wood sculpture of a Mexican peasant mother cradling her infant son. It was two feet high and gloriously done. Sam had expressed an interest in it, and the artist with the weather-beaten face had just named his price.

"I have an aunt who collects primitive art," Anna murmured to Sam. "That piece is worth at least five thousand dollars. He's asking the equivalent of five hundred."

Sam shook her head. "Only one problem. I don't have that kind of cash on me."

It was early afternoon. As planned, the Las Casitas van had dropped them off at the La Trinidad town square. They'd wandered around the small town and stumbled into this artist's studio—basically a hole-in-the-wall. No wonder the sculptor had such an anxious look on his face.

"I can't buy it," Sam realized. "Let's not prolong his agony." She began to tell the artist this in her very fractured Spanish, but Anna interrupted.

"Listen, Sam. I've got an idea. We can call Las Casitas

and have them send out some Mexican pesos with the driver when the van picks us up. I'm sure that would be no problem. They'll just put it on your account."

Sam nodded. "That's a great idea."

Between Anna and Sam, they were able to explain their plan to the artist. At first he wasn't buying it. But eventually, they managed to convince him. He was so pleased about the purchase that he kissed both Anna and Sam on the cheeks like long-lost relatives. Then he reached into his ancient trousers and extracted a business card. Anna examined it when he handed it to her.

"It's a restaurant. El Toreador. The Bullfighter. I think he wants us to eat there."

"*Sí. La comida es muy buena,*" said the artist. "Good. Good."

"Then we should go," Sam agreed. "I'm starved. When you don't eat for three weeks, it's amazing how hungry you get."

"Maybe we should just hang out in the town square until the van comes back," Anna suggested.

Sam gave her a cockeyed look. "Are you crazy? Hang in the town square when we can go be wild women? Where'd you learn all that Spanish, anyway?"

"An extended trip with my aunt to Marbella when I was twelve," Anna explained. "She taught me every Spanish curse word she knew. We worked up from there. Then I took it at Trinity."

"Good. Teach me some good ones at the restaurant so I can shock Eduardo tonight."

Anna agreed to Sam's plan. She wasn't all that hungry, and she thought sitting in the town square and sipping a coffee while the colorful world of La Trinidad passed by would have been fun. But Sam was right—it wasn't all that adventurous.

The artist gave them rough directions to El Toreador, kissed their cheeks again, and the girls walked away. As they departed, Anna tried to call Las Casitas on her cell. No luck. She couldn't even get a signal and realized that there was probably no microwave relay tower in La Trinidad. They'd have to find a landline. Well, that was fine. They could use the phone in the restaurant, if there was one. If not, they'd figure out something.

"Wow, I just bought my first piece of art," Sam realized as they headed down the rough-hewn sidewalk. "That is so cool."

"I think it's this right turn," Anna said, pointing at a narrow side street that went downhill. They followed the street, turned left, right, and left again and finally came upon El Toreador by accident. They tried the front door, but it was locked.

"So much for adventure," Anna said. "No one's here. Should we go back to the town square?"

Sam shook her head and pointed across the street. "Isn't that a restaurant?"

The place was called Los Molinos. The exterior was nondescript: a gray wooden door with a hand-painted sign and the menu tacked to it, a glass window with hand-painted lettering announcing the name of the

restaurant and *BUENA COMIDA, CERVEZA FRIA*. Good
food, cold beer.

They crossed the street and tried the door. Tinkling
bells signaled their entrance. The interior was small, with
a dozen battered tables and wooden chairs, a wooden bar
with a mismatched set of bar stools, and an ancient bil-
liards table. Two old men played dominos at one of the
corner tables; a third snoozed with his head against the
wall. A few younger guys sat at the bar, watching a soccer game on TV. The bartender—a beautiful dark-haired
young woman in American-style clothes—read the
Spanish edition of *Cosmopolitan* magazine. She barely
glanced at the girls before returning to her reading.

A cadaverous elderly waiter with a thick shock of
white hair greeted them effusively in good English,
guessing at their nationality. "Lovely American señori-
tas!" he cried, clasping his hands. "Welcome, welcome!"
He gestured to a table, held out one chair for Anna,
then hurried around the table to help Sam get seated.
"You would desire menus?"

"We would," Anna told him. "But can we use your
telephone first?"

"To where are you calling?" the waiter asked, a bit
wary.

"Las Casitas resort," Sam told him. "We'll pay you
for the call, of course."

"Certainly," he said, with a small bow. "And there is
no charge." He turned to the bartender and barked
out some instructions. She scowled but still got the

old-fashioned rotary phone out from under the bar and dialed some numbers. She talked briefly with the person at the other end, then held the telephone receiver toward Anna and Sam. "*Para usted.*" She gestured.

Sam got up, took the receiver, and had a quick conversation with the Las Casitas desk. A moment later, she was back with Anna. "Done. They're bringing pesos for me. Listen, let's celebrate my purchase." She turned to the waiter, who had waited patiently for her. "A bottle of mescal. Some tapas. No. Lots of tapas. Bottled water. And two glasses."

"*Muy bueno.*" The waiter beamed happily. "We make our own tapas and our own mescal also!" He kissed the tips of his fingers, indicating just how well they had chosen, then hustled behind the bar and told the bartender to prepare what they ordered. She fired a sullen look at Sam and Anna before getting up to work.

"So, mescal." Anna felt a little uneasy. "That's on my long list of new experiences I might try someday, maybe."

"Kind of like tequila, but stronger. Made from the mescal cactus. I crossed it off mine when I was fourteen at this party in Topanga Canyon," Sam recalled. "This guy who was a junior at Harvard-Westlake showed me how to down a shot straight up. He said it made girls sexy. Pathetically enough, I downed seven of them. Cammie rescued me."

Anna raised her eyebrows. "When I think emergency, I don't think of calling Cammie Sheppard."

Sam rubbed a finger along the edge of the rough-hewn

table. "Yeah, well, she'll fool you now and then. Anyway . . ." She spread her arms expansively. "I'd say now's the perfect time to cross it off your list."

Moments later, the elderly waiter returned with a brown bottle, two brown shot glasses, a plate of tapas, and the bottled water. "Enjoy," he said with a slight bow, then retreated to watch the soccer game.

Sam did the honors, pouring generous shots of mescal into Anna's glass and then her own. Anna peered into the bottle from the top. "Do you know that they put moth larvae in the bottle? And that once it dies, they know the alcohol content is sufficient?"

"Well, that's certainly different from the way Cristal is made," Sam declared, raising her glass. "We should christen your mescal-drinking experience with a toast."

"To new experiences," Anna decided, and clinked her glass against Sam's. She watched Sam down her shot in one swallow. Then she did the same. Instantly her throat was on fire.

"Water!" She grabbed one of the bottles, tore the cap off, and guzzled.

"Come on, Anna. Take it like a man," Sam ordered with a laugh. "What kind of party girl are you?"

Tears came to Anna's eyes. "Whew." She fanned her face. There was a mirror on the wall near their table. In it, she could see the female bartender sneering at them. That was enough motivation for her to pour them each another shot. She could prove she wasn't a wuss. This time, she knew what to expect. "Your toast, Sam?"

"To rich girls gone wild," Sam decreed.

They clinked glasses and downed the second shot. This time the heat spread from Anna's throat to her belly and the top of her head; she felt sunburned from the inside out.

Sam nodded. "Whew, baby, that is some potent shit." Sam spun the bottle around and gazed at it. "Brown. No label. Huh. They probably *do* make their own. If we drink enough, maybe we can bring the little sucker back to life."

"Give it mouth to mouth," Anna suggested. Then she laughed, really feeling the alcohol. "That's so funny."

"I know!" Sam chortled. She poured them one more shot, her hand none too steady. "Last one. To . . . to what this time?"

"To Eduardo," Anna decided.

"Eduar-r-r-rdo," Sam repeated, rolling the *r*. "What a hot name. Isn't Eduardo a hot name?"

"Very," Anna agreed

"Why is he into me? That is the question. . . ."

"Why not?" Anna asked.

"He's probably just a guy who wants to get laid," Sam slurred. "I look like an easy mark."

"Sam, think. He's gorgeous. He obviously has money. I don't think he's hurting for female companionship. Besides, he treated you with respect."

"True," Sam agreed. "Drink up."

They clinked glasses and drank. Anna gagged as she felt something slither down her throat. She tried to hock it up, but it was too late. "Yecch!" she sputtered.

"Too strong?"

"No. That larva must have spilled out into my glass. I think I just swallowed it!"

Sam grabbed the mescal bottle and peered inside. "Yep," she pronounced. "You did."

"Great," Anna moaned. "Serves me right."

"Don't flip out. But I should warn you, it's going to get you stoned out of your mind."

"My friend Cyn told me that was a myth."

Sam shook her head. "No, it isn't. I saw a guy at a party down the worm. Fifteen minutes later he was standing on the kitchen table in his mother's high heels, trying to hump his dog."

Anna felt weak in her knees. "But Cyn told me—"

"Don't worry," Sam assured her. "Wherever you're going, I won't leave you stranded." She waved her hand to get the elderly waiter's attention. "Another bottle of mescal, *por favor. Tout du suite.* I mean, *ahora.*"

The waiter stared at her. "You are sure? We make strong mescal here."

"Give the drinks to your friends." Sam gestured toward the men watching the soccer game and playing dominos. "Just bring me the bottle with the worm. Okay?"

The waiter gave her a dubious look and repeated her instructions, as if to make sure he understood them. When he was sure he did, he made an announcement to the customers that resulted in raucous cheering and shouts of, "*¡Olé, la gringa!*"

"The cheers are for you," the waiter told her as he moved off to get the new bottle. "You have . . . how do you say in English . . . made their afternoon."

"Tell them thank you. Don't forget to bring me the worm," Sam reminded.

For the next ten minutes, Sam chowed down on the delicious tapas while the waiter poured shot after shot for his happy customers. Many of them stopped by their table to toast the American girls. Anna, who ordinarily would have been happy for inducing such cross-cultural bonding, just sat there nervously. She was too unsettled to eat and monitored herself to see if—when—she might feel something weird.

Finally the waiter placed the second brown bottle on the table between them. "One bottle, one worm," he said, then hesitated. "Be careful. There are special ingredients in our mescal. From the desert."

"Works for me," Sam told him. Then she tipped the bottle over and let three fingers worth of mescal plopped into her shot glass. Plus one dead worm. "Come on, Anna. Don't make me drink alone."

Anna swallowed hard. Her mouth felt fuzzy, her lips thick. The colors in the room were achingly bright. No. Maybe she was just imagining it. That had to be it; her overactive imagination was at work.

"Okay." She poured one more glassful of mescal from their first bottle. "To what?"

"To the slaves of Beverly Hills; thank God we're not there," Sam pronounced.

"I'll drink to that."

And they did. More than once.

"Hey, Anna! Check out this lizard. Right here!"

Sam pointed to a large iguana that was sunning itself on a large sandstone rock. "C'mere, Bill." She held out her hand toward the reptile. It didn't move.

Anna flew across the sandy landscape toward Sam. At least she felt as if she were flying. She'd been utterly captivated by a purple desert wildflower that had sprouted from the side of a cactus. In fact, she'd gotten her nose practically inside the flower to examine it, amazed by the striations and curves on its interior.

How much time had passed since they'd left the restaurant? Anna wasn't sure. A couple of hours, maybe. Knowing how wasted they were from the mescal, they'd had every intention going directly from the restaurant to the town square to hang out until the van arrived. But at the end of the alley behind Los Molinos, Sam had spotted a trail that headed off into the Mexican desert. And she'd convinced Anna that they ought to take a scenic detour.

That detour had extended as the girls—fascinated by everything they saw—strolled deeper and deeper into the wild, barren landscape.

Anna peered down at the iguana. "Sam? How do you know his name is Bill?"

"He told me," Sam said seriously. "Shhh. Listen, he'll tell you."

Anna cocked her head to listen. The iguana flicked his tongue at her. "Hey," Anna protested. "He hates me. Look what he just did!"

"Maybe he's hungry," Sam said. She reached into her pocket and found a piece of gum. She held it out to see what the iguana would do.

"Sam? I don't think Bill has teeth. To chew gum. Which means he'd have to gum the gum."

Sam found this comment hysterically funny. Anna thought that her finding the comment hysterically funny was hysterically funny. The two girls laughed so hard that the sound echoed off the distant hills.

"Wow, that is so cool," Sam marveled. "It's like our voices are all over the desert." She cupped her hands around her mouth and turned toward the distant, golden hills. "*¡Hola!*"

"Hi!" Anna yelled directly at Sam's face.

Sam reeled backward. "Why are you yelling?"

"You said 'hello' in Spanish. So I said 'hi' in English."

"Oh." Sam nodded thoughtfully. "Right. That makes sense."

Anna pointed at the lizard. It hadn't moved despite their shouting. Maybe he really was magical. "You should give Bill the gum."

"Good idea."

Sam unwrapped the gum and tossed the stick at the iguana. Anna saw an arc trail as the gum flew through the air. "Did you see that?" She pointed at the trail, which still hung in the air.

"What?" Sam responded.

"That!" Anna couldn't find the words, so she trickled her fingers through the air by way of illustration. A trail formed behind them, too.

"Your fingers?" Sam asked.

"What about my fingers?" Anna looked at her hand. "Fingers are so amazing, aren't they?"

"You wanted me to watch your fingers?" Sam asked.

Then Anna remembered. "I meant the trail. Did you see the gum trail when you tossed it to Bill?"

"What's a gum trail?"

"No," Anna said. "In the air. Just before."

Sam looked at her, puzzled.

"Sam. Are we tripping? We can't be tripping. The worm thing is a miss!"

"Well, I think it's a hit," Sam said.

Anna licked her dry lips. "*Myth*, not miss."

"Theriothly?" Sam lisped. That made them both crack up again. When Sam caught her breath, she reminded Anna what the waiter had told them about the homemade mescal. "He said it's got some weird shit that makes you trip."

"Like Don Juan," Anna realized. "And Carlos Castaneda. 'To seek freedom is the only driving force I know. Freedom to fly off into that infinity out there.'"

Sam looked at the iguana. "Bill, what's she talking about?"

The lizard stuck his tongue out at Anna again. Then he jumped down from the rock and scurried away. Sam charged after him as he scampered up a small dirt mound and down into a hole. "See, he hates me," Anna said.

But Sam was too fixated on the sky to respond. "Check it out, Anna."

Anna looked up. Puffy cumulus clouds scudded across the endless blue from east to west, shapes morphing as they did. "I see a lion. And a girl fishing." She turned to Sam—her friend had sprawled in the sand to get a better view of the sky. So Anna dropped down next to her. "This is so great. I haven't done this since I was really young."

"You don't have to stop. You're still really young. And we've got all the time in the world."

Anna checked to see what time it was. Four-fifteen. But when she put her arm down and tried to focus again on the clouds, she was overwhelmed by the sensation of the watch on her wrist. It felt heavy. Really heavy. So she took off the watch and tossed it away.

Much better.

"What are you doing?" Sam said as the wristwatch skittered across some flat rocks.

"Being timeless," Anna explained.

"Great idea. I want to be timeless, too." With a few quick movements, Sam removed her own wristwatch, then flung it off into the desert.

"We should just be here now," Anna pronounced. "Where no one can get to us. Nothing from civilization. No watches, no rings, no jewelry, and definitely no cell phones." Following her own advice, she methodically took off her earrings and her rings, dug her cell out of her pocketbook, and heaved it all off the mound. "Yep. Castaneda would approve."

"Didn't he make half that shit up?" Sam asked rhetorically. "Oh, what the fuck." She took off her necklace and rings, found her cell phone, and threw them each into the desert in a different direction.

"Bravo," Anna told her as an overwhelming sense of freedom washed over her. No baggage. No worries. Just herself, her friend, and the cerulean sky.

Dinner With Eduardo

"It's a beautiful sunset," Anna said. "Amazing, really."

"Yeah," Sam agreed.

They were sitting together on a boulder not far back from the edge of a cliff that dropped down to the ocean. The cloud-strewn western sky was on fire from the setting sun. At least that's how it looked to Anna, who recognized that she was still in an extremely altered state. She felt fine, though. Absolutely serene. She was not at all concerned about a bank of dark clouds that loomed on the opposite horizon. From the beatific smile on Sam's face, she could only assume that her friend felt the same way.

Anna sighed contentedly. Maybe she needed to drink homemade mescal more often. Her mind wasn't racing, worrying about her family or her love life.

"Life is so great," she declared.

"I know," Sam agreed, closing her eyes. "I think you're right, Anna. About Eduardo. I mean, he really is into me. Isn't that so awesome?"

Anna thought for a few moments. Eduardo. There was a guy named Eduardo. Wasn't Sam supposed to meet this guy, Eduardo? And wasn't she supposed to meet Kai?

"Sam?"

"Uh-huh?"

"How long have we been here?"

Sam shrugged. "A while."

"Aren't you supposed to have dinner with Eduardo tonight?"

"Yeah," Sam replied. "Fine, no problem. What time is it?"

Anna looked down at her wrist. No watch.

"I had a watch. Didn't I?"

"I think so. Yeah." Sam stood up and stumbled a little. "Whoa. That was some intense mescal. Check the time on your cell."

Anna reached into her bag for her cell. No cell.

"Check yours," she told Sam. But Sam didn't have a watch or a cell, either.

"I think we need to go back to that town," Anna said as she stood up.

"Sure," Sam agreed. "Sounds good. Which way?"

Anna looked behind her. Then to the right and to the left. She had absolutely no idea of the direction from which they'd come, and it was getting darker by the moment. "I don't know. Do you?"

Sam gazed around. "Clueless."

"I think we're stuck," Anna realized.

"We can't be stuck. We just have to figure out how we got here."

"That's easy. We walked," Anna said. The comment started them both on a laughing jag, which was interrupted by a slash of lightning in the sky behind them. And then, seconds later, thunder.

"Thunder. That means rain," Sam reckoned.

"You're right," Anna agreed. She held her hand out. "Not yet, though. That's good." An instant later, there was another lightning-thunder combination. "Not good."

"We need a plan," Sam decided.

"Shelter."

"Good, Anna." Sam peered around. "What shelter?"

Anna could feel normalcy dig its way through the fog of her brain as she glanced back at the gathering storm and then scanned the terrain in the murky twilight. She couldn't see much. Of what she could see, there was nothing taller than they were.

"This is dangerous," she told her friend, and strode off into the desert. "We're human lightning rods out here. Come on."

"Come on *where*?" Sam called, but hustled after her friend.

Anna jogged south, hoping to find something—a hut, a lean-to, even a depression in the ground—that might provide some kind of shelter from the storm. She picked up her pace as another lightning bolt split the sky and cast an otherworldly glow on their surroundings.

"Anna, would you fucking wait!"

"No. Come on, Sam. Move it!"

Anna broke into a run; Sam followed. It was hard to see; they stumbled over rocks and bushes as the storm rushed in and the rain came—splatters at first, followed by a steadier flow. Then a bolt of lightning struck a cactus not three hundred feet from them, splintering it.

"Shit!" Sam bellowed.

"Over there!" Anna pointed. The lightning had been terrifying, but it had briefly illuminated something a few hundred yards to the left. Anna thought she had seen some white buildings. But now, in the pounding rain, she couldn't see anything. Still, they had no other hope. "Go!"

They dashed in the direction that Anna had indicated. Another bolt of lightning lit up what Anna thought she'd seen—a compound of low-slung white buildings, behind a four-foot-high white stone fence. They clambered over the fence and found themselves on a perfectly manicured lawn, not far from a sparking swimming pool, a tennis court, a shuffleboard court, and a white gazebo. Lightning was flashing almost continuously now; they could see the buildings clearly. There were four—no, five of them, all in that same boxy white design. There were no lights. No sign of life. But at least they'd found some semblance of shelter, if they could get inside.

"Amazing!" Sam yelled over the noise of the storm as they ran to the closest of the white buildings. "Out here in the middle of nowhere!"

They circled the low building, looking for a way in. It was about the size of the largest of the guesthouses on the Sharpe estate in Beverly Hills, but it didn't appear to have a door. Finally they came to what was obviously a garage door. Anna tried it; it wasn't locked. She flung it open—it rolled back easily—and the girls stepped inside. As they did, a bank of automatic overhead lights came on.

"Whoa," Sam said, checking out the contents of the building. "Check this out."

They were indeed in a garage. One that housed five cars. A pearl gray 1932 Rolls-Royce. A cherry red Ferrari. A yellow Lotus. A metallic blue DeLorean. And a classic black Ford Model-T, perfectly restored. All of them had Mexican license plates.

Anna wrung out her wet hair. "Do you see what I'm seeing, or am I still hallucinating?"

"If you are, we're sharing a three-million-dollar-auto vision," Sam surmised, dripping water as she walked around the DeLorean. "This puppy is even more loaded than my father's. Let's check for keys. Maybe we can drive back to Las Casitas."

"Don't you think we should ask whoever lives here first?"

"Oh yeah. That," Sam reluctantly agreed.

They went to the open garage door and peered out into the night. The storm was still raging; thunder shook the night. Anna pointed across the lawn toward where she thought she'd seen the biggest structure.

"I think the main house—whatever it is—is over there. Ready to run?"

Sam nodded.

"Okay, then . . . .go!"

Anna charged into the storm as yet another lightning bolt illuminated the sky. She saw the main building— low-slung and pure white, just like all the others—about two hundred feet away. She made it to the front door in record time, with Sam not far behind. She immediately leaned on the doorbell but heard nothing.

"The power must be out!" she yelled toward Sam over more rolling thunder.

Sam answered by pounding on the ornate carved-wood front door. No answer.

"There's no one here!" she shouted. "Let's go back to the garage!"

They went back and searched each car for keys. But they came up empty-handed. The only useful thing they found was a flashlight.

Wherever they were, they were there for the night. Alone.

The Great Wizard

Jackson Sharpe was a man used to getting what he wanted. What he wanted right now was to locate his daughter, which was why he was furiously pacing back and forth in his bedroom, watching the clock tick down to seven o'clock. The same time they were scheduled to leave to make it to the NBC studios in Burbank for Leno's show.

The search for Sam was making his life difficult. All through his workout with Billy Blanks and his session in the new tanning booth, he'd worried that he was wasting his time. Both activities were designed to make him look properly buff and golden on *The Tonight Show*. But unless they found Sam, that appearance was going to be ruined. What would he tell Jay to explain why his daughter was missing? And what if something truly bad had happened to Sam and her friend? What then?

Poppy sat on the bed, shredding a Kleenex into little pink balls. "She did this on purpose, I know she did." She sniffed. "I knew she was planning something when she skipped my baby shower."

"Can we just make sure she's okay before we beat her up?" Jackson snapped.

Poppy put her hands protectively over her massive belly. "Please, sweetie. Indoor voice. You'll upset Ruby Hummingbird."

"Sorry." Jackson paced some more until his cell phone rang. He flipped it open. It was Kiki, who'd finally tracked down the father of Sam's new friend from New York. She announced that she had Jonathan Percy on three-way at a bed-and-breakfast up in San Simeon.

When Jackson told Jonathan what was going on, Jonathan reported that his daughter Anna was at the Las Casitas resort in Mexico.

Bingo. Jackson asked Jonathan to call his daughter and see if Sam was there, too. A few minutes later, Jonathan rang back.

"Good news. I think your Sam is with my Anna," he told Jackson. "One of my junior execs is at Las Casitas and says that Anna was with a friend who calls herself Mary Poppins."

Double bingo. Jackson remembered that when Sam was little, she adored the movie *Mary Poppins.* So much so that she insisted that the family hire a British nanny. Then she insisted that Jackson fire the nanny because she couldn't fly.

"Evidently Anna and Mary went shopping at some town called La Trinidad. I left a message for her to call me immediately," Jonathan reported. "And for Mary to call her father, too. We good?"

"Yeah, great. Thanks for the help, Jonathan."

"Keep me posted, okay?"

Jackson hung up, somewhat relieved. At least he knew Sam was safe. But why did his daughter pull this shit? Maybe they needed to reconnect. He'd have to get Kiki to book a family day, just him and Poppy and Sam and prenatal Ruby Hummingbird. That would make a great photo op. And make up for whatever joke Leno was bound to make tonight at Sam's expense.

Sam. Samantha. Samantha Sharpe.

Eduardo ruminated on her name as he dressed for his date. A sexy name for a sexy girl. He loved the way she looked. And he loved her outspokenness. Wimpy girls had never appealed to him.

For the evening, Eduardo decided to go simple but elegant: a handmade suit from a Hong Kong tailor that he favored and a plain black Gap T-shirt.

His thoughts went to Sam again. The curves of her body—lush and full and womanly—made his heart pound. When he'd caught a glimpse of her skinny dipping that night with her friend, she'd looked so amazing in the moonlight. She seemed full of joy, whooping with delight in the waves. He remembered everything: the line of her profile, how her eyes shone, the cascade of dark hair flowing down the lush curve of her back. Lunch with her on the island had sealed it. She'd been so funny, so charming. It had been all he could do not to ask her to cancel her shopping trip so they could be together for the rest of the afternoon.

Instead he'd played golf on the wonderful Las Casitas course. He'd been placed in a foursome with a vacationing South African pro who'd competed at the Masters. Normally he would have been thrilled. But instead he found himself thinking about her instead of his swing. Same thing later, when he was sailing one of the resort's catamarans. Even back in his casita when the big rainstorm had blown through from the southwest.

He'd called Las Casitas' florist and ordered two dozen tangerine blood roses to be sent to Sam's casita with a note that read, LOOKING FORWARD TO TONIGHT. EDUARDO. The florist had called to tell him that no one had answered the knock, so they'd used a passkey to leave the roses in a vase on her coffee table. Eduardo was pleased; he hoped Sam would also be pleased when she returned from shopping.

Seven o'clock. Finally.

Eduardo walked the three hundred yards to Sam's casita and knocked on her door. No answer. He knocked again. Nothing. This was curious. But perhaps she'd misunderstood, thinking they'd meet at the French restaurant.

But she wasn't there when Eduardo checked. Nor in the main lobby. So he waited patiently at the lobby bar. Seven-fifteen P.M. Seven twenty-five P.M. Seven-thirty P.M.

Then the resort's surfing instructor—Eduardo couldn't recall his name, but he'd taken an excellent lesson with him a couple of days before—strode into the lobby, obviously looking for someone.

"Get stood up?" Eduardo asked, only half joking.

Kai looked at Eduardo closely. "Didn't I see you this morning? With Anna Percy and her friend?"

Eduardo nodded. "Saman—Mary. We were supposed to have dinner at seven. But she's not in her casita. And she's not here, either."

Kai shoved his hands into the pockets of his loose chinos. "I was supposed to meet Anna for sushi at seven. But she's a no-show, too. And she strikes me as the prompt type. I've looked everywhere for her."

"They went to La Trinidad this afternoon. Just a moment."

Eduardo left the bar to ask the diminutive French concierge what time the resort van had returned from La Trinidad with Anna Percy and Mary Poppins.

The concierge kept his voice confidential, but his hands fluttered as he answered. "It seems there is a bit of confusion, Mr. Munoz. The young ladies never met us. Nor have they called the hotel, to our knowledge. We're looking for them as we speak."

"*What?*" Eduardo was incredulous.

The concierge winced and made a placating gesture. "Please, sir. We are doing everything possible to ascertain their whereabouts. Perhaps the young ladies decided to dine in La Trinidad and neglected to call the hotel."

"I was to meet one of those young ladies for dinner," Eduardo declared apprehensively. "And your employee over there was supposed to meet the other." He nudged his head toward Kai.

"We are not in the habit of babysitting our guests, Mr. Muñoz," the concierge explained, careful to keep his tone polite. "We very much respect privacy here at Las Casitas. But I assure you, we *are* looking for them."

"You pride yourself on having the world's best security!" Eduardo exclaimed. "How could this have happened?"

The concierge, none too tall to begin with, seemed to shrink. "Sir," he explained, "our security is unparalleled. But it is designed to keep those not registered as guests *out.* Not to keep registered guests *in.*"

Eduardo forced himself to calm down. "I understand. But you must call the local police. No. Call the Mexican *federales.* In the meantime, I'm going to telephone their families. Let's start with Miss Poppins. Her number, please. Now."

Several hundred miles to the north, there was a knock at Jackson's door. Kiki stuck her head in. "We have to leave for the studio if we're going to make the taping."

Jackson peered into the mirror over his dresser and brushed some lint from the collar of his jacket. "Christ. What a mess. Where are her friends?"

"Dee's in her room. Adam and Cammie are watching TV downstairs. They say they're not going home until we hear from Sam."

Jackson turned to Kiki. "That's nice, anyway." He shook his head. "How can she be so damn flaky? What the hell am I paying that quack Dr. Fred for, anyway? How can—?"

His phone rang—the landline, not his cell. He picked it up. "Yeah?"

"Mr. Jackson Sharpe?"

Jackson didn't recognize the British-accented male voice. "Who's calling?" he asked warily. Sometimes the oddest people managed to unearth his unlisted home phone number.

"My name is Eduardo Muñoz. I am a friend of your daughter, Samantha. We met here at Las Casitas resort in Mexi—"

"Where is my daughter?" Jackson demanded.

"That's why I am calling, sir. I don't work for the resort. I'm a friend." Quickly Eduardo filled Jackson in on the few facts he knew.

"You mean they're *missing?*"

"I don't mean to alarm you. Perhaps the girls are off having a marvelous time. But perhaps not."

An unfamiliar feeling began in the region of his Jackson's heart. A tightening of the chest. It was fear. But he knew instantly that fear would not locate his daughter. That would require decisive action. He had the young man ask for the chief of resort security. But the chief of security was out in the field, searching for Sam and Anna. An underling was put on the phone.

"Have you brought in the police?" Jackson barked.

"Yes, of course, sir, it's already done," the underling reported. "And might I add that it is a pleasure to speak with you, Mr. Sharpe. I am a big fan. I have seen all your movies."

Jackson closed his eyes and rubbed the bridge of his nose. It never failed to amaze him how people would go into that I'm-your-biggest-fan thing at the most inappropriate times. When he was taking a piss at the Ivy. At the memorial service for Christopher Reeve. And now, while his daughter was missing in a foreign country.

"Thank you. Now go to work. I want my daughter found, and I want it to happen immediately. Am I clear?"

Jackson hung up, unsure what to do next. It was so much easier when someone else wrote the lines. Then he always did the right thing. He won the fight, caught the bad guys, and got the girl. But there was no script for this. An unfamiliar insecurity washed over him. It reminded him of *The Wizard of Oz;* he felt like the small man behind the screen instead of the great wizard who awed everyone. That small man was no hero. At the moment, Jackson didn't feel like one either.

"Sweetie?" Poppy stepped back into the room. "How do I look for *Leno?*"

Jackson glanced at his young wife, who'd made a quick change into a different outfit: a sleek black off-the-shoulder top that fell to her hips and covered the stretch waistline of a pair of black palazzo pants. The hair and makeup people had spent two hours buffing, painting, and spraying her to perfection. But Jackson didn't give a damn. He got up from the bed.

"No *Leno*. Poppy."

Poppy's jaw fell open. "We can't just blow off Jay Leno at the last min—"

"Yeah, we can," Jackson interrupted. He knew exactly what he had to do. He gathered up his wallet and rummaged in the bedside drawer for his passport. "In fact, we just did. Kiki, call Jay and apologize. Say I'll come on another time. Anytime he wants. Send a hefty donation to that charity his wife started. Make sure he knows about it."

"But—"

"But nothing. And call my pilot. I'm going to Mexico."

Hot Tub

It wasn't any harder to get into the main house than it had been to get into the garage—when they tried the front door, it was unlocked. But the inside was pitch-black, and Anna had to use the flashlight they'd found in the garage to search for a light switch. She found one and flipped it on. Nothing happened.

"Great." Sam groaned, shivering in her wet clothes.

"Power's got to be out," Anna mused. "A place like this, I bet they have an emergency generator."

"What about the lights in the garage?"

"Battery-powered, set off by motion detector?" Anna guessed. "Come on. If there's a generator, we need go out and find it."

"What the hell." Sam sighed. "We can't get any wetter."

Guided by the flashlight and the occasional bolt of lightning—the storm had moved off to the north, leaving only steady rain behind—Anna and Sam searched the spacious grounds of the estate. Not far from the

house, they found a small white shed. Inside was a
gas-powered generator. Anna found the main switch,
flipped it, and a gas-powered engine roared to life. A
moment later, lights went on inside the main house and
a few of the outbuildings.

"Your mind is an impressive thing," Sam marveled.

"I bet the lightning knocked out their security system, too," Anna guessed. "That's why the doors were
open and there was no alarm."

"Thank you, Madame Genius."

They ran back to the house and pushed through the
front door. What they saw inside—the kind of splendor
that confronted them—made even Sam and Anna stop
and take notice.

The interior walls were adobe, hung with framed
artwork: Anna recognized originals by Diego Rivera,
Frida Kahlo, Milton Glaser, and Romare Bearden. All
worth a mint. Wall lizards in silver and gold crawled up
the corners of the massive entryway. Rough-hewn pine
furniture—Anna could tell that it was in fact all handmade and doubtless cost a fortune—sat upon Navajo-
patterned rugs. Celestial chimes of moons, suns, and
stars hung in the arched doorway that led to the rest of
the house. But there'd be time to admire that stuff
later. What Anna was most interested in now was finding a phone.

She spied one on the pine chest, went to it, and
lifted the receiver to her ear, mentally rehearsing her
Spanish for the operator.

The mental rehearsal was pointless. There was no dial tone. "Dead," she reported.

"Of course," Sam told her. "That would have made it much too easy."

"No kidding. Are you as freezing as I am?"

Sam nodded. "Let's find clothes."

Anna hesitated. "But what if someone is here? It's called breaking and entering."

"Yeah, and if we take their clothes, it's called stealing," Sam said, rubbing her arms. "But we're rich. We can buy our way out of trouble if need be." She led the way through the room with the wonderful artwork and down a long hallway. Anna pushed open a door as they passed it and ducked inside.

It was a bathroom the size of a New York studio apartment; inlaid Mexican tiles surrounded a sunken tub big enough for four people. The water spigots were shaped like lizards. Anna spun one of the spigots, and water flowed out of the lizard's mouth. Then, as Sam joined her, she opened one of the closets and discovered a stack of white terry-cloth robes.

"Let's change," she told Sam. They stripped off their wet clothes and hung them on pegs, then wrapped themselves in the robes and towel-dried their hair. For the first time since getting caught in the storm, they were something approaching comfortable.

"Know what's weird?" Sam asked. "I haven't seen a photograph of anyone. It's like no one lives here."

"Or whoever lives here doesn't want their pictures around," Anna added.

The mystery of the place continued as they found a second great room that was furnished in high-end desert chic: pine tables surrounded by taupe carpets and aqua couches piled with Navajo-print pillows. There was a large-screen TV and state-of-the-art sound system, plus hundreds of CDs stacked in a glass-doored CD tower. But still no photographs.

"I'm guessing drug lord," Sam said, opening doors to various closets and cubbyholes. She found a photo album, but it contained nothing but pictures of expensive cars. No people. Then Anna spotted another telephone on the second level of an étagère. On the off chance that it was a second phone line, she picked it up. Nothing.

"So much for a night rescue," Sam said. She hoisted her robe and tied it more tightly. "This is kind of creepy, don't you think?"

"Very."

"Like a B-grade horror flick," Sam went on, "and the reason no one knows our names is because Freddy or Jason or whoever offs us during the first ten minutes of the film."

Anna shuddered. "Okay, let's not make ourselves paranoid."

"Sometimes when you're paranoid, it's because someone is really after you."

"And sometimes when you're paranoid, it's because

you're coming down from hallucinogens. No one is after us. No one even knows we're here."

"Right," Sam hissed. "Except Jason."

"Cut it out," Anna commanded. "We're not flipping out. We're looking for a bedroom, and actual clothes, remember?"

The search took them all through the one-story structure. First they discovered a game room that had a pool table, an air hockey table, table tennis, and a bank of pinball machines from the 1950s as well as Japanese pachinko and every game system known to mankind. Off of it was a home screening room that rivaled the one in the Sharpe mansion, complete with THX surround-sound capability. Near the projection area were racks of DVDs in English, Spanish, French, and German, including six starring Jackson Sharpe. Just down the hall from the screening room was an art gallery that featured only twentieth-century paintings; Anna recognized priceless works by Picasso, Mondrian, and Clyfford Still.

Anna, no stranger to luxury, was stunned. *Whose place is this?*

Finally they reached an oversized bedroom. It was dominated by a king-sized round bed covered in Blackglama mink. The bed was reflected in a ceiling mirror.

"Forget drug lord," Sam opined. "This place has to belong to a rap artist. Or a porn star who likes to watch himself in action."

Anna gazed at her overhead reflection. "Makes it kind of hard to get lost in the moment, don't you think?"

Sam chuckled. "Since when did the snooty New York rich girl get so bawdy?"

"I am trying to goeth with the floweth and not creep myself out in this place," Anna told her. She opened various closets—men's clothes only and yet another media system. "I'm still surprised there isn't a watchman."

"Definitely. With an M-16. And snapping rottweilers, frothing at the mouth." Sam rushed at Anna, panting like a rabid dog.

"Stop it!" Anna said. "That's not funny."

"Yes, it is."

"Sorry." Anna shuddered again because she really was concerned about a watchman who might shoot first and ask questions later. Anyone who had a spread like this had to have some kind of security. "I'm trying to be a model of calm. But it isn't working."

"Take a deep breath. We're fine. If the telephones aren't working, no alarm system can work, either."

This was true. And it did get Anna to relax a little as Sam went to a chest of drawers and opened the top one.

"Oh yeah. Someone has taste. Someone female." She extracted a gray triple-ply Anouk Ferrier cashmere sweater and tossed it at Anna. "These puppies go for two grand a pop. Put it on."

Anna held up the sweater. "I don't feel great about helping myself to the owner's wardrobe."

"Anna. Think about it. Mrs. Rap Artist Porn Star

Cocaine King with a secret estate in the middle of
Nowhere, Mexico, is not going to leap from under the
bed and ax us to death because we wore her clothes
overnight." She went to the last closet that Anna hadn't
checked, opened the double doors, and started pushing
hangers around. "Sweet. Armani. Hugo Boss. Versace.
Dolce and Gabbana. Roberto Cavalli. Can't a girl just
find a pair of jeans and—aha!" She stopped at a black
Juicy Couture warm-up suit and took out the hanger.
"This'll do. So last season, but you can't have everything. Put the sweater on, Anna."

Anna hesitated. "Are you sure? We're in enough
trouble already."

"Fine. Stay in a robe. I don't know about you, but
I'm still cold."

Sam doffed her robe and stepped into the warm-up
suit. Anna shivered and considered. The cashmere she
was clutching looked really warm, and she was really
freezing. If the mystery owner showed up, they'd just
have to find a way to explain themselves. Before she
shot them.

No. Stop, brain, she commanded herself, and pulled
on the sweater, luxuriating in the rich, soft fabric. Sam
found some jeans for her in a drawer. They were too
big, but a Chanel scarf snaked through the loops was a
decent improvised belt. Then Anna cocked her head at
a set of double doors. "I wonder what's through there."

It was an indoor pool surrounded by lush tropical
foliage and a smaller hot tub. The ceiling was glass—

Anna gazed up at the dark sky and the falling raindrops. "Amazing. This is an amazing house."

"Hey!" Sam exclaimed. "There's a bar and a fridge over there. Let's see what they've got." She padded over to the thatch-roofed bar and opened the refrigerator. "Oh yeah. We've just hit the jackpot." She held up a bottle of chilled champagne. "Taittingers."

Anna groaned. "How can you think about doing any more drinking?"

"Life is short, Anna. But we can hold this in reserve. Meanwhile, check out all this food!"

Anna realized how hungry she was. She went to the fridge. It was well stocked with delicacies from all over the world. A tin of smoked salmon from Norway. Almas beluga caviar from Vishny Volochek, Russia. Confiture de groseilles with red currants from Bar-le-Duc, France. A jar of capers with Spanish onion peeled and fried in hundred-year-old extra-virgin olive oil from Barcelona. Foie gras in a tin. Even a box of Goo Goo Cluster candies from Tennessee. "You know what this means," she told Sam.

"That we're about to feast?" Sam asked as she plucked up a jar of caviar.

"Someone has been here recently," Anna corrected. "Why else would the fridge be stocked?"

"I don't know, Nancy Drew, and I don't care. And it's all packaged, nothing fresh. It could have been here for a year." She waved the caviar jar under Anna's nose, then cracked it open. "Ever taste this stuff? It's better than sex, I swear."

Anna's stomach rumbled. So she dipped her index finger into the caviar and then licked it clean. The little eggs melted into her tongue. "Mmmm."

"My sentiments exactly." Sam opened the champagne.

"I'm not drinking," Anna declared.

"Just one toast," Sam said. "To one of the best weeks of my life." She passed the bottle to Anna, who shook her head. "Hey, we haven't seen anything else liquid except what comes from the tap, and I know you aren't drinking water that isn't bottled."

"Good point." Anna took a swig and then passed the bottle back to Sam. They finished the caviar and several pieces of salmon. Then Sam spotted a bank of buttons on the opposite side of the room. "I wonder what those are."

"Sam, don't touch . . ."

But Sam was already bounding over to the control panel. She pushed a button at random. The lighting in the room shifted from bright and yellow to red and moody. "Cool." She pushed another button. A booming female voice wailed through the hidden sound system.

"That's 'Redneck Woman'!" Sam said, laughing. She started to dance around to the catchy song. "Who would have thought our mystery owner would be a country fan?"

"Who would have thought *you'd* be a country fan?"

"I'm not. But they play this at my aerobics class," Sam explained. "I get it stuck in my head, it's so hokey.

'Let me get a big hell yeah from the redneck girls like me. Hell, yeah!'" she sang out.

"We aren't redneck girls," Anna pointed out.

"Oh, loosen up, Anna." Sam kept on dancing. She pulled Anna to her feet. Sam's joy was infectious; so was the music. Anna gave herself up to it. The girls danced together, losing themselves in the rowdy female anthem. "Hell, yeah!"

When the song ended, it segued into a country ballad neither of them recognized. They took the moment to plop down by the side of the hot tub and dangled their feet into the warm water.

"This is so cool," Sam pronounced. "I would have said, 'That's hot,' but did you know that Paris Hilton actually trademarked the phrase?"

"Not really," Anna said.

"Really. Is that sad or funny or both?" Sam splashed Anna with her toes. "The only thing lacking at the moment is male scenery."

"I'm sorry you missed your date with Eduardo. But he'll understand."

"Just my luck. I finally meet a hot guy with a brain who likes me, and I stand him up."

"Once you explain—"

"I doubt it." Sam yawned. "He goes back to Paris tomorrow. It's probably better this way. It's not like it was going to work out."

"How do you know?"

"Okay, let's say I went out with him and I started to

really, really like him. He'd either stop liking me or I'd find out that he's actually an asshole. Either way, I lose."

"Why so defeatist?"

"It's called experience." Sam went back to the food stash and got the jam, some crackers, and a knife. She brought it all back to Anna. "Hot tub?"

Sans bathing suits, obviously. Well, it didn't really bother Anna. She was comfortable with her body. And she thought it was a good sign that Sam seemed to be growing more comfortable with her own.

"Why not?"

Anna stripped off her borrowed clothes. Sam did the same, and they lowered themselves into the steaming water. "Bliss." Sam sighed, leaning her head against the lip. "Sheer bliss."

Anna reached for the jar of jam. Instead of spreading it on a cracker, she used her finger as she had in the caviar. "Mmmm. You can't just give up on love, Sam. You're seventeen."

"The only thing that's true about love is that true love doesn't exist," Sam declared.

"Yes, it does," Anna insisted.

"Well, if you're right, I'd like to experience it. Just once." Sam slid lower into the water and closed her eyes.

Anna wondered if she'd ever really experienced it herself. Was love finding the right person to have children with, to grow old with? Or was love the way a boy made you feel when you were in his arms and the world was absolutely, completely perfect? She couldn't imagine having children right now, and she definitely couldn't imagine growing old. But she remembered only too well what it had felt like to be in Ben Birnbaum's arms.

"With Ben, it felt like love," she said softly. She waited for Sam to scold her for talking about Ben. When nothing happened, she extended her foot underwater and tapped it against Sam's leg. "Sam?"

"Wha?" Sam asked blearily. She seemed only half awake.

"Don't fall asleep."

"Why not?"

"Jason? Freddy? The owner of this place walking in on us?" Anna prompted.

"Please. What do you expect us to do, stay awake all night?"

Anna realized that was ridiculous. Besides, she was exhausted. Then a plan came to mind.

"Maybe I should write a note and leave it downstairs explaining things so that if someone comes home, they'll see the note before they see us."

Sam gave her a baleful look. "Dear crazed mystery owner, we broke in, we ate, and now we're upstairs asleep in your kinky bed under the mirror. Love, Anna Percy. And you'll write it in English *and* Spanish, of course."

Anna let her head loll back against the rim of the hot tub. "You're right. Dumb idea.

"Come on. Let's call it a night."

Anna climbed out of the hot tub; Sam followed.

They went back through the double doors into the bedroom, where Sam started to snore the moment flesh met mink quilt.

But Anna, tired as she was, couldn't sleep. What an amazing, impossible day. Tomorrow they still had to find their way back to Las Casitas. In the meantime, someone could still come in and catch them. Anything could happen.

She turned over and closed her eyes. It was scary.

But it was also wonderful.

"Seat belts fastened? Seats upright?" The prematurely gray, uniformed captain of Jackson Sharpe's private jet—a fifteen-seat Gulfstream III that had belonged to John Travolta before Travolta bought his Boeing 707—stood outside the cockpit and did a quick safety check.

"Let's go, James," Jackson snapped.

"You got it, sir."

Dee could see that Sam's father was in a bad mood. It had taken three hours for Kiki to track down Jackson's pilot, Captain James McGill, and get him to Van Nuys airport, where Jackson kept his private jet. Jackson kept bitching to Kiki about how he paid James a small fortune and expected his pilot to be on call. In fact, Kiki herself had decided not to make the trip. She'd claimed to be staying behind to do damage control with Leno, but Dee thought maybe it was because she didn't want to get yelled at anymore. In Dee's experience, Jackson Sharpe wasn't a yeller. Dee chalked it up to his concern for Sam. It was sweet, really.

Poppy wasn't on the plane, either. She didn't want to be far from her obstetrician. At first, Dee had wanted to stay with Poppy to support her. But then Dee found out that Cammie had insisted on flying to Mexico with Jackson. Dee knew that if Cammie went and she stayed with Poppy, it would seem as if Cammie cared more about Sam than Dee did. Dee couldn't let that happen. Everyone knew she was a nicer, more caring person than Cammie. She had a reputation to uphold, even if she did feel guilty as hell saying goodbye to Poppy before climbing into Jackson's limo to the airport.

Captain McGill finally closed the cockpit door. Five minutes later, they were airborne from Van Nuys and quickly reached their cruising altitude. It would be merely an hour's flight to the small Las Casitas airstrip—the Gulfstream could fly at nearly six hundred miles an hour.

Dee had brought a copy of the *Tanya*, the classic Chassidic Jewish text on Kabbalah, but found herself too anxious to read. It was like the farther the plane got from Los Angeles, the more she found herself reliving all the good times she'd had with Sam. What if Sam had been kidnapped? That would be horrible.

So instead of reading, she just gazed around the cabin, which was more like an expensive living room. The leather seats and sleeper couch were custom-made, the entertainment center had a plasma high-definition television and state-of-the-art sound system; there was even a DVD library of the five hundred best movies of all time as selected by Peter Bart at *Variety*. Dee saw that Jackson was trying to distract himself with one of those DVDs—*It's a Wonderful Life*. But he kept drumming his fingers on the leather arm of his chair and checking his watch every other minute.

Dee was thirsty. A pick-me-up wouldn't hurt. She unhooked her seat belt, went forward to the galley, and found a can of Red Bull. She was trying to wean stimulants from her diet, so she now rationed herself to two Red Bulls a day. As she drank, she studied the framed photographs mounted on the interior walls of the galley. Jackson and Poppy's wedding photo. Jackson with Tom Hanks. With Harrison Ford. With Robert Zemeckis. With Nicole Kidman. On the prize committee at Cannes. Holding his Golden Globe award.

"Is there a Diet Coke in there?"

Dee turned to Cammie, who'd joined her in the galley. "Yeah, lots. I have to say, Cammie, I'm surprised you actually came."

"Why? Sam's my best friend."

Dee always felt anxious when Cammie said that. Sam was *her* best friend.

"I thought you'd want to stay with Adam," she explained.

"I'm totally confident about Adam," Cammie

insisted, taking a can of Diet Coke from the refrigerator and popping the top.

Dee found that comment interesting. Usually Cammie really *was* totally confident. But Dee didn't believe she was all that confident about her relationship with Adam. Yes, Dee had walked in on them about to do the deed, but everyone knew that Adam had been crazy about Anna in the not-so-distant past. And Anna Percy was the only girl who had ever given Cammie Sheppard true competition. It was one of the few things Dee really liked about Anna. She took a sip of her Red Bull. The temptation was certainly there, to rub salt into Cammie's wounds. The Kabbalah rabbi she'd heard with Poppy last Saturday had termed it in Hebrew the *yetzer hara*, the evil impulse. But she was trying to become a more evolved person, to listen to her *yetzer tova*, the good impulse. So she changed the subject.

"You remember the first time we were on this plane? Right after Jackson bought it?"

Cammie chuckled softly. "Oh yeah. When we were—"

"Thirteen," Dee filled in.

"All the kids at school were having their bar and bat mitzvahs," Cammie recalled. "When Sam found out you had to be Jewish to get one, she was ready to convert. So Jackson flew about a dozen of us to the Bahamas instead."

"After he left, we stayed with those boring Jamaican nannies. Remember?" Dee asked, picking up the story.

"And one of them kept praying for us and telling us to repent our evil ways—"

"Right!" Cammie exclaimed, laughing. "The others didn't seem to care what we did. But that older woman kept saying, 'If you do dat, you'll go to hell, children.' Which didn't stop us from scoring some killer island ganja." She smiled at Dee. "I swear, they get the best reefer there."

Dee grinned. Maybe the *yetzer tova* was working. She hadn't felt so close to Cammie in quite a while. And to think it was all because Sam had gone missing and they were on a rescue mission.

"You know, Cammie, if anything happened to Sam . . ."

"We'll find her." Cammie gave Dee a little hug. "I know we will."

Wow. Dee was impressed. Maybe Cammie's *yetzer tova* was at work, too. Or else Adam was improving Cammie's personality. Still, she didn't doubt for a moment that Cammie really was worried that Anna was competition for her with Adam, that if Anna wanted Adam back, she could get him quicker than Dee could whip out her MasterCard at Trashy Lingerie on La Cienega Boulevard in West Hollywood. Which meant that deep in Cammie's heart of hearts it was *yetzer hara* all the way. Cammie probably hoped that Sam would be found and Anna wouldn't.

Dee couldn't decide how she felt about finding Anna. Anna had stolen her place on Sam's A-list, that was for sure. Anna had also stolen the boy they all wanted, Ben Birnbaum. And then she'd dropped him, too.

A girl that fickle deserved whatever the gods dished out to her.

Well, if Anna wasn't found, there would probably be a memorial service. Dee could wear her black Pamella Roland wrap dress and her new Alberto Ferretti slingback pumps with the leopard-print lining. She'd keep her makeup really pale, with maybe a touch of MAC Prrr lip gloss. Or maybe she'd buy all new stuff to honor Anna's memory.

Not that Dee wanted anything really bad to happen to Anna. That would be truly bad karma. But she figured she should cover all the fashion bases, just in case.

¡Ay, Caramba!

Ben was kissing Anna everywhere; pure bliss. Back in New York, she'd dreamt of finding a boy who would make her feel like she felt this very moment. These kisses proved that dreams really could come true. They were lying on a gentle hillside, the lush grass underneath was so soft, so luxurious, almost like mink—

Anna's eyes snapped open. Her mind went into instant overdrive.

Mink. She was sleeping under mink.

Where was she?

She looked around the dimly lit room as she heard Sam snore next to her. That's right. They were in the lavish master bedroom of the estate they'd discovered the night before during the storm. Ornate hand-painted tiles bordering the room, hand-knotted rugs resting on burnished wood. She glanced straight up and saw herself in the mirror, Sam curled up to her left. Right. Mirrored ceiling.

Ouch. Her hand went to her head; she had the worst

headache, and she saw now that she looked as bad as she felt. Well, first things first. Get up and check the telephones, see if they were working and—

Wait.

Had she just heard something?

Voices. In the house. She froze, listening carefully. Two of them. Male. Gruff. Spanish. Coming closer to the bedroom.

Anna jostled Sam. "Sam, wake up!"

Sam snored and rolled over. The voices got louder.

Anna shook Sam again. "Wake up *now!* Someone's here! And we're naked!"

Anna scrambled for something to wear. The clothes and the robes from the night before were in the room with the hot tub. No time to get them. She grabbed the Mexican shawl off the back of a white rocking chair and threw it at Sam. "Put this on! Hurry!" Then, as the male voices got still louder, she dove back onto the bed and pulled the mink throw around herself.

Suddenly the door burst open and the lights snapped on. Two armed men in khaki uniforms pointed Uzis at the girls.

"*Quien están ustedes? ¡Sus manos al cielo!*" the taller of the two men yelled.

Anna flung her hands toward the ceiling, following the man's instructions. "Do what I'm doing, Sam. Dammit!" Anna told Sam, her voice cracking with fear. She tried to hold onto the mink comforter with her chin to cover her nakedness and racked her brain for the Spanish to say, "We're naked under these blankets." But she drew a blank. She did manage, *"Somos norteamericanas. Somos turistas a Las Casitas."*

Neither of the men seemed interested or impressed.

"Rich Americans! From Beverly Hills, California," Sam shouted in English. "My father is Jackson Sharpe. The famous actor!"

"Nosotros no hablamos ingles. ¡Español solamente!"

"They don't speak English," Anna reported. "Let me try to find out who they are. *Ustedes son con el gobierno?"*

"No!" the tall man bellowed. *"¡Securidad!"*

Anna's heart sank. "They're security guards, Sam. Not official."

But Sam wasn't deterred as she pleaded with the men. *"¡Por favor! Mi papi* Jacksono Sharpo. Mee *papi* Jacksono Sharpo, from *los* movies!"

"Ella se llama Samantha Sharpe," Anna translated. *"Su papá se llama Jackson Sharpe. ¡El grand hombre norteamericano de los peliculas! ¡El jefe!"*

But the guards didn't seem to care. *"¡Ustedes! ¡Vienen con nosotros!"* the taller one insisted, pointing toward the door with his rifle butt.

"Sí, sí," Anna said, trying to placate them. "We'll come with you. *Uno momento, uno momento."*

She caught a glimpse of a clock in the nightstand. Six-thirty A.M. The storm was over. Surely people from Las Casitas had to be looking for them. Probably even the Mexican police. But if these men took them away, they were ruined. Who knew what they wanted or where they wanted to go?

There was absolutely nothing in the *This Is How We Do Things* Big Book, East *or* West Coast edition, that covered being confronted at gunpoint by uniformed men who didn't speak English when you were completely nude in a mansion that you had broken into. Anna glanced at Sam and saw she was at a total loss now that the usual "I'm Jackson Sharpe's daughter" thing hadn't worked. In fact, Sam looked petrified.

Shit.

Anna took a deep breath. She knew that panic would be disastrous. The best thing she could do, she realized, was stall until help came, thin a hope as that might be.

"*Por favor,*" Anna asked. "*Useme nuestra ropas. Estos son en el cuarto de baño.*"

"What'd you say?" Sam demanded.

"I asked if we could get dressed."

The guards discussed this. After much consultation, they told Anna that they would follow her and the other girl to the bathroom. If the girls were not dressed in thirty seconds, the guards would shoot their way in. Anna told Sam the plan, skipping over the shooting part. Sam was freaked out enough already.

Rifles at their backs, blankets and shawls wrapped around them, the girls edged out of bed. They shuffled to the bathroom and changed as quickly as they could. Fortunately, their clothing had dried overnight.

"We are so fucked," Sam muttered darkly as she

pulled on her Mexican skirt. "Tell them in Spanish who I am, Anna."

"I did. They didn't give a shit." Then Anna had an idea. "Look. Maybe they have a radio in their car. They can check with their boss, who can check with Las Casitas."

The guards were waiting when the girls came out. Thankfully they didn't have the rifles pointed at their chests anymore. That was progress. Anna turned to the shorter, marginally less threatening of the guards.

"*Yo tengo una idea,*" she said. "*Vete al carajo, y—*"

She never got the rest of sentence out. He slung the gun up to his shoulder and aimed it directly at her chest, suddenly infuriated.

"*¡Vamanos, vamanos!*" the taller one shouted, glowering. "*Le estamos llevando a nuestra jefe. ¡Ustedes están en apuro importante!*"

"What the hell happened?" Sam whispered desperately as the guards marched them out of the house, hands in the air. "I thought you were telling them something *good.*"

"I was trying!"

"Then why are they using our hearts for target practice?"

"I don't know," Anna admitted, hoping that Sam didn't notice her voice cracking. Parked directly in front of the white mansion was a single black Hummer with tinted windows. That the grounds surrounding the mansion were utterly magnificent barely registered on Anna when she saw the sinister-looking vehicle.

"*¡Salen la puerta y en nuestra Hummer!*"

"He wants us to get in the Hummer," Anna translated. "They're taking us to his boss."

"Dead or alive?" Sam asked, her voice choked with tears. "How do we know they aren't kidnapping us or something? We have to *do* something! Maybe we should run."

"And get shot?" Anna hissed. She willed herself not to cry. "What do you think they'll do when they see us . . . ?"

Her words were drowned out by a whup-whup from above. A helicopter. It was circling above the estate at about a thousand feet.

"Shit," Sam cried. "They've called in reinforcements!"

The guards looked up, too. Then they started chattering in Spanish, pointing to the chopper and arguing vehemently. Anna couldn't understand a thing over the noise of the chopper.

"We've got to run!" Sam yelled.

"No! That's crazy, Sam!"

Anna's heart hammered as the helicopter descended and landed a hundred yards from them in the middle of the estate's front lawn. Were they going to be taken away in the helicopter to God knew where?

The helicopter shut down its engines, and a door popped open. Two men leaped out, ducking their heads so they wouldn't be decapitated by the still-whirring blades. One of the men was Latino and wore a Mexican military uniform; the other one was light-skinned, in jeans and a blue shirt. The man in civilian clothes strode toward the girls, tall and purposeful. The guards' rifles fell to their sides as they stared in awe.

Anna could not believe what she was seeing. It couldn't be.

"Dad?" Sam asked.

"Sam!"

It was like a scene from a movie. Jackson stopped and held out his arms. Sam ran toward her father and flung himself into his embrace as the two security guards looked on, gape-mouthed.

"Sam," Jackson exclaimed. "Thank God!"

"How did you—?"

"It doesn't matter. You scared the hell out of me."

Now that they were apparently safe, Anna realized how frightened she'd been—her hands were still shaking, and she felt weak in the knees. She didn't think she'd ever been so happy to see anyone as she was to see Jackson Sharpe at that moment.

"*Oye*, Jackson Sharpe!" one of the security guards cried. "*¡Ay, caramba! ¡Usted es mi estrella de las peliculas preferida! Que hace usted aquí en México, Señor Sharpe?*"

The helicopter pilot, who wore the uniform of the Mexican army, had joined Sam and Jackson. "He says you're his favorite movie star," the pilot reported to Jackson.

"*Gracias*," Jackson told the men, keeping an arm around his daughter. "Now if we could—"

"*¡Uno momento!*" One of the guards scurried to the Hummer and came back with a disposable camera, which he handed to his partner. Then he parked himself next to Jackson. "*Una fotografía para nuestras esposas, por favor, Don Jackson?*"

"He wants some pictures for their wives," translated the pilot.

"And just like that, we're their new best friends," Sam chortled ecstatically, throwing her hands in the air in an expression of both joy and frustration. "What was the last half hour all about?"

But she stepped away from her father; the taller guard put his arm around Jackson's shoulder and beamed, and his partner snapped a quick photo. Then they switched. They were starting to hunt for paper for autographs, but the Mexican pilot called them off. So the men got into their Hummer and drove away, seemingly the two happiest private security guards south of the border.

The girls boarded the helicopter with Jackson and the pilot. As the helicopter took off, Jackson craned around and reached for his daughter's hand.

"You're lucky that I'm too frightened to be angry at you, Sam."

"What do you mean?" Sam asked.

"You really scared me," her father told her reflectively. "I know the new baby has been hard on you, but you can't just pick up and leave town without telling me. If you need a time-out, just let me know. I'll understand. And if I'm not acting like I understand, remind me. Deal?"

"Deal," Sam responded.

Watching Sam and her dad, Anna got a lump in her throat. Silly as it was, she wished it were her father, tall and strong and sure, who had marched off that helicopter to save her.

"Hey, Anna." Sam nudged her.

"What?"

Sam was beaming. "How cool is this?"

Anna had to smile back. "Very."

"I just can't figure out why the guards didn't leave us alone once we told them who my dad was. At first I thought maybe they were the two people in the world who weren't fans," Sam started. Then she leaned over toward Jackson. "Sorry, Dad."

"That's all right, sweetie," he replied with a wink.

"I don't get it, either," Anna added.

"Do you think it had something to do with what you said to them in Spanish?" Sam asked.

"No way," Anna answered. "I just told them to call Las Casitas."

"Uh, excuse me, sir," Sam said to the pilot.

"Yes?" the pilot responded.

"Can you translate something for my friend here?" she asked. Clearly she had grown suspicious of the accuracy of Anna's Spanish. "Anna, tell them what you said."

"What?" Anna asked.

"Tell them what you said, Anna," Sam repeated with mock impatience.

"Fine," Anna said. She wasn't used to being challenged, nor was she sure if she liked it. *Vete al carajo—*"

The pilot burst out laughing.

"Why are you laughing?" Anna asked, utterly bewildered.

"Go out to the car is *'vete al carro.' 'Vete al carajo'*

is . . . how do you say it in English? Go fuck yourself."

Sam roared with laughter, as did her father, and the pilot. Anna joined in. It *was* pretty funny, and probably they were both laughing from relief. "You know, I don't know which is more surprising," Sam declared. "That Anna Percy used the F word, or that Anna Percy made a mistake."

Next Time We'll Surf

Freaky. An hour later, Sam was reunited with Dee and Cammie at the Las Casitas pool while Anna was packing her stuff in her room. Everything at the resort was normal—or as normal as life got at a two-thousand-dollar–a-night resort. People were sunning, crowding the swim-up bar for their first cocktails of the day, and having breakfast at one of the many poolside tables. It was so normal that Sam found it difficult to believe that her adventure with Anna in the desert had actually happened.

Cammie hugged Sam hard. "How dare you go off to Mexico without me, you bitch," she teased.

Sam couldn't be sure, but she thought she saw actually saw tears in Cammie's eyes. Was Cammie actually touched? Really and truly touched? Wow. This was an emotion that Sam had rarely in her life seen Cammie display.

"I can't believe you guys came with my dad," Sam marveled.

"I can't believe your dad came here when he was

supposed to appear on *Leno*," Cammie shot back. "Or that he forgave you for skipping out on the appearance."

Sam shrugged. "What's he got to worry about? Now Leno probably just wants him even more."

Cammie looked impressed. "That's true."

Next it was Dee's turn to hug Sam. "Wow, I'm so glad you're okay. And Poppy wants you to know she's here in spirit."

"Which is actually the way I prefer it," Sam said, laughing.

"We were out all night looking for you," Cammie told her. "With the Mexican police."

Sam was amazed. "You did that, for me?"

"Not really *all* night," Dee put in, her face very serious. "We took breaks. Cammie more than me."

"It wasn't a contest, Dee," Cammie pointed out, then turned her attention back to Sam. "I did walk miles looking for you. Don't let it happen again, because it was hell on my new Sigerson Morrison heels."

Sam grinned happily. She could read between the quips; Cammie really did care.

Dee looked around. "Wow, if it wasn't for Poppy, I'd want to stay for a while. This place looks awesome."

"Another time. My dad wants me to pack up and check out," Sam complained. "There's another storm coming. Can you guys hang out here for a bit? I'll be right back."

Cammie smiled. "As long as they keep those mimosas coming."

Sam hugged her friends again—it really was touching that they'd flown down with her dad to look for her—and then headed for her casita. Yet she had a niggling feeling at the pit of her stomach as she walked back to pack. Too bad she'd never had a chance to say good-bye to Eduardo before he went back to France. Not that it mattered. It wasn't like they really knew each other. He was just a cute guy with a cute accent who for some unfathomable reason had wooed her like someone out of a *telenovela*. Whatever. Like she'd told Anna, it was probably better this way. It wasn't like they were going to fall in love. Because that shit never happened to her. So why obsess about—?

There he was. Waiting on the front step of her casita.

"Hi," she mustered, suddenly feeling shy.

"Hello."

She couldn't read his face. "Are you mad?"

He looked very serious. "Let's start with relieved."

"No shit," Sam told him, going for blithe. "We almost got shot by these two guards. They pointed some big-ass rifles at us."

Eduardo's brows knit together. "Why do you say it like it's a joke?"

"Why not? It's over, we're fine, the end." When he didn't speak, she shrugged. "It's not like I intended to stand you up last night. My friend Anna and I drank this vicious mescal and she accidentally ate the worm and then I—"

"You don't have to justify yourself to me," he interrupted.

Sheesh. He seemed so stiff and formal. Where was the charming, sexy guy she'd met the day before? Maybe she'd just imagined that he was wonderful because she so wanted it to be true. It was amazing—and sad—how her own mind could fool her so badly.

"Okay." Sam didn't quite know what to say. "It was almost fun. I . . . um . . . have to go. So I guess we're victims of premature evacuation."

He didn't laugh. "I'm glad you're all right, Samantha."

"Oh, sure. No problem. Well . . ."

"Well . . ."

God. She had to end this and put them both out of their misery. She'd go inside, pack up, and be on the way back to Beverly Hills inside of twenty minutes. Stupid, stupid, stupid, that's what she was. Stupid for having hopes that some guy who'd picked her up in Mexico could be special.

"So, 'bye, Eduardo." She made herself step past him to the front door of her casita. Once inside, with the door safely shut, she added, "I am such an asshole. And that is the end of that sordid little tale."

"Anna? Excellent!" Anna was sitting alone at the lobby bar, eating eggs Benedict—she was ravenous—and drinking French-press coffee. She turned to see Lloyd hurrying toward her, a huge grin on his face.

"Hello, Lloyd," she said in a monotone, forcing herself not to actually roll her eyes.

He lifted his sunglasses and stuck them in his hair. "I heard you were back. Good thing. Your father was ready to kick my butt for losing you."

"You didn't lose me, Lloyd," Anna assured him, trying to hold on to civility. "I'll make sure he knows."

"Bad, bad girl." Lloyd wagged a finger at her. "Now, if you had stayed and played with me last night, you would have avoided all this drama."

Play with Lloyd? How revolting was *that* idea?

Anna sipped her fresh-squeezed juice before she replied. "Lloyd, how can I say this so it won't hurt your feelings? I'd rather stay lost in the desert and subsist on roasted iguana for the rest of my life than play with you. Ever."

Lloyd scratched the copious dark chest hair that bloomed from his open Hawaiian shirt. "Well. You don't need to share any of that with your father, of course. Right?"

"I think this would be an excellent time to excuse yourself, Lloyd," said a voice with an Australian accent.

"Hey, you work here." Lloyd rose and pointed at Kai. "Meaning you work for me."

"I'll certainly keep that in mind," Kai replied as he slipped onto the bar stool next to Anna. Anna hugged him. Lloyd took the hint and slunk away.

"Saved by the Aussie," Anna thanked him gratefully.

"Welcome back. Whatever happened to you two, I hope it was a wild ride."

"Wild doesn't even begin to describe it."

Kai put a hand on her arm. "I'm sorry you're leaving."

"I bet you say that to every girl you share a hot tub with," Anna quipped.

"Actually, no," Kai admitted.

She studied his handsome face a moment. "Tell me honestly, Kai. Do you think you'll even remember that we met?"

"If I passed you on the street in New York, say?"

"Right."

"Of course I would."

Anna was surprised. "What happened to 'fun is fleeting'?"

"Even the paradise clause has an out in it," he said wistfully. Then he lifted her coffee cup in a toast. "Here's to meeting up again, Anna. Next time, we'll surf. And anything else you want to do."

She clinked her crystal juice glass against the coffee cup. So. Even Kai wasn't completely satisfied with living only in the moment. Well, maybe she needed to do more of it and he needed to do less. In any event, she didn't regret her decision to forgo a fling with him. Danny might be right: Lust between near strangers wasn't necessarily wrong.

But for right now, at least, it was wrong for her.

With All Her Heart

While Sam spent most of the flight catching up with her friends, Anna was lost in thought. Yes, she'd had an amazing adventure. But now that she thought about it, things were not terribly different than when she'd left Los Angeles a few days before. She was no clearer on how she felt about Ben or her sister Susan's disappearance. And if what she'd wanted at Las Casitas had been a do-it-and-forget-it with a gorgeous guy, well, she'd underachieved in that area, too.

The flight from Mexico to the Van Nuys airport was just over an hour. She was the first person down the steps from the plane, and the first person she saw was her father, who stood at the edge of the tarmac. This was no surprise; she'd called him from Las Casitas and he'd promised to meet her at Van Nuys. But how he appeared, standing alone in jeans and a wool sweater just outside the utilitarian concrete building that served as the airport's terminal, was a little shocking. There was a day's growth of stubble on his chin; there were bags under his eyes. He looked exhausted.

"Anna." He hugged her hard. "You scared the hell out of us."

"I'm sorry. I didn't mean to, it just . . . happened." She peered around. "And just where is the other half of 'us'?"

Jonathan rubbed his chin. "Long story. Your mother—"

"Just a sec." Anna saw Jackson, Sam, and the others come out of the plane and waved to them. "Excuse me, Dad. You never actually met Sam's father. Let me introduce you. You remember Sam, right?"

"Of course."

Sam called to her. "See you at the Polo Lounge?"

"Definitely," Anna agreed. Sam had called Jackson's Kiki and had her arrange a homecoming luncheon at the Beverly Hills Hotel's flagship restaurant for that afternoon.

"Great, see you there. I'll take Cammie and Dee to my dad's limo. Kiki brought it over."

Anna nodded. She didn't bother with Cammie and Dee, who were already on their way into the terminal. But she did bring her father over to Jackson. The two handsome men shook hands, taking each other's measure.

"I can't thank you enough," Jonathan told Jackson.

"All's well that ends well, huh?" Jackson replied. "I was crazy at that age myself."

"Oh yeah," Jonathan agreed, and they shared a chuckle at their misbegotten youth. "Listen, I want to thank you for going down there right away. I tried, but . . . anyway, thanks."

"No problem," Jackson replied, smoothing over

Jonathan's discomfort. "Glad to help. You've got a ride back over the hill?"

Jonathan nodded.

"Great. You know, my daughter really thinks a lot of your daughter. Now that I've spent some time with her, I can see why." With one more quick handshake, Jackson departed into the building.

"Nice guy," Jonathan commented, making no move to leave.

"Can we go, Dad?" Anna asked, wondering why they were still standing on the tarmac. "I'm a little tired."

"Actually, we've got to chill," Jonathan said. "I sent Django to deliver some papers to a client in Studio City since we were in the neighborhood. He should be back soon—he'll pick us up in front." He shook his head. "Can't deal with the terminal. This airport is so damn ugly, it's depressing."

Anna longed for a hot bath and a long nap before Sam's party, but it wouldn't kill her to hang out for a while. "Fine. Where do you want to wait?"

"In front," her dad decided. He took her luggage, and they walked through the ramshackle terminal and through the front doors.

Her father had it right—the place could use a renovation. Anna donned her tortoiseshell Kate Spade sunglasses before they took seats on the single stone bench by the passenger drop-off circle.

"So, what happened down there?" Jonathan asked in a serious tone, crossing one leg over the other.

Anna sighed. She really was tired, definitely not in a mood to give him a blow-by-blow. "Sam and I went shopping. We took a walk. We got lost in the desert. That's all."

"Hey, don't make light of this," her father chided. "You put a whole lot of people out."

"I didn't mean to, and I wasn't making light of it," Anna protested.

Jonathan shook his head. "It doesn't add up. You are the most responsible person I know."

"Well, this time it didn't work out," Anna said flatly, her voice colder than she'd intended. It had to be because she was so exhausted.

Jonathan regarded this carefully. "You're pissed at me," he surmised.

"No."

"Yeah, you are," he insisted. "But I'm not the one who screwed up here. . . . Anna, would you take off the glasses so that I can see who I'm talking to?"

Anna pushed the glasses into her hair. As she did, she realized that her father had never answered her original question. And she realized something else, too.

"I was just thinking," she began. "When we went to meet Susan's plane, you made such a big thing about all three of us being at the airport. Now here I am. But where's Mom?"

Her father gazed at his suede Calvin Klein driving mocs, unable to meet Anna's eyes. "Milan, probably," he finally muttered. "Who the hell knows with her?"

Anna shook her head. "I don't understand."

"Three days into our trip down memory lane, we both remembered why we can't stand each other." He looked up at her again. "She had me drop her at the Santa Barbara airport."

A private jet roared down the runway and into the sky. Jonathan gazed upward, following its flight into the wild blue yonder, then smiled sadly. "Ever wish you could just fly away, Anna? Oh, wait, you just did."

He looked so wistful. One part of Anna felt sorry for him—he'd obviously been hurt by his ex-wife's abrupt departure. But another part of her couldn't believe his naiveté.

"Did you really think that some quick romance with Mom would make it all better?" she asked him softly.

"I don't know what I thought." He rubbed his face wearily. "Anyway, after she was gone, I just . . . I needed some time alone, to think." He ran a hand through his already mussed hair. "There's just so damn much pressure now. Your mother only added to it."

It's always someone else's fault with them both, Anna thought. She had no doubt that her mother—wherever she was—was complaining about the pressure and blaming the whole mess on her father.

"Ah, it's so much clearer now," Anna commented, her tone even chillier than before.

Jonathan pointed at her. "You sound just like Jane." Then a thought flitted across his face. "Did anything bad happen in Mexico? With Lloyd, maybe? He's a quirky guy. Brilliant, but quirky."

"Quirky" didn't begin to cover it. For one brief moment, Anna was tempted to give her father the complete rundown on Lloyd's dubious achievements in Mexico. But no. Except for one weak moment when Ben Birnbaum had broken her heart, she wasn't in the habit of sharing with her father.

"Lloyd is just fine. He thinks you should buy the resort and the place is spectacular. End of report."

"I know exactly what Lloyd thinks; he e-mails me twice a day. But I don't care about that. What I care about is that you're okay."

Anna folded her arms. Her father's solicitousness was getting tiresome. "Yes, well, we've covered that ground already."

"No, we haven't. You've come back with this major attitude. I don't get it."

Maybe it was a delayed reaction to her scary encounter with the over-armed Mexican rent-a-cops. Maybe it had something to do with whatever had been in the homemade mescal she'd downed in La Trinidad with Sam. But just when she thought she had everything under control, something inside Anna cracked like an overstressed fault line.

Attitude? He thought she had an attitude? Everyone in her damn family did whatever they wanted whenever they wanted to do it. She was the only one who ever felt any responsibility to anyone else!

"How worried could you have been, Dad?" The words poured out of her. "Sam's father dropped everything and flew to Mexico. But not you. You were too busy in San Simeon dealing with the pressure."

"I couldn't get there—"

"Because you didn't *want* to. Not enough. I guess it doesn't really matter where I live. My parents are bi-coastal no-shows."

Hot tears rolled down her cheeks. Embarrassed at losing control, Anna fisted them away. Her father dug the monogrammed handkerchief he always carried out of the pocket of his jeans and offered it to her, but she wouldn't take it.

"I'm sorry," he murmured as he pushed the handkerchief back into his pocket. "Shit, Anna. What do you want me to say? I know I've sucked as a father in the past. I want to change all that."

She opened her purse to rummage for a tissue of her own. "Those are just words, Dad."

He looked defeated, arms dangling. "Yeah. I guess so."

Anna found a Kleenex, wiped her eyes, and blew her nose. She struggled for composure. "The thing is, Dad, I've figured out how things work in your world."

"Great. Explain it to me."

"Everyone is expendable. Mom. Margaret. Susan." She swallowed back a lump in her throat. "And me."

Her father leaned forward and touched her arm. "Never you, Anna. I swear."

The lump in her throat welled back up. "Then why . . . why didn't you come for me?"

"I'm so sorry, Anna. I'm so damn sorry."

He held out her arms to her; she let him comfort her. And she told herself that he was there right now, even if he hadn't come to Mexico.

But the image of Jackson Sharpe striding toward Sam to save the day was forever etched in Anna's mind. With all her heart, she wished that it been her father jumping down from that helicopter to rescue her. But like so many of her wishes when it came to her family, she knew this one was never going to come true.

Balance

A few hours later, Anna sat at a round table in the Polo
Lounge at the Beverly Hills Hotel with all of Sam's
closest friends, plus assorted wannabes and hangers-on.
There were Cammie and Dee. Adam, who had an arm
draped around Cammie. Parker Pinelli, who sat to the
left of his latest girlfriend, Krishna, while Krishna's ex, a
guy named Bennett, sat to her right. Anna was almost
certain that he had his hand on her thigh under the table.
There was a girl named Skye, recovering from her second
nose job to fix her cocaine-habit-induced deviated sep-
tum. A guy named Blue and a handful of others.

Anna had come because she'd promised Sam that she
would. But she really had no more use for this crowd—
with some notable exceptions—than she'd ever had.
Cammie was a viper waiting to strike. And Dee was a
jacket short of a Chanel suit. Adam, however, was one
of the truly good guys. And Sam . . . Well, other than
Cyn back in New York, Sam was as close to a best friend
as Anna had. Tripping in the desert and facing down
M-16s had been a bonding experience, to say the least.

Anna's eyes slid to Adam, who was looking at Cammie with something approaching adoration. Cammie gazed at him the same way. Which was *way* stranger than fiction. Maybe they really did care for each other. Anna could stake no claim on Adam; that she knew. She'd treated him badly. He'd moved on. But she still hoped, cliché as it might sound, that one day they'd be friends again.

As for the others, maybe she could learn something from her experience in the desert: to be less judgmental and just *be*—to live and let live. Besides, everyone at this little gathering had been perfectly decent to her, hugging her and gushing about how glad they were that she was back. Not one bitchy word had passed anyone's lips, not even Cammie's. In fact, they were all rapt as Sam finished recounting the story of their odyssey.

"Wow, a psychedelic experience in the desert," Bennett gushed. "That could be life-changing."

"It was almost life-ending," Sam joked.

Skye sipped her Evian. "But wait. You're telling me that after all that, you and this Eduardo guy never hooked up?"

Sam shrugged. "Whatever."

Anna could tell that Sam was feigning nonchalance. Eduardo had seemed so terrific. She was sincerely sorry that Sam hadn't gotten the happy ending she deserved.

"Did you buy any cute clothes while you were there?" Krishna asked, apropos of nothing.

"Tons of them. From all of the top Mexican designers." Cammie tilted her head back and laughed.

"Like who?" Dee asked, wide-eyed.

"Like none, Dee," Cammie explained slowly. "That's the whole point."

Dee twirled some hair around a finger. "I like southwestern-style clothes. Remember that really cute silver serape thing I got a couple of years ago at Cinnamon's? And then Fergie from the Black Eyed Peas wore the exact same one at the MTV Music Awards?"

"We didn't buy any designer silver serapes," Sam stated. She was methodically buttering a fresh-baked roll. Anna could see her fighting the urge to take a huge bite.

"So, what did you buy?" Skye asked.

Anna's memory was jogged. "A sculpture."

Sam met her eyes with something approaching amazement. She, too, had obviously forgotten the old Mexican artist. In a way, Anna thought, he was the whole reason they'd ended up in the desert.

"A what?" Cammie scoffed.

"A sculpture," Sam told her with dignity.

"A primitive. By a native artist. It's being shipped to her," Anna jumped in, exaggerating the truth only a tiny bit. After a phone call or two to Las Casitas, she had no doubt that the sculpture would be en route to Beverly Hills in a matter of days.

"Wow," Dee breathed. "I need to get a sculpture by a native artist, too."

Across from Anna, Cammie laced her fingers

through Adam's and shook her curls off her face. "Before you two got lost, some of us had a fantastic time back here." She leaned over to kiss Adam.

Oversharing, Anna thought. Maybe Cammie and Adam had swung naked from the chandeliers, but there was certainly no reason to broadcast it.

"I know that's true," Dee squealed. "I walked in on them." Then she clapped a tiny hand over her mouth. "Oops. I probably wasn't supposed to say anything."

"That was the general idea," Adam jested, but he didn't sound mad.

"Sorry," Dee chirped. "I'm just glad you guys found true love, that's all."

Could that be real? Anna wondered. She wanted Adam to be happy. But with Cammie Sheppard?

"So Anna, what did you do that was fun?" Krishna asked, breaking into Anna's thoughts. It was clear from her tone of voice that she couldn't care less.

"I learned to surf, actually," Anna offered.

"Oh yeah?" Parker asked, focusing his megawatt smile on Anna. Considering that he resembled a young Brad Pitt, that could have been an intense experience if Anna hadn't known he was as dull as he was good-looking. "We should drive down to Newport sometime. Or to Zuma."

"Um, maybe," Anna responded lightly.

Krishna shot Parker a dirty look. "*We* never go surfing."

"You said it wrecks your hair," Parker reminded her.

"So?"

The waiter set a tuna Nicoise down in front of Anna. She took a halfhearted bite. What was it about this crowd that seemed to bring out the absolute worst in her? She'd just lied and said that she'd learned to surf. For what reason? To impress them?

"I thought you were on a diet, Sam." Skye smirked when she saw Sam put a forkful of the Polo Lounge's homemade ketchup on the cheeseburger she'd ordered.

"I never said that."

Skye shrugged. "Dee told me."

"No, I didn't," Dee insisted. She looked at Sam with her big blue eyes. "I said that I read about this man who lived on air because he was able to transcend the physical needs of his body. And I said that you should try meditation. But I never said you were on a diet. I really didn't."

"The burger would work, minus the bun," Krishna suggested. "The South Beach Diet is the only one that works. My sister lost six pounds in a week. She bought the most adorable Valentino skirt to wear to the Olsen twins' birthday party at Pastis, remember? She was, like, as skinny as Mary Kate."

Anna glanced over at Sam, who was chewing a small bite with the most morose expression on her face. All the energy and joy Anna had seen in Mexico was gone. And these people were Sam's friends.

"Samantha?" Anna heard a voice behind her. British accent.

"Omigod." Sam literally dropped her burger.

Everyone at the table turned toward a sharply dressed gorgeous guy, with copper skin, curly black hair, twinkling dark eyes, and a perfectly chiseled chin. He crossed toward Sam and took her hands as the table fell completely silent.

"Samantha," he repeated. His smile displayed two perfect dimples. Then he nodded to Anna. "Hello again, Anna."

"Hi, Eduardo." Anna kept her voice calm for her friend's sake, but she felt like jumping up and down with happiness.

"But—but . . ." Sam stammered. "You were on your way to Paris."

"True," Eduardo confirmed. "I took the puddle jumper to LAX, where I would change planes. And then . . . I never got on the other plane."

Like my sister, Anna thought. But better.

"For me?" Sam asked in a small voice.

"I called your home. Your stepmother was kind enough to tell me where I could find you," he went on. "And here I am."

Sam shook her head. "But you seemed annoyed when I left."

"I was being an ass when you left, actually. So do you have plans for the evening? We never did have our dinner date."

"Let me introduce you." Sam turned Eduardo so he faced the table. "Eduardo, these are my friends. Everyone, *this* is Eduardo."

"Hello, all," he greeted everyone with perfect grace. "I hope I'm not intruding."

"My God, you really *are* hot!" Skye exclaimed.

"And he seems like he's really into her," Dee added supportively.

"Yes, he really is," Eduardo confirmed. As if to punctuate his words, he took Sam into his arms and gave her the most tender kiss on the lips Anna had ever witnessed. Then he whispered something in her ear.

Sam beamed and turned to her friends. "I hope you guys will excuse me. We've got plans."

"Wait!" Krishna demanded. "You can't leave your own welcome-home party."

"Oh, I'm sure you guys will be fine without me." She laughed, getting up from the table and taking Eduardo by the hand.

For a long moment, the table was silent. Finally Bennett broke the quiet. "Well, hell, anyone can change planes." He sniffed.

Everyone began to eat and talk again. But Anna was lost in thought. Sure, any guy with the right credit line could buy a ticket wherever he wanted to go. But not just anyone would do what Eduardo had just done. And no amount of money could make a boy look at a girl the way he had looked at Sam. Maybe Sam was about to experience love. Or it could turn out to be just lust. But she'd never know unless she put her heart out there. Took risks. Followed through.

Suddenly Anna pushed out of her chair. "I have to

go," she announced to the table. "There's someplace I have to be. Right now."

Anna got her Lexus from the valet and headed west on Sunset Boulevard to the Pacific Coast Highway, then up the coast to Zuma Beach. At Diego's Surfing Emporium, she rented a wet suit and a longboard. She changed in the back room and then lugged her board across the PCH and down the long wooden staircase to the beach.

She surveyed the water. The waves were breaking evenly, about three feet, with plenty of time between sets. There were just a few surfers in the water. Conditions were ideal. It was now or never.

Anna carried the board into the water. Paddled into the surf the way Danny and Kai had taught her. Stopped out where the waves were beginning to break. Turned toward Hawaii and waited for perfection to arrive.

And there it was. She spun her board toward shore, paddled like hell, and felt the water rush under her. She rose to her feet.

Be the wave. Be the wave.

Arms out, knees bent, totally concentrated on the moment, Anna Percy rode the wave. She laughed with joy as the wall of water powered her toward shore. Life, love, boys—it was all about balance.

Welcome to Poppy.

A poppy is a beautiful blooming red flower
(like the one on the spine of this book). It is also
the name of the new home of your favorite series.

Poppy takes the real world and makes it
a little funnier, a little more fabulous.

Poppy novels are wild, witty, and inspiring.
They were written just for you.

So sit back, get comfy, and pick a Poppy.

poppy

www.pickapoppy.com

gossip girl

THE A-LIST   THE CLIQUE

the it girl   POSEUR